THE WILDCATS
OF EXETER

By Edward Marston

THE RAILWAY DETECTIVE SERIES
The Railway Detective • The Excursion Train
The Railway Viaduct • The Iron Horse
Murder on the Brighton Express • The Silver Locomotive Mystery
Railway to the Grave • Blood on the Line
The Stationmaster's Farewell • Peril on the Royal Train
A Ticket to Oblivion • Timetable of Death
Signal for Vengeance • The Circus Train Conspiracy
A Christmas Railway Mystery • Points of Danger
Fear on the Phantom Special • Slaughter in the Sapperton Tunnel
Tragedy on the Branch Line
Inspector Colbeck's Casebook

THE HOME FRONT DETECTIVE SERIES
A Bespoke Murder • Instrument of Slaughter
Five Dead Canaries • Deeds of Darkness
Dance of Death • The Enemy Within
Under Attack • The Unseen Hand • Orders to Kill

THE BOW STREET RIVALS SERIES
Shadow of the Hangman • Steps to the Gallows
Date with the Executioner • Fugitive from the Grave
Rage of the Assassin

THE DOMESDAY SERIES
The Wolves of Savernake • The Ravens of Blackwater
The Dragons of Archenfield • The Lions of the North
The Serpents of Harbledown • The Stallions of Woodstock
The Hawks of Delamere • The Wildcats of Exeter
The Foxes of Warwick • The Owls of Gloucester
The Elephants of Norwich

THE RESTORATION SERIES
The King's Evil • The Amorous Nightingale • The Repentant Rake
The Frost Fair • The Parliament House • The Painted Lady

THE BRACEWELL MYSTERIES
The Queen's Head • The Merry Devils
The Trip to Jerusalem • The Nine Giants
The Mad Courtesan • The Silent Woman
The Roaring Boy • The Laughing Hangman
The Fair Maid of Bohemia • The Wanton Angel
The Devil's Apprentice • The Bawdy Basket
The Vagabond Clown • The Counterfeit Crank
The Malevolent Comedy • The Princess of Denmark

THE CAPTAIN RAWSON SERIES
Soldier of Fortune • Drums of War • Fire and Sword
Under Siege • A Very Murdering Battle

PRAISE FOR EDWARD MARSTON

'A master storyteller'
Daily Mail

'Packed with characters Dickens would have been
proud of. Wonderful [and] well-written'
Time Out

'Once again Marston has created a credible
atmosphere within an intriguing story'
Sunday Telegraph

'Filled with period detail, the pace is steady and
the plot is thick with suspects, solutions and clues.
Marston has a real knack for blending detail,
character and story with great skill'
Historical Novels Review

'The past is brought to life with brilliant
colours, combined with a perfect
whodunnit. Who needs more?'
The Guardian

THE WILDCATS
OF EXETER

EDWARD MARSTON

Allison & Busby Limited
11 Wardour Mews
London W1F 8AN
allisonandbusby.com

First published in Great Britain in 1998.
First published by Allison & Busby in 2021.
This edition first published by Allison & Busby in 2021.

A CIP catalogue record for this book is available from
the British Library.

10 9 8 7 6 5 4 3 2 1

ISBN 978-0-7490-2645-5

Typeset in 11/16 pt Adobe Garamond Pro by
Allison & Busby Ltd.

The paper used for this Allison & Busby publication
has been produced from trees that have been legally sourced
from well-managed and credibly certified forests.

Printed and bound by
CPI Group (UK) Ltd, Croydon, CR0 4YY

The king, however, closely besieged the city, attempting to storm it, and for many days he fought relentlessly to drive the citizens from the ramparts and to undermine the walls. Finally the citizens were compelled by the unremitting attacks of the enemy to take wiser counsel and humbly plead for pardon. The flower of their youth, the older men, and the clergy bearing their sacred books and treasures went out to the king.

Orderic Vitalis

Prologue

While he put on his apparel again, Nicholas Picard deliberately kept his back to her. It was not the only thing which peeved her about his visit.

'What is wrong?' she asked.

'Nothing, my love.'

'Why do you turn away from me like that?'

'No reason,' he said, making the effort to face her again and managing a token smile. 'Is that better?'

'Something has happened,' she decided. 'What is it?'

'I called to see you and taste the sweetness of your company. That is what happened. Have you so soon forgotten?' he teased her. 'Five minutes ago, your lover lay in your enchanting arms.'

'He did not,' she complained, sitting up on the bed and pulling a robe around her naked shoulders. 'That was not my lover I held in my arms. It was a complete stranger. His body was like yours but his mind was a hundred miles away. And he had no heart whatsoever.'

'My love!' he protested.

'What is going on?'

'I have told you – nothing!'

'Do not try to fob me off with lies.'

'They are not lies.'

'I know you too well, Nicholas,' she reminded him. 'Better than any woman knows you. Far better than that ice-cold wife of yours.'

'Leave her out of this,' he warned.

'I was hoping that you would do the same,' she said crisply. 'But you seemed to be looking over your shoulder all the time, as if she was in here watching us. Is that your fear? Discovery? Are you afraid that Catherine will find out about us?'

'Silence!'

Nicholas Picard spoke with more anger and authority than he intended, using the peremptory tone he normally reserved for erring servants or irritating Saxons. She was cowed by the force of his command and lowered her head in submission. Picard was at once irked and guilt-stricken, annoyed by her questions but sorry to have snapped at her with such open contempt. He wanted to make amends by putting a comforting arm round her but something held him back. She was deeply hurt and he was unable to soothe her in the way he had done so many times before. The rift between them widened still further.

While he finished dressing, Picard studied her carefully and tried to reconcile the competing emotions in his breast. Did he still love her? He was not sure. She was still very beautiful and he felt a faint stirring of lust as his eye roved over her sensuous body once more, tracing its graceful curves and caressing its silken skin. No woman had pleased him like this one though many had tried. With the signal exception of his wife. Mention of Catherine cut him to the quick. He rode into Exeter to escape her indifference, not to be forcibly reminded of it. Until today, his mistress had completely understood the terms of their relationship. Now she had broken the rules. She talked about his wife.

Head still bowed in contrition, she murmured her apology. 'I am sorry, Nicholas. Forgive my folly.'

'You were provoked,' he admitted.

'I was frightened.'

'By what?'

'Your behaviour towards me,' she whispered, looking up at him with a wan loveliness that almost made him reach out for her. 'I count the hours until your visits. They have been few and far between of late which means that each one is more important to me than the last. I expect too much, I know. It is a grievous fault. But I was so disappointed today. I am bound to wonder if it is because of some failure on my part.'

'No, my love.'

'Do I not attract you any more?'

'Of course you do.'

'Can I not delight you?'

'Blissfully.'

'Then why do I feel so inadequate?'

He fell back on the charm which had served him so well in the past. 'You are the most wonderful lover in Creation,' he said with a flattering smile, 'and any man would envy me for possessing you. The fault is not in you, my sweet. I was distracted, I confess it. I have much on my mind at the moment. When I come to you I can usually shake off my worries, but they were too tenacious this time. It is I who should be asking for your forgiveness.'

'There is nothing to forgive,' she said, judging it the right moment to rise from the bed and step into his embrace. 'I am honoured that you come to me. All that I strive to do is to make it a special occasion for you.'

'And you do,' he assured her. 'Every time.'

'Until today.'

'My mind is troubled.'

'About me?' she asked in mild alarm. 'Am I the cause of your anxiety?'

'No, no,' he said but his denial carried no conviction. 'It is another matter which weighs upon me. Royal commissioners are due in the city any day. Amongst other things, they will investigate my affairs and may even challenge my right to certain of my holdings.'

'How can that be?'

He shook his head dismissively. 'Let it pass.'

'I will let nothing pass when it preys upon you so,' she said, kissing him on the cheek. 'If you have worries, share them with me. Everything that touches upon your life is precious to me. Surely you realise that by now?' Another kiss, softer and more lingering. 'I love you.'

The warmth of her body was exciting him again. Holding her tight and stroking her hair, he tried to work out what to say and do. She was not making it easy for him. He had come to Exeter in order to tell her that they had reached the parting of the ways. On the ride to the city, he had rehearsed his speech a dozen times. He vowed to be firm but considerate, making a complete break but doing so as gently as possible. A letter would have been cruel. After all this time, he owed her an explanation to her face. It was the only fair way to end their romance.

But he reckoned without her charms. Instead of spurning them for ever, he yielded to them again in the misguided belief that he was doing her a favour rather than satisfying his own primal urges. In the intimacy of the bedchamber, he felt, he could break the news to her in a less painful way, but he had done the opposite. His desultory lovemaking was a declaration of intent. Sensitive to his moods and responsive to every motion of his body, she knew what he was there to tell her. Fear of losing him made her give herself more eagerly than ever before. She pleasured him until they neared exhaustion.

Yet it was not enough. She must be told. For a number of reasons, Picard simply had to walk away from the house in Exeter for good. Their relationship was too dangerous to continue. He searched for the words to bring it to a conclusion but it was she who spoke first.

'Do you remember how we first met?' she said, looking up at him.

'By accident.'

'Happy accident.'

'Yes,' he said gallantly.

'I was about to leave the cathedral as you were about to enter. You looked so proud, so upright, so handsome. I have never had such sinful thoughts on consecrated ground.'

'Nor I.'

'Every time I go to the cathedral, I think of you.'

'That is good.'

'It has such significance for me.'

'And for me, my love.'

'Is that the truth?'

'Yes.'

'Are you glad that we met that day?'

'Of course.'

'How glad?'

'What do you mean?' he said defensively. 'You've had ample proof of my gratitude. I have come to see you whenever I could and brought occasional gifts for you as a token of my devotion. What more do you want?'

'The fulfilment of your promise.'

'Promise?'

'You see,' she said, breaking away from him, 'you have forgotten already. A promise made in the throes of passion is worthless. Easily given but just as easily abandoned. I do not believe you ever meant to keep your word. Did you, Nicholas? It was a ruse.'

'No, it was not.'

'A cunning way to worm yourself into my affections.'

'That is not what I did.'

'Then why not honour your promise?'

He hesitated and bit his lip. 'It is difficult to explain,' he said at length. 'Circumstances have changed.'

14

'Yes,' she accused him. 'You no longer love me.'

'I do!'

'Then why do I not feel loved? Why do you take me to bed when you do not really want me any more? I am not blind. I am not stupid. Why did you come here today, Nicholas?'

It was the perfect moment to tell her the truth but it died on his lips. Picard lost his nerve. He persuaded himself that it would be too brutal to part in this way and tried instead to calm her, pulling her to him again and burying his intentions in a long kiss. She responded willingly, but there were tears in her eyes when she stepped back from the embrace.

'Ignore my complaint,' she said. 'I spoke too hastily.'

'Not at all.'

'You owe me nothing. I absolve you from your promise.'

'I will be indebted to you for ever,' he said with more sincerity than he actually felt. 'It is impossible for me to repay you in full for the love and the happiness you have given me here.'

'Do you really mean that, Nicholas?'

'Why else should I say it?'

'And will you come again?'

'Yes.'

'Soon?'

'Very soon,' he affirmed.

But they both knew that he was lying. Their final embrace was perfunctory. Her eyes were still moist as she walked across to the door with him. There was a valedictory kiss, then she ran her hands round his face and down his body as if trying to memorise every last contour. Picard smiled bravely but his stomach was churning. He was betraying a woman whom he

15

once loved and who clearly still doted on him. Other mistresses had been discarded with relative ease, but this one had a deeper hold on him. He was in pain.

'Farewell!' she said.

'*Adieu.*'

He let himself out and descended the steps at speed, leaving by the back door of the property and collecting his horse from the stables. A sense of relief welled up in him, but it was tempered by regret. He would miss her badly. The loss, however, was outweighed by several gains and he tried to concentrate on those. As he rode through the busy streets at a brisk trot, Picard fought off the impulse to look back. She belonged to his past now. Other priorities would take her place.

He had business in the city with the town reeve and headed for the man's house. When he was offered a cup of wine by his host, he downed it in one gulp. More wine was served. Memories of his earlier visit soon began to fade. It was some hours before he was ready to begin the homeward journey and it took him past her house once more. Picard did not even give it the tribute of a glance. Untroubled by sorrow or remorse, he went on through the North Gate and breathed the clean air of freedom.

Evening shadows were starting to dapple the grass and there was a hint of rain on the wind. He was in a buoyant mood. The town reeve had complied with his requests and been a generous host. Picard had achieved all that he had set out to do, ridding himself in the process of a lady who was starting to become an encumbrance. He was so pleased by his visit to Exeter that he did not even think about the bleak welcome which awaited him from his wife. For the first time in years, he rode home with a degree of real pleasure.

He was still congratulating himself on his success when he entered the wood. Shadows turned to patches of darkness. Leaves rustled. Branches creaked gently in the breeze. Picard felt no fear. Other Norman barons always travelled with an armed escort, but his was too short a journey to merit company and he had been very keen to arrive in Exeter alone so that he could call on his mistress unseen. A noise in the undergrowth made his horse shy, but Picard controlled the animal and nudged it forward with his knees. The wine was making him feel drowsy.

It was when he approached a beech tree that misfortune struck. A thick bough, festooned with leaves, was overhanging the road and swaying slowly to and fro. There was no suggestion of peril until he rode directly beneath the branch. A loud snarling noise took his gaze upward then, and he caught a glimpse of a wildcat, hurtling towards him with bared teeth and murderous claws. Landing on his face, the creature sank its angry fangs into his cheek and attempted to gouge out his eyes. The force and suddenness of the attack knocked him from the saddle. Nicholas Picard was soon squirming in the dust as he tried to fight for his life.

Seated at the table, she was working at her tapestry by the light of the candle when the servant burst in. She looked up in surprise, but her deft fingers continued to sew on. The servant was trembling under the weight of the tidings he bore.

'Yes?' she said with a note of disapproval. 'Why do you disturb me so?'

'The master's horse has just come back to the stables, my lady,' he gabbled. 'On its own. There is no sign of the lord Nicholas. We fear the worst.'

'Why?'

'Your husband is a fine horseman. He would not easily be thrown.'

'Is that what happened?'

'We do not know, my lady.'

'Then do not jump to foolish conclusions,' she said, putting her needle aside and rising from the chair. 'There are many reasons why the horse might have returned without its rider and they do not all have sinister import.'

'We are concerned for his safety, my lady.'

'My husband is well able to look after himself,' she said complacently. 'I have more faith in him than you. Well, do not stand there gibbering, man,' she added with a gesture. 'Send out a search party. They will need torches at this time of night. Bring me word of what they find.'

'Yes, my lady.'

'And whatever it is,' she emphasised, 'knock on the door before you enter. If you charged in on the lord Nicholas like that, you would have your ears soundly boxed. Now, be off with you!'

The servant nodded and raced off to obey her order. The lady Catherine resumed her seat and took up the tapestry once more. While the rest of the manor house was in a state of turmoil, she was curiously uninvolved. Her needle was continuing its delicate work when the search party thundered from the stable yard and set off down the track.

* * *

It did not take them long to find him. The wood was a favoured spot for robbers and more than one traveller had been ambushed there. Picard had ridden through it a hundred times alone without incident, but it still remained the most likely place for any assault. There were six of them, knights in Picard's retinue, holding flaming torches and scouring the land on either side of the winding road. When they reached the wood itself, they spread out to widen their search. It was over in minutes.

'Here!' cried a voice. 'Here! Ho! I have found him.'

The others quickly converged on the speaker and six torches illumined the sorry scene. Nicholas Picard lay on his back, his body twisted into an unnatural position, his hands covered in gore, his face lacerated beyond recognition and his eyes no more than two bleeding sockets. By the dancing light of the flames, they saw that his throat had been cut from ear to ear.

Chapter One

Brother Simon was in great distress. He led such a spiritual existence and devoted himself so wholeheartedly to the Rule of St Benedict that he hoped to shed the inconvenience of bodily functions and float in a more cerebral sphere. It was not to be. He was shackled to the physical world and could not escape its dictates. The wants of nature had to be satisfied on a daily basis. Within the enclave, where his routine was supremely ordered, it was a simple enough matter to slip off to the latrines at given moments. When he was dragged into lay company and forced to travel across three whole counties, it was a different matter. Embarrassment quickly turned into humiliation. When a female was present — a species which Brother Simon regarded with fear and distaste – his humiliation became a continuous ordeal.

Fortunately, the understanding Canon Hubert was there to help. 'Where are you going, Brother Simon?' he enquired.

'For a walk, Canon Hubert.'

'A *long* walk?'

'I fear that it may be so.'

'Do not rush back on our account.'

'Thank you.'

'I will keep the others distracted.'

'You are very kind, Canon Hubert.'

'Even a saint has to take an occasional walk,' said Hubert in his homiletic vein. 'It is the Lord's way of reminding us that we are human and, as such, subject to human restraints. Do not be ashamed, Brother Simon. You merely walk where apostles have walked before you.'

Simon's walk was more of a frightened scamper into the bushes than an apostolic saunter. Hubert smiled and looked across at the others. There were eighteen of them. They had broken their journey to rest and take refreshment. Ralph Delchard, the leading commissioner, had brought his wife, Golde, on the expedition. Gervase Bret, his young friend and colleague, lent the commission legal expertise and it had been given further authority by the addition of Hervey de Marigny, a Norman baron with extensive holdings in Derbyshire. Eight knights from Ralph's personal retinue acted as a bodyguard and the escort was swelled by the six soldiers whom de Marigny had called into service.

None of them had seen the emaciated monk disappearing and Hubert wanted to make sure that Simon's absence went unnoticed. The latter had already suffered some jovial mockery at the hands of the escort and Ralph took a pleasure in bringing a blush to the pale cheeks of their scribe. Canon Hubert saw it as his duty to protect his fellow Benedictine from as much sniggering as he could. He waddled across to the others and lowered his bulk gingerly down onto the trunk of a fallen tree.

'How much further, my lord?' he asked Ralph.

'Put that question to Hervey,' suggested the other. 'He has been in Devon before and I have not. If it were left to me, I would not be visiting this county now, but the king must be obeyed.'

'We have already spent far too long in the saddle.'

'There speaks a man of God,' observed Ralph with a chuckle. 'Had you been a soldier like Hervey and me, you would be used to spending a whole day astride your horse. The worst that you have to suffer is an ache in the knees from all that prayer. Hervey and I had blisters in much more testing placcs.'

'True,' agreed de Marigny. 'We spent so much time in the saddle that we felt like centaurs. But it was all to good effect in the end. With God's good grace and Duke William's inspired leadership, we conquered this beautiful island.'

'Parts of it,' corrected Gervase. 'Wales and Scotland are not subdued.'

'Not wholly,' conceded Ralph. 'But they will be.'

'I beg leave to doubt that.'

Ralph grinned. 'You lawyers must quibble over details.'

'To answer your question, Canon Hubert,' said de Marigny with a glance up at the sky, 'we should arrive in Exeter well before nightfall.'

'Thank you, my lord. What shall we expect to find?'

'A warm welcome for weary travellers.'

'I was really asking what sort of place Exeter was.'

Hervey de Marigny shrugged. 'Then the truthful answer is that I do not know. It is almost twenty years since I was last in Devon and places can change much in that length of time. I was part of the army which besieged Exeter for eighteen days before it finally capitulated. The Saxons of Devon were doughty fighters and clever politicians. The king had to make several concessions before the gates of the city were opened to him. That did not please the Conqueror.'

He went on to give them a concise account of the siege and its main consequences. They listened with interest. Hervey de Marigny was not a typical soldier. There was no arrogance in his manner and he did not lapse into the boastful reminiscences which so many Norman barons enjoyed. He talked quietly and honestly, acknowledging the qualities of worthy foes and showing a respect for their customs. A stout man of middle height, he was shrunken by age and his hair was peppered with silver, but he retained all his faculties and would patently be an asset when he sat alongside the others in the commission.

He was such an amiable man that he had befriended everyone in the short time they had been together. Golde had developed a real fondness for de Marigny. He was courteous, attentive and genuinely interested in her. Canon Hubert and Brother Simon were strongly opposed to the idea of including her in the party, but de Marigny believed that she added a sparkle to the company and helped to soften the unthinking coarseness of soldierly banter. Golde looked forward to spending more time with the new commissioner when they reached their destination.

'How long will we stay in Devon?' she asked.

'Too long!' grumbled Ralph.

'A week? Two? Three?'

'Who knows, Golde? The size of our task is daunting. Our predecessors identified over a hundred estates with contested ownership. It will take us an age to sit in judgement on all of them. We may well be here for a month. A year. A decade even.'

'Ralph exaggerates,' said Gervase. 'If we are expeditious, we should dispatch our business in a couple of weeks. And we must do so,' he stressed. 'An important matter awaits me in Winchester.'

Golde smiled. 'Alys is much more than an important matter,' she scolded playfully. 'You make your marriage to her sound like yet another assignment.'

'Why, so it is,' said Ralph jocularly. 'Gervase will approach his wedding day with the same zeal which he displays as a commissioner. Alys is one more case which comes before him for judgement. When they stand at the altar, he will deal justly with her.'

'He will love and honour her,' chided Golde.

'Indeed, I will,' said Gervase seriously. 'But first, I have to return to Winchester in time for the wedding. Alys will feel neither loved nor honoured if I am trapped in Devon and she is left standing alone at the altar.'

'We will do our utmost to oblige you, Gervase,' said de Marigny.

'Yes,' said Ralph, taking charge. 'The sooner we get to Exeter, the better. I have no wish to stay in this benighted county a moment longer than I have to. Mount up, friends! We will set off. Canon Hubert?'

'My lord?' said the other.

'Go and retrieve Brother Simon from the bushes. He has had time enough to lift his skirts and place a holy sacrament on the ground.'

Hubert bristled. 'That is blasphemous!'

'Then tell him to desist from blasphemy.'

'Your comment was profane, my lord.'

'And quite uncalled for,' said Golde softly.

'Then I withdraw the remark at once,' offered Ralph cheerily. 'Fetch our scribe from his prayers, Canon Hubert, and we will ride on.'

At that moment, Brother Simon emerged furtively from the bushes. Hoping to attract no attention, he was horrified to find every pair of eyes in the whole party turned upon him. Some faces were merely curious but others bore a knowing leer. Simon was mortified. His cheeks turned crimson, prickly heat broke out all over his body and he fled back into the bushes as if pursued by the hounds of hell.

Baldwin the Sheriff was in a testy mood. Instead of being able to enjoy a day's hunting, he was forced to remain in the castle to lead the inquiry into the murder of Nicholas Picard. He was curt with the first witness he examined.

'What is your name?' he asked.

'Walter Baderon, my lord sheriff.'

'You were on duty in the city last evening?'

'I was.'

'At the North Gate?'

'Yes, my lord sheriff.'

'Then you must have seen the murder victim leave.'

'I believe that I did.'

'Believe!' snapped Baldwin. 'You only believe? Give me no beliefs, sir. I want the facts of the case, quickly and honestly. Did you or did you not observe Nicholas Picard when he left Exeter by the North Gate?'

'Yes, my lord sheriff.'

'At what time was this?'

'I am not sure.'

'Why not?' roared the sheriff, slapping the table with an angry palm for emphasis. 'Were you drunk? Had you fallen asleep? Did you desert your post? What excuse do you have to offer for your incompetence?'

Walter Baderon took a deep breath before answering. He had been hauled out of bed to face the interrogation and was still not fully awake when he arrived. The sheriff's ire concentrated his mind. Baderon was a stocky man of middle height in the helm and hauberk of a Norman knight. Even though he was seated, the intimidating figure of the sheriff seemed to loom over the man who stood before him.

'Well?' prompted Baldwin.

'I was at my post, my lord sheriff, alert and watchful.'

'Then tell me when the lord Nicholas went past you.'

'Light was fading,' recalled the other. 'I waved to him as he rode out through the gate but he was too deep in thought to acknowledge my greeting. The bell for Compline soon began to ring.'

'Now we are getting somewhere!'

'But that is all I can tell you.'

'There is more to be squeezed out of you yet,' said Baldwin grimly. 'You say that he was deep in thought. Could you discern the nature of those thoughts from his expression? Did he seem worried? Afraid? Rueful? Was he in a hurry to quit the city?'

'No, my lord sheriff. He seemed pleased about something.'

'Pleased?'

'He was smiling to himself.'

Baldwin sat back and pondered, drumming his fingers on the table.

'Do you know why I sent for you?' he said at length.

'I think so, my lord sheriff.'

'If you watched Nicholas Picard ride out through the North Gate, you may well have been the last person who saw him alive. Apart from his killer, that is. Was anyone following him?'

'No, he was quite alone.'

'Did anyone leave the city soon afterwards?'

'Not by the North Gate.'

'Let us go through it once more,' said Baldwin, sensing that the man might be holding something back. 'When did you come on duty?'

'When the bell was ringing for Vespers.'

'Describe what happened between then and the time when Nicholas Picard rode past you with a smile on his face. And, Walter Baderon . . .'

'Yes, my lord sheriff?'

'Tell me the truth.'

The warning was accompanied by a long, searching stare. Baderon remained calm. He told the sheriff most of what he could remember and embellished the bare facts with a few significant details. Baldwin listened intently and frequently interrupted. When the interrogation was over, he dismissed his

28

witness with a brief nod, then reviewed the evidence he had gathered. He was not left alone for long. There was a tap on the door and his steward entered.

'My apologies for disturbing you, my lord sheriff,' he said.

'What is it, Joscelin?'

'The royal commissioners.'

'They have arrived already?'

'No, my lord sheriff, but they may be here at any moment. Their apartments are ready and the town reeve is standing by to await their orders. I wondered if there had been any change of plan.'

'Change of plan?'

'Yes,' said Joscelin smoothly. 'You bade me organise a feast here at the castle to welcome them to Exeter. I have set everything in motion. But this murder investigation now claims your attention. Do you wish me to postpone the banquet? Or shall we hold it and apologise to them for your absence?'

'Neither. I will be at the head of my table to welcome my guests.'

'Yes, my lord sheriff.'

'This murder is an unfortunate business but it should not delay me long. I have every confidence that the killer can be tracked down with due celerity. With luck,' he continued, 'I may even have the villain behind bars before Ralph Delchard and his colleagues reach Exeter. I want them to see what a law-abiding city we have here. That is why the stain of murder must be removed as swiftly as possible. Prepare the feast!'

'Everything is in hand, my lord sheriff.'

Joscelin the Steward gave a faint bow and withdrew.

* * *

They made good time and came within first sight of the city sooner than they expected. Ralph Delchard and Hervey de Marigny rode at the head of the cavalcade, exchanging memories of battles in which they had fought and mutual friends whom they had lost in combat. Canon Hubert and the suffering Brother Simon were at the rear of the column as it wended its way along, grateful that the soldiers in front of them had at last tired of making ribald comments about Simon's disappearance into the bushes. Golde rode behind her husband and alongside Gervase Bret. She was keen to discuss his forthcoming wedding.

'It has been a long betrothal,' she noted.

'Far too long!' he sighed. 'Had it been my decision, we should have been married six months or more ago.'

'Did Alys resist that suggestion?'

'She did not but her parents did. They felt that we needed more time to get to know each other properly.'

'That is sound advice,' said Golde. 'Not that I heeded it myself. Ralph and I were too impatient to wait until we knew each other better. We married as soon as we could, but then we had no parents to hold us in check. Your case is different, Gervase. You will not be as reckless as we were.'

'More's the pity!' he said. 'If recklessness leads to the kind of marriage that you and Ralph enjoy, then I wish that I had taken Alys to the altar within a week of meeting her.'

'Ralph and I were fortunate.'

'And well-suited. Like Alys and me.'

'Not exactly, Gervase,' she said with a wistful smile. 'We had both been married before, remember. We have a past. You and Alys still have the freshness of youth and the joy of innocence.'

He raised an ironic eyebrow. 'That is not what I would call it.'

They shared a laugh. Golde was strongly drawn to Gervase. Conversations with him were not only a pleasure, they were usually conducted in her native tongue. Born of a Saxon mother and a Breton father, Gervase was able to speak both languages fluently and he had been a patient tutor to Golde as she tried to master the Norman French spoken by her husband.

'What do you hope from your marriage?' she wondered.

'What everyone hopes for, Golde – love, happiness and children.'

'Ralph and I have found two of those. The third, alas, eludes us. But that is God's will and we accept it. Besides,' she added, glancing at her husband, 'Ralph is like a big child at times so I am able to mother him.'

'I will not tell him that you said that.'

'He would not be offended if you did. Do you miss Alys?'

'Painfully.'

'It will make your reunion all the sweeter.'

'I hope so,' said Gervase. 'But I would sooner fret away the time before our wedding in Winchester than in Devon. I have a strange feeling that I will somehow be detained here against my will. Alys would be livid.'

'At first, perhaps,' said Golde. 'Any bride would chafe in such trying circumstances. But I am sure that Alys would understand and make due allowance. She knows the importance of your work and appreciates the honour which is bestowed upon you by the king.'

'I would prefer a little less honour and a little more time in Winchester,' said Gervase. 'No sooner do I return to the city than we are dispatched on a new assignment.'

'That is a sign of the king's faith in you.'

'My absences put a strain on our betrothal.'

'That strain will soon end, Gervase,' she assured him. 'In a month's time, you and Alys will be living in wedded bliss with no thought of the frustrations which you endured beforehand.'

'That is my dearest wish.'

'There is only one decision you will have to make.'

'What is that?'

'The same decision which confronted Ralph and me. If the call comes once more from the king – as assuredly it will – do you leave your wife at home or take her with you? I was only too eager to come with Ralph. But what of Alys?' she probed. 'Would she put up with a long ride to Exeter in order to be close to her husband?'

'Naturally!'

'Have you discussed it with her?'

'Not yet, Golde, but I know what her choice would be.' Gervase fell silent, doubting the confidence in his own reply. A new anxiety assailed him. What if Alys refused to travel with him and the others to distant shires of the realm? She was not as robust a woman as Golde nor as seasoned a rider. It would be galling if he finally married her, only to continue their regular periods of separation. It all served to increase his anxiety to return to Winchester as soon as possible.

Ralph and his companion were more concerned with the work which awaited them in Exeter than a marriage which lay beyond it. Hervey de Marigny was the oldest of the commissioners but the least experienced.

'You will have to guide me, Ralph,' he said.

'There will be little need of that.'

'You and the others are veterans. I am a novice. What must I do?'

'Look and listen,' advised Ralph. 'You will soon pick up the rudiments of our trade. We are here to sit in judgement and to collect taxes. That means we shall be very unpopular.'

'I am used to that. It is in the nature of conquest. After twenty years, the Saxons still do not accept us.'

'It is not the Saxon population who cause the problems,' warned Ralph with a faint grimace. 'It is our fellow Normans. Devon has more than its share of robber barons, Hervey. We must call them to account.'

'A final reckoning?'

'Indeed. A Domesday Book.'

They skirted a copse and crested a rise to be given their best and most striking view of their destination. Exeter was a handsome, prosperous, compact city, encircled by a high wall above which the tower of its cathedral, the massive fortifications of its castle and the roofs of its taller buildings rose with evident pride. Situated on the River Exe, it occupied a strategic position and was easily defended from attack. Seeing it so close once more reminded de Marigny of his earlier visit.

'There is something I did not mention,' he said, keeping his voice low so that nobody but Ralph could hear him. 'An aspect of the siege too indelicate to discuss in front of Golde and Canon Hubert.'

'Go on,' urged Ralph.

'The reason they held out for so long was that they were

emboldened by the presence of Gytha, mother of their late king, Harold.'

'*Earl* Harold. He was no king but a vile usurper.'

'The Saxons recognised him as their monarch and his mother shared in the lustre of his name. They flocked to her banner accordingly.'

'A forlorn enterprise.'

'Give them their due, Ralph,' said the other. 'They held us at bay for eighteen days and might have done so even longer had we not come to composition. But what I felt too improper to recall earlier was this. One of those hairy Saxons was bolder than the rest.'

'What did he do?'

'Mounted the ramparts to show his defiance to our army.'

'In what way?'

'He lowered his breeches, bared his buttocks and let out such a fart of contempt that it was heard a mile away.'

Ralph was torn between anger at the insult and amusement at the sheer bravado of the man. He found it difficult not to laugh.

'Was the rogue caught and punished?'

'I do not know, Ralph.'

'Farting at the king? He should have been soundly whipped for his effrontery.' He began to shake with mirth. 'Then given a second beating for his backsidery. It was a savage weapon to use against us.'

The two of them laughed all the way to Exeter.

Joscelin the Steward prided himself on his efficiency. Tall and slim, he cut an elegant figure as he glided around the castle to check on the preparations for the guests. He was relatively young to hold such a position – still in his late twenties – but he discharged his varied duties with a quiet industry that left no room for complaint. Baldwin de Moeles, sheriff of Devon, came to rely on his steward more and more, delegating tasks to him which would normally have been outside his remit. Joscelin coped admirably with all that was thrown at him. No matter how onerous the work that was piled upon him, he managed to retain his poise and good humour.

He was in the kitchen when the guests arrived. As soon as he caught a glimpse of them through the window, he abandoned his inspection and headed for the courtyard. Ralph and the others had dismounted. Relieved to be out of the saddle at last, they were stretching their legs and taking stock of their surroundings. Joscelin sailed across to them, surveying the company as he did so and forming a favourable impression of them. There was a sense of order and discipline about them which was apparent even at a cursory glance.

'Welcome to Exeter, my lord!' he said, identifying Ralph Delchard as the obvious leader and heading for him. 'I am Joscelin the Steward and I will see to all your needs while you are here in the city.'

'Thank you,' said Ralph. He introduced his wife, Gervase Bret and Hervey de Marigny before indicating the two monks. 'Canon Hubert and Brother Simon will sit with us on the commission but they will not lay their heads beneath the same roof. They will be staying as guests of Bishop Osbern and would appreciate a guide to take them to their host.'

Joscelin flicked his fingers and a servant trotted across to him to receive his instructions. After bidding farewell, Hubert and Simon rode out of the castle on the heels of the servant. Another gesture from the steward brought a soldier to his side. The man was told to take charge of the escort, to see to the stabling of their horses and to show them to their lodging. In less than a minute, Joscelin had cleared the courtyard of all but Golde and the three commissioners. Ralph was struck by his easy authority and imperturbable manner.

'I hope that we meet with the same willing co-operation from everyone in this county,' he said with a grin.

'Do not count on that, my lord,' said Joscelin tactfully. 'Commissioners from the king mean taxes on property. You may encounter resistance.'

'That is nothing new, my friend. We are inured to it.'

'What manner of man is the town reeve?' asked de Marigny.

'Saewin?' said the steward. 'He is a good man and a diligent reeve. Saewin also has another distinction. He is one of the few Saxons in whom you can place absolute trust.'

'Take care what you say,' warned Ralph with a jovial nudge. 'My wife is the daughter of a Saxon thegn and Gervase here, too, has Saxon blood in his veins. They will take you to task for any aspersions you may cast upon their forebears.'

'I meant no disrespect,' said the other calmly, 'but you must remember our history. Exeter was the site of a major rebellion soon after we took possession of this island.'

'I know it well,' said de Marigny with a nostalgic grin. 'I was part of the army which laid siege to this city. It took us almost three weeks before we persuaded Exeter to submit.'

'Yes, my lord,' continued Joscelin, 'but that was not the end of the matter. When you departed with the rest of the army, four more attempts were made to stir up a revolt and expel us. It has made the lord sheriff view the Saxon population with some degree of suspicion. However,' he said, waving an arm towards the inner bailey, 'you are completely secure here and I will be happy to escort you to your apartments. A feast has been prepared in your honour and the lord sheriff will be there to give you a more formal welcome to the city.'

'Thank you,' said Ralph.

'He had intended to be here when you arrived, but the investigation took him out of the castle this afternoon.'

'Investigation?'

'Yes, my lord. A man was brutally murdered last night.'

Golde was shocked, Gervase curious and Ralph alerted, but it was Hervey de Marigny who pressed for the salient details.

'Has the killer been apprehended yet?' he said.

'No, my lord,' replied the steward.

'Is his name known?'

'The lord sheriff is at present seeking to identify him.'

'Who was the victim? Norman or Saxon?'

'Norman, my lord. And well respected in the county. His name was Nicholas Picard.'

'Picard?' echoed Gervase with slight alarm. 'But he is involved in one of the major land disputes we have come to settle. Only last night, I was studying the documents relating to his case. Nicholas Picard was to have been called before us on several counts.'

'That will no longer be possible,' said the steward discreetly. 'But you will glean fuller details from the lord sheriff over the banquet. He knows far more than I may tell you. Come,' he added, 'you must be tired after your journey and in need of rest. Please follow me.'

'Lead on,' said Ralph.

The four of them were led across the courtyard, noting how neat and tidy it was kept and how well-drilled the guards appeared to be. Exeter Castle felt completely safe, yet its garrison seemed to be poised to fight off an imminent assault. The visitors suddenly became aware of how isolated the city was and how they were part of a small Norman minority in a city that was still essentially Saxon in tone and atmosphere.

Golde felt once more the pull of conflicting loyalties, her instinctive sympathy for the indigenous population offset against the vow of obedience she had given to her husband and the ties of love which bound the two of them so indissolubly together. It put her in an anomalous position and she wondered whether it had been altogether wise to accompany Ralph on this particular assignment. Holding her arm as they walked towards the inner bailey, he sensed her misgivings.

'What is the matter, my love?'

'It is nothing.'

'Something is troubling you.'

'I am fatigued.'

'Are you not glad that we have arrived?'

'Yes,' she said. 'Glad but . . . unsettled.'

'You cannot be both, Golde.'

'Yet I am.'

'That does not make sense,' he argued. 'Do you still feel guilty about being the wife of a Norman? Is that it?' He gave a chuckle. 'I thought you had learnt to live with that disability.'

He squeezed her arm and gave her an affectionate kiss on the cheek. Golde relaxed. Her doubts vanished and she thought only of the more pleasant aspects of their stay in Devon, reminding herself that she was merely a passenger and had no official function. It was not her place to introduce any personal qualms. Golde was there to support her husband and to share the few private moments they would contrive together.

The keep was a tall, square, solid structure, perched on the high mound which was a characteristic feature of a Norman castle. They went up the steps which had been cut into the grass and entered through the door. A staircase faced them but they were not allowed to ascend it. Blocking their way and beaming inanely at them was a short, round individual with an unusually large head from which hair sprouted wildly like weeds in a neglected garden. He was dressed in the garb of a Saxon peasant and wore a full beard. In his hand he bore a stick with an inflated pig's bladder at the end of it.

When the group appeared, he let out a cackle of joy and brought them to a halt with a wave of his stick. Without warning, he then pretended to fall down the steps before he pulled himself to his feet, went through the door and somersaulted down the mound. They watched in amazement.

'Who, in God's name, was that?' spluttered Ralph.

'Berold,' explained the steward.

'Berold? Is he a madman?'

'Of a sort, my lord. He is a jester.'

Chapter Two

Canon Hubert and Brother Simon did not feel entirely safe until they entered the cathedral precincts and saw black Benedictine cowls moving about with Christian assurance. Travel was a source of great discomfort to Hubert, whose portly frame was always balanced precariously on his long-suffering donkey, and it was a continuous agony for Simon, who had committed himself to the monastic life partly in the hope that he would escape lay company and the affairs of the workaday world in perpetuity. Thrust into royal service, the two of them were caught between a sense of duty and a profound discomfort. While Hubert veered towards self-importance and regarded each new assignment as a recognition of his considerable abilities as a jurist, his companion viewed their work as a kind of martyrdom and prayed daily for release.

The cathedral church of St Peter soared above them like a huge protective hand and their spirits were immediately lifted. It was a Saxon foundation, distinguished more by its sheer size than by any architectural merit, but they surveyed it with a mixture of relief and awe. A certain amount of rebuilding had taken place in recent years, but there had been no major additions to the basic structure and its essential simplicity set it apart from the elaborations of Canterbury Cathedral and York Minster, both of which the newcomers had visited in the course of their duties.

They felt at home. As they made their way to the cloister, a figure emerged through the stone arch and came towards them with measured tread. Dean Jerome was a tall, spare man in his forties with a long, rather lugubrious face and a tonsure so perfectly suited to the shape of his skull that he seemed to have been born with it. He introduced himself, bade them welcome and showed them where they could stable their mounts. His voice was deep and reassuring.

'We have been looking forward to your arrival,' he said.

'Brother Simon and I are grateful to be here,' said Hubert. 'The journey was interminable and the conversation not always fit for monastic ears. Now that we have found you, we feel cleansed.'

'That is as it should be, Canon Hubert.'

'I bear a letter of greeting to Bishop Osbern from our own dear Bishop Walkelin of Salisbury,' said the other, tapping the leather satchel slung from his shoulder. 'I hope to be able to deliver it in person.'

'And so you shall,' said Jerome. 'We had notice of your coming in a letter from the king himself, and Bishop Osbern left instructions that you were to be admitted to him as soon as you reached us. Let me first show you to your lodgings then I will take you both to meet him.'

Hubert was delighted at their reception. No less a person than the dean himself had taken the trouble to greet them and the bishop was treating them like visiting dignitaries. Simon was thrilled to be included in the audience. The spectral monk was accustomed to fade into anonymity whenever they encountered a prelate, leaving Hubert to speak for both of them. To be summoned to the presence of so illustrious a bishop as Osbern of Exeter was an honour to be savoured.

When they had deposited their satchels at their lodgings, they were conducted across the cloister to the bishop's quarters. Dean Jerome tapped on a door and waited for the invitation to enter. As he went into the room, he beckoned the others after him.

'Our guests are here, Your Grace,' he said deferentially, indicating each in turn. 'This is Canon Hubert and this, Brother Simon.'

'A hearty welcome to you both!' said the bishop. 'I thank God for your safe arrival in Exeter. We are pleased to have you as our guests.'

'Thank you, Your Grace,' said Hubert with an obsequious smile.

'Yes,' added Simon nervously. 'Thank you.'

'I trust that your journey was without incident?' said Osbern.

'Happily, yes,' replied Hubert.

Unhappily, no, thought Simon, recalling his ordeal amid the bushes.

'It is a tiresome ride,' said the bishop, 'and must have left you both fatigued. Do sit down and rest your aching bones.'

The visitors lowered themselves onto an oak bench along one wall and beneath a crucifix. Bishop Osbern was opposite them, seated at a table where he had been studying the Scriptures in preparation for a sermon he was due to deliver. He was an elderly man of medium height but he exuded such a sense of religiosity that he appeared to fill the whole room. His round face had a beatific smile which robbed him of a decade or more. A network of blue veins showed through the luminous skin of his high forehead. But it was the kindness and compassion in his blue eyes which most impressed the travellers. They knew that they were in the presence of a truly holy man.

Hubert was pleased to have the opportunity of meeting someone who had been chaplain both to Edward the Confessor and to King William yet bore such a daunting pedigree so lightly. For his part, Simon was so overwhelmed by his proximity to a legendary churchman that he did not hear Dean Jerome leave the room and close the door behind him.

'This is your first visit to Exeter?' enquired Osbern.

'Yes, Your Grace,' said Hubert, answering for both of them.

'It is a pleasant town though not without its faults. My predecessor, Bishop Leofric, came here almost forty years ago to find the minster in a sorry condition. All that remained of a monastic community was a set of Mass vestments and a few sacred books. Leofric had to start afresh, renovating a dilapidated building and creating an establishment of canons and vicars.' There was little enough money to spare on such worthy projects,' said Osbern with a sigh, 'but Leofric put what there was to the best possible use. He is buried in the crypt and I offer up a prayer of thanks for his episcopate whenever I visit his tomb.' A smile played on his lips. 'But there was one idiosyncrasy.'

'What was that, Your Grace?' said Hubert.

'When Bishop Leofric installed canons, he made them subject to the Rule of St Chrodegang.'

Hubert frowned. 'A curious decision, indeed.'

'You are familiar with the Rule?'

'No, Your Grace,' muttered Simon.

'Yes,' said Hubert, grateful for the chance to display his intellectual credentials. 'Chrodegang was bishop of Metz over three centuries ago. He had a distinguished political career, but his ecclesiastical achievements were even more impressive. He founded the abbey of Gorze and devised the Rule by which his name is remembered.'

'That is true,' said Osbern. 'The canons of his cathedral lived a community life devoted to the public prayer of the Church but in close association with diocesan officers. They were also – and this is what makes the Rule so odd in my view – authorised to own property individually. I incline strongly to the more stringent dictates of Benedict.'

'So do we, Your Grace,' said Hubert.

'A vow of poverty leaves no place for ownership of property.'

'We are glad that you have righted your predecessor's error.'

'It was not an error, Canon Hubert,' said the other tolerantly, 'but merely a difference of emphasis. God may be worshipped in many ways, all of them equally valid. I have knelt in prayer beside a Saxon and a Norman king of England. Their language, upbringing and attitudes separated them but their devotions united them as one.'

'Yes, Your Grace. But I forget myself,' said Hubert, realising that he was still holding something in his hand. 'Bishop Walkelin sends his warmest greetings and bids me deliver this to you.' He crossed to the table to place the letter upon it. 'He has fond memories of your last meeting.'

'I share those memories,' said Osbern. 'When you leave Exeter, you will bear my reply to the good bishop of Salisbury. But tell me,' he added as Hubert resumed his seat, 'are you aware of the outrage which occurred on the eve of your arrival?'

'Outrage?' repeated Simon. 'No, Your Grace.'

'A foul murder was committed not far from the city.'

'This is grim news,' said Hubert.

'I fear that it may complicate your own work here, Canon Hubert,' said the bishop with a shrug of resignation. 'The unfortunate victim was Nicholas Picard. I believe that he was involved in a property dispute when the first commissioners came to Devon so I suspect that his name is not unknown to you.'

'Indeed, it is not,' confirmed Hubert. 'His death makes a difficult case even more intractable. What was the motive for the murder?'

'That has not yet been established.'

'It may have some bearing on our investigation.'

'In what way?'

'The lord Nicholas had substantial holdings, Your Grace, many of which are contested. Now that he is no longer here to defend his title to the property, it may go elsewhere. Someone will gain handsomely by his death.' His face puckered with concern. 'The timing of his murder can surely be no coincidence. Hearing of our visit, someone may have been prompted to kill him. It is almost as if we instigated this crime.'

'Dear God!' cried Simon, studying his palms in horror. 'What a disturbing thought that is! We have blood on our hands.'

Ralph Delchard liked the town reeve from the moment he made his acquaintance. Saewin was polite without being servile and confident without being brash. The reeve would be in a crucial position during their stay, making the shire hall ready for their use and summoning all the witnesses whom they needed to examine. Ralph was pleased that he called at the castle to pay his respects and to collect his instructions. It showed diligence. Saewin was a big, broad-shouldered man with rugged features half hidden behind a beard. He wore the cap, tunic and cross-gartered trousers favoured by the Saxons but spoke French fluently and even with a certain pride.

Their conversation took place outside the hall and they had to raise their voices above the clatter from within. Preparations for the banquet were becoming increasingly noisy.

'Is there anything else, my lord?' said the reeve.

'No,' said Ralph. 'Obey the orders I have given you.'

Saewin nodded. 'I will detain you from the festivities no longer.'

'It sounds more like a siege than a banquet. What are they doing in there?' Ralph asked as a grating sound jarred on his ears. 'Using a battering ram on the venison? Or are they knocking down a wall in order to bring in a fatted calf or two?'

Saewin smiled and made to withdraw, but the other plucked at his sleeve. 'One moment, my friend. I wanted to ask you about this foul murder that has been committed.'

'A sad business, my lord.'

'And a highly inconvenient one. The lord Nicholas was to have been called before us to contest the ownership of several manors.'

'I know,' said Saewin. 'It was at the forefront of his mind.'

'What makes you say that?'

'He mentioned it to me as he left my house.'

'When was this?'

'Yesterday evening, my lord.'

Ralph's interest quickened. 'You saw Nicholas Picard yesterday?'

'Yes, he came to discuss some business with me.'

'Not connected with the property under dispute, I hope.'

'No, no,' said the reeve. 'It was a separate matter, a small favour which I was able to grant. But he was looking forward to your visit so that he could attest his right to the land in question and put an end to the hostility which it has provoked.'

'Hostility?'

'There are other claimants, I understand.'

'Two at least.'

'I think you may find that there is another, my lord.'

'You seem remarkably well informed.'

'I only repeat what the lord Nicholas told me,' said Saewin. 'He was very bitter about it. This new claimant made no appearance before the first commissioners who visited the county. He only announced his intention to enter the fray a few days ago.'

'Then you know more than we ourselves. Who is the fellow?'

'The abbot of Tavistock.'

'Saints preserve us!' moaned Ralph. 'Do I have to endure another pompous prelate? I will have to set Hubert on to him.'

'Hubert, my lord?'

'Ignore what I said. I was talking to myself.'

'I see.'

'Let us come back to the lord Nicholas. At what time did he leave you?'

'Not long before Compline, my lord,' said the other. 'He told me that he would ride straight home to his manor house. Unfortunately, he had to go through a wood on the way. That is where they attacked him.'

'They?'

'His killers.'

'There was more than one of them?'

'That would be my guess,' ventured Saewin. 'The lord Nicholas was a strong man, an experienced soldier with many campaigns behind him. I do not think that a solitary attacker could have easily overpowered him.'

'Have you put that argument to Baldwin the Sheriff?'

'Yes, my lord.'

'What was his reply?'

'That he would reserve his judgement until he had more evidence.'

'A sensible course of action,' said Ralph, stroking his chin thoughtfully. 'So you were the last person to see the lord Nicholas in Exeter?'

'No, my lord.'

'Then who was?'

'The guards at the North Gate.'

'The exit by which he left the city? Who was the captain of the guard?'

'A certain Walter Baderon.'

'What does he remember?'

'You will have to ask him that yourself, my lord. I know only his name and that of his master.'

'His master?'

'Yes,' said the reeve. 'The guard is provided by a succession of barons and other notables. The knights who were on duty last evening came from some distance away to stand vigil at the city gates.'

'Whom do they serve?' asked Ralph.

'The abbot of Tavistock.'

Overshadowed by an unsolved murder, the banquet that night was a strangely muted affair. The food was rich, the wine plentiful and the entertainment lively but a pall still hung over the event. It was not a large gathering. Some twenty or more guests had come to the castle to join the sheriff in welcoming the visitors. At the head of the table, Ralph and Golde sat either side of their host and his wife, Albreda, a gaunt beauty who did little beyond smiling her approval at everything her husband said. Even the smooth tongue of Hervey de Marigny was unable to entice more than a few words from the mouth of their hostess. Gervase Bret was also present and Canon Hubert had been lured from the cathedral by the promise of a feast, but Brother Simon felt unequal to the challenge of such a gathering and spent the time instead in restorative meditation.

Gervase found himself sitting next to de Marigny. The latter was an agreeable companion and diverted his young colleague with endless stories of his military career.

'Have you seen much of the city?' said Gervase.

'I have not yet had time to do so. A walk along the battlements is all I have been able to manage, though that taught me much and revived many memories. But,' said de Marigny, 'I have already seen what I hoped to find in Exeter.'

'What is that?'

'One of our tunnels, Gervase.'

'Tunnels?'

'Yes,' said the other with enthusiasm. 'I noticed it when we entered through the East Gate. When our siege failed to bring the city to its knees, the king ordered tunnels to be built under the walls. The intention was to weaken the foundations and – with the aid of a fire in the tunnel – to bring about a collapse of the stonework. In the event, they were not needed. Exeter surrendered and work on the tunnels was abandoned. A sad moment for those who had laboured so hard to dig it,' he observed. 'They spilled blood and poured sweat while clawing their way through the earth.'

'Was the tunnel you saw not filled in?'

'Apparently not, Gervase. It did not undermine the walls so it is not a potential danger. Besides, there has been enough damage and decay within the city to repair. That is where all the efforts have been directed. That hole in the ground is exactly where it was almost twenty years ago.'

'A bleak memento for Exonians.'

'Perhaps that is why they have retained it,' suggested de Marigny, sipping his wine. 'To remind themselves of the fateful day when they finally accepted Norman overlordship. My lord sheriff would be able to tell us,' he said, nodding towards the head of the table, 'but I fear that he is not in the mood for conversation tonight.'

Gervase looked across at their host. Baldwin de Moeles, sheriff of Devon and castellan of the fortress in Exeter, was clearly not enjoying the occasion. Chewing his meat disconsolately, he was gazing into space with an expression of severe disappointment. Ralph Delchard was trying to talk to him, but his words were going unheard. Angered by his inability to bring the murder investigation to a swift conclusion, Baldwin was caught up in bitter self-recrimination. It took a nudge from his wife to bring him out of his fierce reverie.

'What is it?' he said, rounding on her.

'Our guests are being ignored,' she whispered.

'Guests?' He made an effort to pull himself together. 'Why, so they are,' he said with forced joviality. 'What kind of host forgets such important visitors? More wine, ho! Let it flow more freely.'

'It has flowed freely enough, my lord sheriff,' said Ralph with a grin. 'We have had both wine and ale in abundance.'

Baldwin was startled. 'Ale? Someone is drinking ale at my table?'

'I am, my lord sheriff,' admitted Golde. 'From choice.'

'You choose English ale over French wine? That is perverse.'

'Not if you appreciate the quality of the ale.'

'Golde is an expert on the subject,' boasted Ralph. 'I have tried to coax her into drinking wine but her fidelity to ale is

51

impossible to breach. When we first met, she was in the trade. You will find it hard to believe, but this beautiful creature beside me was once the finest brewer in the city of Hereford.'

Baldwin was amused enough to smile but his wife curled her lip in distaste. Albreda's only trade consisted of being wife to the sheriff. The smells and toil involved in brewing would be anathema to her. Golde was upset by her reaction and by the supercilious lift of her chin which followed. She sensed that Albreda would not be the most affable hostess during their stay at the castle.

'It is a fine banquet!' continued Ralph. 'Thank you, my lord sheriff.'

Baldwin scowled. 'It would be a more lively occasion if the spectre of Nicholas Picard was not sitting at the table with us. I have spent a whole day on the trail of his killer without picking up a whiff of his scent.'

'In what state was the body found?'

'Too gruesome to discuss here, my lord.'

'Where does the corpse lie?'

'In the mortuary.'

'Here at the castle?'

'Yes.'

'May I see it?'

'Not if you wish to keep any food in your stomach,' said Baldwin with a grimace. 'I have looked on death a hundred times but never seen anything quite as hideous as this. Whoever murdered Nicholas Picard did so out of a hatred too deep to comprehend.'

'I would still like to view the body, my lord sheriff.'

'This murder need not concern you.'

'But it does,' argued Ralph. 'We have already made the acquaintance of the lord Nicholas in the returns for this county. It is a name which recurs, often. He was due to appear before us. We are anxious to know why he was prevented from doing so – and by whom.'

'So am I,' grunted the other.

'Where was the body found?'

'In a wood not far from the city.'

'Could someone take me to the place?'

'I am the sheriff, my lord,' said Baldwin with a proprietorial glint in his eye. 'Let me deal with this crime. I will soon track down the villain and I will brook no interference. Look to your own affairs.'

'I will,' said Ralph, backing off at once. 'I sought to help rather than to interfere. But you are right, my lord sheriff. My nose has no place in this inquiry. I will sniff elsewhere.'

'Please do.' He turned to Golde and forced another smile. 'You hail from Hereford, I hear?'

'That is so, my lord sheriff,' she said.

'Then you must meet Bishop Osbern.'

'It would be an honour to do so.'

'It is, it is, I assure you,' said Canon Hubert, seizing a chance to get into the conversation. 'We spent an hour with the bishop ourselves. It is a privilege to be in the company of such an exalted being.'

'His brother, William FitzOsbern, was earl of Hereford,' said Baldwin.

Golde smiled. 'I remember him well as a just and upright man.'

'Osbern has spoken of happy visits to the city. He will be interested to hear that we have a guest from Hereford.'

'From Hereford by way of Hampshire,' Ralph corrected him. 'I tempted her away from her native city to live with me. Not that we have spent much time on my estate. But Golde and I are together and that is the main thing.'

She squeezed his hand under the table and caught another unfriendly glance from Albreda. It was proving to be an uncomfortable feast. Their host was distracted and his wife either meek or disdainful. Golde began to question her wisdom in travelling with the commissioners. Exeter Castle looked to be a cold and friendless establishment.

Joscelin the Steward tried to introduce some vitality into the scene. Watching from the edge of the hall, he saw with dismay the dull faces and lacklustre gestures of the guests. The long silences which fell on them were all too eloquent. Since the tumblers, the musicians and the conjurer had failed to hold the interest of the assembly, Joscelin turned to a novel form of entertainment. Clapping his hands to attract the attention of the whole room, he gave a signal to the musicians who began to play their instruments with more gusto than they had hitherto shown. A door opened and four dancers came whirling into view, spinning nimbly on their toes and drawing a momentary applause for their colourful attire and spirited performance.

Three of the dancers were men, but it was the sole woman who caught the eye. Short and plump, she was yet remarkably lithe and led her partners in a merry jig up and down the hall. She had long fair hair that hung down her back and a thick veil which hid the lower half of her face. While the three male dancers had great vigour, she had both grace and effervescence, eluding them as they tried in turn to grab at her and jumping up onto the table at one point before stealing a cup of wine and leaping high into the air.

The listless atmosphere was completely dispelled. Within a short space of time, the four dancers had reminded the guests that they were there to enjoy themselves and even enticed the sheriff into pounding on the table in appreciation. When the music reached its height, the three men converged on the woman and formed such a close ring around her that she disappeared from sight. As the applause rang out, the men sprang suddenly apart, but there was no sign of the woman. Her wig, dress and veil had been shed in an instant to reveal a weird creature with a bulbous head, a bushy beard and a mischievous grin.

Cries of astonishment went up as the guests realised how cunningly they had been fooled. The woman who led the dancing with such verve and femininity was none other than Berold the Jester. He dropped a curtsey to his audience then held his arms wide in acknowledgement of the gale of laughter which ensued. Even his master was sharing in the general hilarity. Berold had banished all thought of Nicholas Picard.

Golde stood open-mouthed in amazement and clapped her hands.

'Is he really a man?' she asked.

'No,' said Ralph. 'He is a magician.'

Catherine sat in her accustomed position with the tapestry across her knees. What had once been an art in which she excelled had now become a chore which did not bring any pleasure. Her needle was plied without any sense of purpose and her mind was drifting. It was almost twenty-four hours since they brought news of her husband's death on the road home from Exeter and she was only just beginning to feel the full impact. Unable to grieve for a man she never truly loved, she instead mourned the wasted years she had spent as the wife of Nicholas Picard.

As she worked on, she grew careless and the needle jabbed her thumb. She sat up with a sharp intake of breath and sucked the blood which oozed from the tiny wound. Her companion, an old servant who had been with her since she first married, looked up from her seat in alarm.

'Are you hurt, my lady?'

'No,' said Catherine. 'It was only a prick.'

'You are too tired to work at that tapestry.'

'I must have something to do.'

'Would you like me to sew it for you, my lady?'

'No,' said her mistress firmly. 'It is mine and only mine. Nobody else must ever touch it. Do you understand?'

'Yes, my lady.'

'What are you doing here?'

'You asked me to sit with you.'

'Did I?'

'Yes, my lady,' said the other softly. 'You felt the need for company.'

'Well, I no longer do so,' announced Catherine in a tone which brought the servant instantly to her feet. 'You may go and attend to your duties.'

'Is there anything I can fetch you?'

'Nothing.'

'Then I will leave you here alone.'

After a moment's hesitation, the servant headed for the door, her face etched with concern. A household which was known for its calm was suddenly in turmoil. Anxious for her mistress, the woman was also fearful about her own future. When she opened the door to quit the room, she was stopped by a sudden call.

'Wait!' said Catherine. 'Has Tetbald returned yet?'

'I believe that he has, my lady.'

'Find out for me at once.'

'I will.'

'If he is here, ask him to come to me.'

The servant nodded obediently and withdrew. Catherine began to sew again but she swiftly lost interest and tossed the tapestry aside. Rising to her feet, she paced the room as she considered the options which now confronted her. She did not hear the tap on the door. When she turned back towards it, she saw the steward standing just inside the room.

'You sent for me, my lady?' he said.

'Close the door.'

He did so then faced her again. 'What is your wish?'

'I need your advice, Tetbald.'

'That is always at your command,' he said with an oleaginous smile, moving in closer to her. 'How may I help?'

'First, tell me what has been going on. Have they searched?'

'Throughout the day.'

'What have they found?'

'Very little, my lady. Darkness forced them to break off.'

'Did you speak with the lord sheriff?'

'I did,' said the steward evenly. 'He vowed that he would track down the murderer but admitted that the trail was cold. He returned to the castle to feast with the royal commissioners.'

'How can he revel at a time like this?' she said with asperity.

Tetbald said nothing but he smiled inwardly. He was a fleshy man in his late twenties with dark wavy hair framing a countenance that was slowly yielding its good looks to the encroaching fat of his cheeks. He stood in an attitude of deference, but there was a familiarity in his manner which Catherine seemed to accept rather than condemn.

'What am I to do, Tetbald?' she asked.

'Wait until the funeral is over, my lady.'

'But the commissioners begin their deliberations tomorrow. My husband was to be among the first to be called before them.' She bit her lip with indecision. 'Should I go in his stead?'

'That would not be seemly, my lady.'

'I will not sit idly by while others fight over my land.'

'Then let me go in your place,' he volunteered. 'The lord Nicholas would have had me at his side in the shire hall because I know all the particulars of his manors and the lands appertaining to them. Employ me as your ambassador, my lady. I will not let you down.'

'That is true,' she said with a faint smile. 'I can rely on you, Tetbald. You have been very faithful to me. Faithful, conscientious and discreet.'

'I only wish to please you.'

Their eyes locked for a moment then Catherine broke away to resume her seat. His presence had a soothing effect on her and her composure soon returned. She began to feel in control of the situation.

'Represent me at the shire hall, Tetbald.'

'I will do so gladly.'

'Do not surrender one acre of land,' she insisted. 'It is all mine. I inherit directly from my husband. Nobody else must be allowed to steal the property from me. You must be a persuasive advocate.'

'Right and title are on your side, my lady.'

'My husband feared that they might not be enough.'

'The lord Nicholas is no longer here,' he whispered. 'You do not have to accept his counsel any more. All of his manors now come into your hands, to be disposed of as you choose.'

'I choose to keep them,' she said with emphasis.

'Then that is what will happen.'

'Will you give me your word on that, Tetbald?'

The steward took a step towards her. His smile was at once inquisitive and complacent. 'Do you really need to ask that, my lady?'

Their eyes met again and this time she did not look away.

'No,' she said quietly. 'I trust you. I have to now.'

Chapter Three

Since his marriage, Ralph Delchard slept soundly as a rule, but his first night at Exeter Castle was an unusually restless one. He was wide awake long before the larks were heralding the dawn. Knowing instinctively that something was troubling him, Golde roused herself from her own slumber and rolled over to face him.

'What is the matter?' she murmured.

'Go back to sleep, my love.'

'How can I when you are threshing about in the bed?'

'I did not mean to disturb you. I have been trying to lie still.'

'That is what convinced me that something was bothering you,' she said with a tired smile. 'After twisting and turning all night, you were unnaturally still. That is not like you. I sensed that you were awake. Why?' she pressed. 'What ails you?'

'Nothing that need concern you.'

'I want to know, Ralph.'

'There is no point in the two of us losing our sleep.'

'Tell me,' she said with a playful punch. 'I insist.'

'Very well. I was thinking about that jester. Berold.'

'And do not lie to me,' added Golde, jabbing him harder. 'This has nothing to do with the jester, amusing as he was. You are still perplexed by this murder. That is what gnaws away at your mind.'

Ralph grinned. 'I have no secrets from you, Golde. You have learnt to read your husband like a book.'

'Then turn the page so that I may read more.'

'You are right,' he confessed. 'I am sorely troubled by the murder of Nicholas Picard and by Baldwin's reaction to it. Why is he so anxious to keep me out of the investigation? We are interested parties; Nicholas Picard was one of the main people we came all this way to see. I want to know what happened to him. Yet the lord sheriff will not even let me view the body.'

'Why should you want to, Ralph?'

'Because I may learn things from it that have eluded Baldwin's eye. I have buried many friends in my life, Golde, brave soldiers who were cut down in battle. I can tell if a wound was inflicted by sword, dagger, lance or axe. I can unravel the story of a man's death.' He heaved a sigh. 'But our host spurns my help.'

'For what reason?'

'That is what I have been trying to work out. Is he arrogant enough to believe that he alone can solve this crime? Does he fear that I might find something which has eluded him? Or is there a darker cause?'

'What do you mean?'

'I begin to wonder if the lord sheriff is hiding something from me.'

'Hiding something?'

'You saw his behaviour at the banquet last night.'

'Yes,' she said. 'You did seem to arouse his choler, Ralph. On the other hand, you had more success in talking to him than I did in catching the attention of the lady Albreda. I was snubbed. She obviously regards Saxon women as a lower form of life.'

'So do I,' teased Ralph, slipping an arm round her. 'That's what makes them so appealing. They are wild and untamed.'

'How many of them have you known?'

'Hundreds!' he said airily. 'But you are easily the best.'

She smiled at his empty boast and snuggled up to him. 'I did not like it, Ralph,' she admitted. 'The lady Albreda hurt my pride. I know that she is the king's niece but I refuse to be put down like that. My father was a Saxon thegn who held several manors in Herefordshire. I am used to respect. I will not endure condescension.'

'You will not have to, Golde,' he promised.

'If it continues, I prefer to leave here for more modest accommodation.'

'That will not be necessary.'

'I am not ashamed that I worked as a brewer,' she said. 'It was an honest trade and someone had to carry on the business when my husband died. But the lady Albreda all but sneered at me when she heard that I had actually worked for a living.'

'It was my fault for raising the subject, Golde.'

'You were not to know how she would react.' When he kissed her on the head and pulled her closer, she went on: 'What puzzles me is why she was so meek with her husband yet so tart with me. I did nothing to offend her.'

'But you did, Golde. You shone with happiness.'

'How could that upset her?'

'Simple envy,' he decided. 'I do not know her well, but my guess would be that the lady Albreda is a lonely and disappointed woman. Baldwin does not have the look of an ideal husband to me. His office takes him all over the shire and he is far too busy to pay much heed to the complaints of his wife. She is afraid of him, we both saw that. She is neglected whereas you are patently not, my love. I think she was consumed with envy.'

'It went deeper than that, Ralph.'

'You were the target for her anger.'

'Anger? She seemed so mild and inoffensive at first.'

'Only in her husband's presence,' said Ralph, recalling her conduct at the table. 'Baldwin keeps her subdued but there must be a lot of anger smouldering away inside her. Some of it was directed at you. That is human nature, alas. Albreda took out her irritation on you.'

'She will not do so again.'

'I will speak to Baldwin about it.'

'No, no,' she said, grasping his arm. 'I will handle this my way, Ralph. I do not expect you to fight my battles for me. I have had my share of dealing with haughty Norman ladies before.' She gave a laugh. 'The irony is that I am sometimes mistaken for one myself now.'

'That is one of the many virtues of marrying me.'

'Virtues or defects?'

Ralph grinned and rolled on top of her. He suddenly became serious. 'Do you know what I am going to do?'

'Make your wife glow with happiness again, I hope.'

'After that,' he said, thinking it through. 'I am going to ignore the wishes of our host and follow my own inclination. The body lies here in the castle. What is to stop me going to the mortuary to examine it?'

'Another body which lies here in the castle – mine!'

Ralph needed no further invitation.

Saewin the Reeve had a long day ahead of him. He rose early and ate a frugal breakfast before addressing himself to his work. He was poring over a document when his servant brought news that a visitor had arrived at the house. Surprised that anyone should call so soon after dawn, the reeve was even more surprised when the visitor was shown into the room. She was a tall, stately woman in her thirties who moved with grace and dressed with elegance. Saewin leapt to his feet at once.

'This is an unexpected pleasure, my lady,' he said, noting her fragrance as she swept in. 'Do be seated.'

'Thank you,' she said, settling down on a stool. 'I am glad to find you at home, Saewin. I feared that you might already have left.'

'I will do so before long. I am needed at the shire hall.'

'That is what I have come to talk to you about.'

Loretta had a poise and confidence which made him feel slightly uneasy. A wealthy widow, she lived in one of the finest houses in the city and had other property further afield. Saewin knew her by sight but rarely spoke to her. Loretta was an intensely private woman who was not often seen abroad. The reeve recalled that the last time he had caught a glimpse of her was at a service at the cathedral.

'How can I help you?' he said.

'By giving me information,' she explained. 'I understand that the royal commissioners have arrived in the city.'

'Yes, my lady. They came yesterday.'

'You have no doubt spoken with them.'

'It was my duty to do so. I had to take my instructions.'

'So you will know the order in which cases come before them.'

'Of course, my lady. I have to ensure that all the relevant witnesses attend. When the first commissioners came, many problems were brought to light and several people failed to appear in order to attest their claims to certain holdings. This second team from Winchester have come to look into the irregularities uncovered by their predecessors.'

'Is Nicholas Picard still on their list?'

'Indeed, it is.'

'Even though the poor man was cruelly murdered?'

'The lord Nicholas may have died,' he said quietly, 'but his land remains and some of it is the subject of bitter controversy. Ordinarily, the holdings would be inherited by his wife but that is by no means certain. Two other claimants came forth at the first hearing and they are now joined by a third.'

'Who is that?'

'The abbot of Tavistock.'

'His claim is of no account,' she said with a dismissive flick of her hand. 'Besides, the abbot has property enough to satisfy him.'

'That does not appear to be the case.'

'He is not a serious contender here. I am.'

Saewin blinked in astonishment. 'You, my lady?'

'I wish to give formal notice of my interest in the holdings under review. Convey it to the commissioners at the earliest opportunity.'

'Why, yes,' he said politely, 'but I am bound to wonder why you did not come forward when the first commissioners were in the county.'

'That is my business.'

'Of course, my lady.'

'Make their successors aware of my claim.'

'I will,' he agreed, 'but they are certain to ask what weight should be attached to it. What may I tell them?'

'Advise them to look into the history of those holdings. They were once in the possession of William de Marmoutier, my late son. He bequeathed them to his mother.' She stood up and moved to the door. 'Tell them that, Saewin. And be sure that they send for me.'

'Yes, my lady.'

'I intend to fight for what is mine by right.'

Without waiting for the servant to show her out, Loretta turned on her heel and made for the door, leaving the reeve to grapple in vain with a number of unanswered questions. Her intrusion into the dispute was far from welcome. It could only make the squabble over the dead body of Nicholas Picard even more acrimonious.

Gervase Bret was kneeling at the altar rail in the chapel when he heard the footsteps approaching. He broke off from his prayer. It was not the steady gait of the chaplain which caught his ear nor the respectful tread of another worshipper. The feet sounded slow and furtive. When the door opened, it did not swing back on its hinges. It inched open so that an eye could scrutinise the interior of the chapel. Gervase rose and stepped back into the shadows, wishing that he was wearing his dagger. It was the last place where he would have anticipated danger, but that is what he sensed now.

Only two small candles burned on the altar, leaving most of the chapel in relative darkness. Gervase flattened himself against a wall and waited. The door opened wide enough to admit a sturdy figure. The newcomer moved stealthily down the aisle. Gervase stepped out to accost him.

'What do you want?' he asked firmly.

Ralph Delchard jumped back in alarm with a hand on his heart. 'Heavens!' he exclaimed. 'You frightened the life out of me.'

Gervase was astounded. 'Is it you, Ralph?'

'Yes. I thought the chapel would be empty at this time of day.'

'I came in to pray.'

Ralph smiled. 'Well, there is no point in pretending that that is why I am here. Nobody would call me devout. Besides,' he said, 'it is not the chapel that I came to see but the morgue.'

Gervase did not need to ask why. The moment he knew his friend's destination, he was a willing accomplice. Both of them were eager to view the corpse of a man who figured so largely in the irregularities which had brought them to Devon. Without any more ado, they crossed to the door in the side wall and went through it. Finding themselves in a gloomy vestry, they were about to withdraw when they noticed a faint glow at floor level on the other side of the chamber. They groped their way to a small door. As soon as they opened it, they knew it led to the mortuary.

The stench of death was sweetened by the presence of herbs but it still rose up to attack their nostrils. Gervase coughed and Ralph turned his face away for an instant. They then went down some steps towards the flickering candle which had cast the strip of light under the door. The corpse was laid out on a stone slab and covered with a shroud. A crucifix stood at its head and the candle burned in an alcove. Ralph exchanged a glance with Gervase, then held the candle over the corpse. They shivered in the dank atmosphere. After bracing himself, Gervase took hold of the shroud and peeled it back from the face. The shock was severe.

'God preserve his soul!' he murmured.

'Poor wretch!' said Ralph.

'Was this Nicholas Picard?'

The sight of such a grotesque visage made them take a step back. Blood had been stemmed, wounds had been bathed and some bandaging had been used but enough was visible to show them what a terrible end the murder victim had met. Skin had been torn from the face, lumps bitten out of it and deep lacerations left in it everywhere. The throat had been cut so viciously that it was surprising the head did not part from the body. Gervase could not bear the sight but Ralph took a more considered inventory. When he had finished, he replaced the shroud over the face.

'This is the work of a fiend,' he decided.

'Who could want to disfigure him like that?'

'I do not know, Gervase, but we now have even more reason to find the villain. That is not a human face. It is a piece of raw meat.

The lord Nicholas looks as if he was attacked by a wild animal.'

'An animal would not carry the knife which slit his throat like that.'

'True. That is the work of a man's hand.'

'Was there only one attacker?'

'Saewin the Reeve felt that there had to be more than one. A trained soldier like Nicholas Picard would not easily be overpowered by a single adversary. Unless,' he said thoughtfully, 'he was disabled in some way. By drink, maybe, or by fatigue. Yet what could have tired such a healthy man? All he had done was to ride into Exeter on business.'

'Something must have thrown him off guard.'

'Why did he not travel with an escort? He had over twenty knights on whom he could call. If the road was perilous, an escort would have been essential. Why did he choose to ride alone?'

'We may never know, Ralph.'

'At least we are aware of what we are dealing with here,' said the other. 'This was no sudden attack by robbers. They would have killed him, taken his purse and fled. And they would certainly have stolen his horse as well. My lord sheriff mentioned that it was the returning horse which alerted the lord Nicholas's household.'

'What are you saying, Ralph?'

'This was a cold, deliberate, calculated act of murder. It was not enough to take the man's life. His face had to be obliterated.' He replaced the candle in the alcove. 'That rules out a random attacker, in my view. This was a person or persons who knew Nicholas Picard and lived close enough to the city to observe his movements. I sense a spirit of revenge here, Gervase. Somebody was paying him back for injuries done to them.'

'No injuries could compare with those we just witnessed.'

'I agree. This is butchery. However,' he said, 'I am glad that my curiosity has been satisfied. The lord sheriff sought to keep this horror from my gaze, but not out of concern for my feelings. I will be interested to learn what his real reason is for shielding me from this murder investigation.'

'Does he have any clues to follow?'

'None that he will disclose to us, Gervase.'

'Why is he so secretive?'

'That is what I intend to find out.'

'Will you tell him that we have now viewed the body?'

'No,' said Ralph. 'Certainly not. There is no need for him to know about our early morning visit. Baldwin the Sheriff would disapprove strongly if he realised that we had gone behind his back. This must be kept from him.'

'That will not be possible,' said a voice behind them.

They turned to see a figure descending the steps from the vestry. Joscelin the Steward had overheard their conversation. His duty to his master outweighed the courtesy he was bound to extend to guests.

'Please leave,' he said. 'I wish to lock the door of the mortuary.'

Canon Hubert and Brother Simon were the first of the commissioners to arrive at the shire hall that morning. They found everything in readiness. Saewin the Reeve was there to welcome them and to invite them into the long, low room in which so much of the civic and legal business was conducted.

The newcomers were pleased to see that the place had been swept clean, chairs and a table had been set out for them and benches had been procured for the witnesses. Refreshments were laid out on a small table in the corner and Hubert could not resist sampling a honey cake, washed down with a cup of water. Simon touched nothing. He put his satchel on the table and began to unload the sheaves of documents which it contained.

Hubert could feel that the reeve was still hovering in the background.

'You may leave us now,' he said over his shoulder.

'I wish to deliver a message to the lord Ralph.'

'Leave it with us and we will see it handed to him.'

'This message came by word of mouth,' said the reeve. 'The lady who gave it to me bade me pass it on to the commissioners. I naturally want to give it to the man who leads you.'

'We all lead in some senses,' said Hubert pedantically, facing him. 'By the same token, we all follow. There is no need for you to linger when you have other business to address. Deliver the message to us and we will give it to the lord Ralph. Will this content you?'

'I suppose so,' said the other uncertainly.

'Who is the lady in question?'

'Loretta, widow of the late Roger de Marmoutier.'

'That name is familiar to me. Do you recognise it, Brother Simon?'

'Yes, Canon Hubert,' said the scribe. 'Certain holdings which came into the possession of Nicholas Picard were at one time part of the manor of Roger de Marmoutier.'

'When he died,' explained Saewin, 'the property was left to his son, William, but he, a headstrong young man, was unfortunately killed in a hunting accident. At that point, the land came into the possession of the lord Nicholas. No claim was made by the lady Loretta when your predecessors compiled their returns for the county but she wishes to press her claim now.'

'Then she may have left it too late,' said Hubert pompously. 'I am not sure that we can allow her to enter the contest at this stage.'

'The abbot of Tavistock has done so,' Saewin reminded him.

'That is a different matter.'

'I do not see how, Canon Hubert. His position is exactly that of the lady Loretta. He waived his right to advance his claim before the first team of commissioners but is ready to come forward now.'

'And must be heard.'

'Will you favour the Church over a private individual?'

Hubert blenched. 'I resent the insinuation behind that question.'

'No offence was meant,' said the reeve, raising an appeasing palm. 'In relaying the message to you, I have done what the lady Loretta instructed. Decisions about who will and who will not come before you are entirely a matter for you and your colleagues. It is not my place to comment in any way. Please accept my apology.'

'Very well.'

'I will detain you from your work no further.'

'Thank you,' said Hubert crisply. He waited until the reeve

went out of the hall before turning to Simon. 'Favouring the Church, indeed! The suggestion is gross.'

'Yes, Canon Hubert. No man is more impartial than you.'

'The abbot of Tavistock will be judged fairly and objectively. He will receive no special courtesies from me or from anyone else. Where the Church has erred – as it occasionally has in some of the disputes we have looked into in other counties – I have been the first to point it out.'

'Your record has been unblemished.'

'And so it will remain.' Hubert chose what he felt would be the most comfortable chair, sitting down like a mother hen settling herself on her eggs. 'But where are the others?' he complained. 'They should have been here by now.'

'The lord Ralph is usually very punctual.'

'He was until he married,' said Hubert sharply. 'This would not be the first time that his wife has made him tarry. I am not at all sure that her influence on him is entirely beneficial. It might be better if the lady Golde did not travel with him on his assignments.'

'That is my feeling,' said Simon, nodding energetically.

'She is an intelligent lady and pleasant company but not an appointed member of this commission. Inevitably, she is a distraction.'

The door opened and they looked up in anticipation, but it was not their colleagues who stepped into the hall. A Benedictine monk shuffled slowly towards them, his hood up and his hands tucked in the sleeves of his cowl. He stood respectfully before the table.

'Canon Hubert?' he asked.

'Yes?'

'I bring word from the lord Ralph.'

'Why is he not here?'

'He has been delayed by the lord sheriff,' said the monk. 'He hopes to be here with the others before too long but sends his apologies in the meantime. The delay was unforeseen.'

'And most unwelcome,' observed Hubert. 'We have an immense amount of business to conduct. An early start is imperative.'

'It will not be possible today.'

'Our deliberations take precedence over conversations with the lord sheriff. Bear that message to the lord Ralph.'

'I would not be admitted to their presence.'

'Why not, brother?'

'Because they have arrant fools enough without me.'

Hubert gaped. 'Fools, did you say!'

'Fools, idiots and mindless soldiers.'

'Such immoderate language for a monk!' said Simon.

'That is why I could never take the cowl for more than a few minutes,' said the messenger, pulling back his hood to reveal the distinctive head and hair of Berold. 'I came in jest but I spoke in truth.'

'To disguise yourself as a Benedictine is an act of sacrilege,' said Hubert in disgust. 'I will make mention of this to the lord sheriff.'

'Then you would be the biggest fool of all, Canon Hubert.'

'Do you dare to mock me?'

'I am only giving you fair warning,' said the other, skipping to the door and divesting himself of his cowl at the same time. 'My master is hot with rage. Only a simpleton

74

would go near him when he is in such a state. Ask the lord Ralph. He is feeling the sharp edge of the lord sheriff's fury.'

'You were expressly told to keep yourself out of it!' roared Baldwin. 'Do you not recognise an order when you hear one?'

'My orders come from the king himself,' said Ralph.

'Devon is under my aegis and you would do well to remember it.'

'A sheriff is still answerable to a higher authority.'

Baldwin turned puce. 'Do you defy me, my lord?'

'I simply wished to view the last remains of Nicholas Picard.'

'Against my wishes.'

'It was too early to seek your permission, my lord sheriff,' said Ralph with a sly wink at Gervase. 'Or we would surely have done so.'

'My permission would have been refused.'

'Then it is as well we did not wait for it.'

'You sneaked into that mortuary like thieves in the night,' yelled their host. 'This is my castle and I expect my guests to respect my authority within these walls. What you did was unforgivable.'

'But within my rights.'

'No, my lord!'

'Yes,' insisted Ralph. 'The lord Nicholas figures so largely in our investigations that we have a keen interest in what happened to him.'

'He was murdered. That is all you need to know.'

'Why are you keeping the truth from us?'

'Do you dare to accuse me of lies?' howled Baldwin as his

anger reached a new pitch. 'Take care, my lord. Men have been thrown into my dungeons for less than that.'

'I did not say that you told lies,' countered Ralph. 'Merely, that you have held back the full truth and tried to prevent us from finding it out. I would respect your authority more if I felt that you were worthy of it.'

Baldwin de Moeles was so incensed that he reached for his sword. Ralph did not flinch but Gervase Bret moved swiftly. Stepping in between the two men, he acted as a peacemaker.

'There is no call for argument here.' He turned to the sheriff. 'We were wrong to disobey your orders, my lord sheriff, and owe you a profound apology. Curiosity got the better of us. We were in the chapel at first light, praying for the success of our work here, when we remembered that the lord Nicholas lay in the mortuary. The temptation to inspect the body was too great to resist, but it was a mistake.'

'No, it was not, Gervase,' argued Ralph vehemently.

'Let me handle this, my lord.'

'We had to see the lord Nicholas.'

'Subject to my lord sheriff's approval.' Gervase shot Ralph such a look of reproof that the latter was silenced at once. When his young friend was in such an assertive mood, it was as well to heed his advice. It was time to let him take over the negotiations. All that Ralph had done was to trade bold words and insults with their host. They had almost come to blows and a brawl would advantage nobody, least of all a commissioner who relied on the sheriff both for accommodation and for help with his office. Gervase's diplomacy would achieve far more than Ralph's plain speaking. Voices which had reverberated around the hall at the castle needed to be deprived of their passion and volume. Gervase shrugged his shoulder and gave a conciliatory smile. 'We were too curious and too arrogant, my lord sheriff,' he said.

'I know it well,' grumbled the other but he sheathed his sword as he did so. 'Too curious, too arrogant and too rash.'

'We had the audacity to believe that we could discover something which your own more experienced eyes had missed. We are royal commissioners who sit in musty halls with our noses in wrinkled documents and ancient charters. What do we know about the pursuit of a killer?' He saw Ralph bite back an interruption and hurried on. 'It was a monstrous folly on our part to imagine that we could do your job in your stead.'

'I am glad that you appreciate it.'

'Appreciate it and acknowledge our fault.'

'I heard no such acknowledgement from the lord Ralph.'

'Nor will you!' Ralph said under his breath, then he felt a sobering kick on the ankle from Gervase. 'He is right, my lord sheriff,' he added aloud. 'I do see the error of our ways now. Gervase speaks for both of us.'

'Would that he had done so earlier!' snapped the other.

'My remarks were intemperate. I take them back.'

'I am glad to hear it.'

'So am I,' said Gervase with feeling. 'Nothing can be achieved by our bickering. We are all on the same side here. Fall out among ourselves and disharmony follows. Pool our resources and work together – under your direction, lord sheriff – and we form an irresistible team.'

'That is so,' said Baldwin, slightly mollified. 'We can join forces but I must be in command.'

'Without question.' Gervase looked meaningfully at Ralph. 'Well?'

'Yes, yes,' came the lacklustre endorsement. 'Without question.'

'Then let us put this aberration behind us,' decided Baldwin, strutting around the room. 'I will forget what has happened if you give me your word not to interfere any more in this murder investigation.'

'We give it unconditionally, my lord sheriff,' said Gervase.

'Do we?' murmured Ralph in dismay.

'It is the only way to proceed.'

'Then let us leave the matter there,' said Baldwin.

'Not until we have given you our opinion,' said Gervase persuasively. 'It was wrong of us to visit the mortuary, but we did reach certain conclusions about the murder victim. They may well confirm your own observations, my lord sheriff, and should be heard for that reason alone.'

Their host pondered. 'As you wish,' he said at length.

'Our feeling was this . . .'

Ralph watched with admiration as Gervase adopted new tactics. Instead of increasing their host's anger with naked defiance, Gervase was subtly flattering him in order to draw information from him. He deliberately altered the deductions they had made about the dead man so that the sheriff would be provoked into correcting him. Ralph and Gervase were learning valuable new details about the case.

'What, then, was your final conclusion?' asked Baldwin at length.

'That the lord Nicholas was killed by someone in order to prevent him from appearing before us to affirm his right to the disputed holdings. One man probably carried out the murder,' said Gervase. 'Someone well known to the lord Nicholas who unwittingly let him get close enough to make a surprise attack.'

'Then you are mistaken on every point, my young friend.'

'How can that be?'

'Nicholas Picard was ambushed by robbers in the wood. His purse was empty when he was found and valuable rings had been taken from his fingers.'

'Could not that have been a ruse on the part of the murderer?' said Ralph, unable to keep silent any longer. 'A cunning villain would do his best to make it look like the work of robbers in order to deflect suspicion away from himself.'

'We *know* that robbers were involved, my lord. Two of them.'

'How can you be so sure?'

'Because my men trailed them to an inn near Crediton,' said Baldwin. 'A messenger rode through the night to bring me word. The robbers had moved on but the innkeeper remembered them well. They spent far too much money for men as poorly attired as they were. He told my officers which way his guests went.' He gave a harsh smile. 'It is only a matter of time before those men are apprehended and brought back here to stand trial for the murder of Nicholas Picard.'

Chapter Four

When the commissioners eventually arrived at the shire hall, they found a number of people awaiting them. Saewin had assembled all the witnesses who needed to be examined on the first day and was standing by to receive further instructions. Ralph Delchard, Gervase Bret and Hervey de Marigny strode into the hall with the speed and purpose of men who wished to make up for lost time. Canon Hubert's protest about their lateness was brushed aside by Ralph. Four of his men were stationed at the rear of the hall while four of de Marigny's knights acted as sentries outside. Ralph had learnt from experience that the presence of armed soldiers tended to encourage a more truthful response from witnesses.

All five of them were soon seated behind the table with documents set out before them. Ralph occupied the central position with Hubert and de Marigny on either side of him. Brother Simon was poised to record the proceedings of the day in his neat hand. Gervase was the most anxious of them all to set things in motion. Though his mind was concentrated on his duties, his heart was still in Winchester with his betrothed. Every delay lengthened the time he would be apart from her and might, he feared, even prevent him from returning in time for his wedding.

Hervey de Marigny looked along the table and gave a chuckle.

'What a daunting tribunal we make!' he observed. 'I would not like to face such an imposing set of judges.'

'We endeavour to frighten the witnesses into honesty,' said Ralph with a grin. 'Only minor cases come before us today so we will not be unduly taxed. I would suggest that you watch us throughout the morning before you join in the merriment.'

'It is hardly merriment, my lord,' said Hubert reproachfully. 'We are royal agents with serious business which must be addressed seriously. May I remind you that one of our principal witnesses was murdered on the eve of our arrival? That is hardly a cause for merriment.'

'No,' agreed Ralph. 'I am justly rebuked. Though our work is not a tale of unrelieved tedium. I am sure that our new commissioner will find some amusement in the lies and evasions which we are bound to hear in the course of the day.'

'Let us begin,' suggested Gervase.

'We have waited long enough to do so!' sighed Hubert.

'Your patience would make Job look restless,' Ralph teased him. 'It is time to let the citizens of Exeter know that we are here and that we will tolerate no false claims to property.' He addressed one of the guards. 'Ask the reeve to send in those involved in the first case.'

'I find this oddly exciting,' said de Marigny.

'So did we at first,' said Ralph. 'Then boredom quickly set in.'

Hubert sniffed noisily. 'The administration of justice is never boring.'

'Speak for yourself, Hubert.'

'I always do, my lord.'

'Much of what we do is bound to be humdrum.'

'Not if you have the intelligence to probe below the surface.'

Ralph laughed at the reproof, then composed his features into judicial solemnity as the reeve brought a number of people into the hall and directed them to sit on the benches. When all the witnesses were present, Ralph introduced himself and his colleagues then called the first man to give his testimony. After taking an oath, the witness launched into a long defence of his claim to some property to the north of the city, plucking charters out of his satchel and waving them in the air. Hervey de Marigny was enthralled. Minor disputes which seemed innocuous on the page took on a colour and vitality which surprised him. Even the most insignificant cases were invested with a bitterness which made them blaze in the shire hall.

The commissioners had complementary skills. Ralph was a stern but just leader, controlling events with a sure hand and giving every person the right to plead his case in full. As befitted a lawyer, Gervase worried away at the fine detail of a claim, haggling over the wording of charters and questioning the legal basis of many assertions. But it was Canon Hubert who most impressed their new colleague. Having found him a learned but vain man, too puffed up with his own importance, de Marigny watched with fascination as Hubert's true mettle emerged. Fair but fearless, he asked the most searching questions and pursued any hint of deceit quite relentlessly. Three of the witnesses were exposed as arrant liars and a fourth was reduced to tears by his persistence.

By the time the cathedral bell gave sonorous warning of Nones, de Marigny felt able to take a more active role in the process, asking for elucidation, questioning witnesses directly and studying their faces for tell-tale signs of their true character. Under the pressure of examination, few of them maintained their composure throughout. Hervey de Marigny soon learnt how to sow discomfort with an artless query and he was eventually repaid with a moment of triumph. At the end of the day's proceedings, Ralph was the first to congratulate him.

'Who are the teachers and who the pupil here?' he said. 'That was masterly. You had that fellow squirming like a fish on a hook.'

'He was obviously lying,' explained de Marigny.

'But how did you know?'

'He all but took me in,' admitted Gervase.

'And me,' said Hubert. 'I have never met so plausible a rogue.'

'It was his very plausibility which alerted me,' said de Marigny. 'If his argument was as strong and irrefutable as he alleged, why did it not convince our predecessors? They smelt an irregularity. So did I.'

'And unmasked the man for the perjurer he was.' Ralph gave him a pat on the back. 'Excellently done, Hervey! You are indeed a worthy commissioner and need no more instruction from us.'

'Tomorrow, you may think otherwise,' said de Marigny modestly.

'Why?'

'Because we only dealt with the most paltry cases today, Ralph. Small disputes which could easily be settled. Tomorrow, I believe, we are due to tackle something far more substantial and complicated.'

'The case involving the late Nicholas Picard.'

'Yes.'

'I have a suggestion to make,' said Hubert in a tone of voice which made it sound more like a decree than a proposal. 'Let us postpone that dispute until a fitter time and deal instead with the many others which await our judgement.'

'That is eminently sensible advice,' said de Marigny.

Hubert was pleased. 'Then it is settled.'

'No,' said Ralph, 'it most certainly is not, Hubert. Our schedule has been worked out and we will keep to it as planned.'

'But the lord Nicholas's death alters everything,' returned Hubert.

'The only thing that it alters is his chance of appearing before us.'

'The case must be postponed out of respect.'

'To whom?'

'His family.'

'That will not be necessary.'

'His widow will be prostrate with grief.'

'Then why did she send word to me through Saewin that she wished the dispute over her husband's property to be settled as soon as possible? The town reeve gave me this message as we arrived here.'

'He delivered another message for you,' suddenly recalled Brother Simon.

'Indeed?'

'It seems that there is a further claimant in that dispute.'

'One more reason to tackle it at once,' decided Ralph. 'The longer we delay, the more time we give for new people to contest those holdings. We already have three in addition to the widow of the lord Nicholas, who would normally be expected to inherit his estates. Postpone this case indefinitely and we will find that half the county wish to lodge a claim.' He rose from the table. 'Who is the latest to be added to the list?'

'The lady Loretta,' said Hubert. 'Widow of Roger de Marmoutier.'

'That is a name of importance in Devon,' noted Gervase. 'The lord Roger held property scattered throughout the county and did at one time hold the land at the centre of this dispute.'

'So did the abbot of Tavistock,' Hubert reminded him.

'And so did everyone else south of Bristol!' said Ralph with sarcasm. 'The next person who will assert his right to those holdings will be Berold the Jester! This dispute trembles on the edge of absurdity.'

'It is a major case,' said Gervase calmly, 'and should be heard sooner rather than later. Many different interests are involved here. If we settle this dispute with firm authority at the start of our sojourn here, it will act as a salutary warning to those involved in later cases. It will set the standard for all else that follows.'

'I could not agree more, Gervase,' said Ralph.

'Nor I support you less,' added Hubert. 'There are questions of taste and delicacy here. We must not be seen to incite an argument over the bones of a man who has not yet been buried.'

'I side with Canon Hubert,' said Simon loyally.

'And I incline to his view as well,' confessed de Marigny. 'Can the widow of the lord Nicholas really wish us to proceed so soon?'

'According to Saewin,' said Ralph. 'He received a personal visit from her steward, urging that there be no delay. This same steward, Tetbald, is to represent the widow before us. He has full authority to act in her stead so the case will proceed.'

'Against my better judgement,' noted Hubert.

Ralph beamed. 'As usual.'

'I find this very perplexing,' said de Marigny, scratching his head. 'If I was brutally murdered, I am certain that my wife would not wish to continue any litigation in which I was involved until a decent interval had elapsed for mourning. Can this lady be so heartless that she does not need to weep over her husband's tomb? Or is there another reason why she wishes to hurry this matter through?'

'The explanation has already been given, my lord,' said Gervase. 'This dispute hangs over his widow like a black cloud. Until it is dispelled, she is not able properly to mourn the deceased. And is it so surprising that a wife should fight for something which she believes is part of her rightful inheritance?'

'Golde would do so in the same position,' said Ralph.

'I doubt that,' returned de Marigny.

'So do I,' supported Hubert.

'You forget that the lord Nicholas's widow will not be here in person,' said Gervase, keen to terminate the debate. 'While she grieves in private, her steward can speak for her in public. If he can report to her that we find in her favour, I am sure that it will be a balm to her troubled mind.'

'No more argument,' announced Ralph. 'It is agreed.'

Canon Hubert grumbled, Brother Simon rolled his eyes in despair and Hervey de Marigny still had reservations, but all three accepted his decision. As they left the shire hall, Ralph fell in beside Gervase.

'Thank you for backing me, Gervase.'

'I thought it important to settle this dispute while it is still within our power to do so,' said the other. 'It was tangled enough before we arrived but it has grown infinitely more complicated since we have been here. If we delay a judgement, we may find that its intricacies only multiply and that it takes an eternity to resolve.'

'With you stuck in Devon while Alys pines in Winchester.'

'That thought was at the back of my mind.'

'So it should be, Gervase,' said Ralph jovially. 'Our work is of the highest importance but we must not let it keep you away from the altar. I share your fears that this case could increase in size and complexity until it dominates all the rest and ensnares us for weeks. On the other hand, it may soon be simplified for us.'

'Simplified?'

'Yes. Remember what Baldwin told us. Arrests are imminent. When we know why Nicholas Picard was killed, we will have a much clearer idea of what this dispute is all about.'

'The lord sheriff said that he was murdered by robbers.'

'I know,' said Ralph. 'But who hired them?'

It was the smoke which gave them away. Breaking their journey for refreshment, they lit a fire to roast one of the chickens they had stolen from a farm. It made a tasty meal and they ate it between long gulps of ale. Their fortunes were improving. As they counted out their takings once more, they realised that they could afford to buy what had hitherto only been within reach by theft. The two of them sniggered complacently.

The posse comprised a dozen men, veteran soldiers who knew how to work together. They trailed the robbers all the way from Crediton until they reached the copse where the couple was hiding. A slow curl of smoke rose above the trees. It was all the encouragement they needed. Under the guidance of their captain, the soldiers separated to surround the copse. When the signal was given, they moved slowly in.

The robbers were dozing beside the fire when they heard the crack of a twig beneath a hoof. It brought them awake at once and both reached for their daggers. They were far too late. The clearing was suddenly boiling with the sheriff's officers. The robbers were knocked to the ground by lances, disarmed and pinioned. Dismounting from his horse, the captain searched their purses and found them bulging with money. He also found some gold rings which had once adorned the fingers of

Nicholas Picard. When the men tried to protest, he beat each of them into silence with a mailed fist.

'Tie them to their horses!' he ordered. 'The lord sheriff wants them taken back to Exeter to face his wrath.'

Asa sat beside the window in her bedchamber and stared sadly out through the shutters. Perched on a low hill, the house gave her a clear view over the thatched roofs of the city to the twin peaks of castle and cathedral, but she was impervious to both. Though her eyes looked out, her gaze was turned inward. Memories surged through her mind in a confusing mix of nostalgia and remorse. She was a short, slender young woman in fine apparel more suited to a Norman lady than to a Saxon. Her chemise and gown were of white linen, her girdle a long silken rope with tasselled ends. Coiled at the back, her long black hair fell in curls at the front. Her face had a quiet loveliness in repose and a vivacity that was captivating when she was animated, but there was no sign of it now. As her mind dwelt on the past, a deep frown bit its way into her brow.

The knock on her door brought her out of her daze.

'Yes?' she called. Her servant entered. 'What is it, girl?'

'The town reeve has sent word.'

'What is the message?'

'You are to appear at the shire hall tomorrow.'

'So soon?'

'That is what I have been told.'

'But the funeral is tomorrow. I must attend that.'

'I am only passing on the message I was given.'

'Why did you not call me to hear it in person?'

'You warned me not to disturb you.'

'Did I?'

'Yes,' said the servant softly. 'You told me to turn away any visitors.'

'Why, so I did,' remembered Asa, trying to gather her thoughts. 'You were right, Goda. Had you tried to call me downstairs, you would have been given a flea in your ear for your pains. I am sorry to be so vague. My mind is elsewhere today.'

'I understand.'

Goda was a plump woman in her thirties with bright green eyes and a large nose which turned a pleasant face into an unattractive one. As she studied her mistress, her expression bordered on maternal concern.

'Is there anything that I can fetch you?' she offered.

'No, Goda.'

'Some food perhaps? You must eat.'

'I am not hungry.'

'You have touched almost nothing for days.'

'I will eat when I wish to and not before.'

'Yes,' said the other deferentially.

'But I thank you for worrying about me.'

Goda gave a wan smile and turned to leave the room. Asa fell back into her reverie. Stirring herself out of it once more, she walked to the stairs and descended to the kitchen. Goda was about to fill a cooking pot with water from a wooden pail. She looked up inquisitively.

'You are ready to eat something?'

'Not yet, Goda. I have an errand for you.'

'I will do it at once.'

'Run to Saewin's house,' ordered Asa. 'Explain my situation. Tell him that, whatever happens, I must not miss the funeral tomorrow. That takes priority over all else. I will gladly appear before the commissioners after the funeral.'

'What if they call you for the morning?'

'I will not go.'

'That will not help your cause,' warned Goda.

'I shall put myself in Saewin's hands,' said Asa. 'He must contrive it so that I can attend both the funeral and the shire hall. A town reeve has some influence in these matters. Ask him to use it on my behalf.'

'I will.'

'And Goda . . .'

'Yes?'

Asa gave a distant smile which brightened the whole of her face. 'Tell him that I will be most grateful.'

'What makes this case so unusual, Ralph?' she asked. 'You have talked of nothing else since you returned.'

'I am sorry, my love,' he said, giving her an apologetic kiss. 'I did not mean to bore you with my problems.'

'They do not bore me at all.'

'Tell me about your day.'

'When you have satisfied my curiosity,' said Golde. 'I know that the lord Nicholas's death has given this dispute more intensity, but I do not understand why it rates above all the others.'

'Two reasons.'

'What is the first?'

'Money,' said Ralph. 'The holdings in question run to several hides and contain some of the richest farmland in the county. Whoever inherits that property from Nicholas Picard will become quite wealthy.'

'And the second reason?'

'Women, my love.'

'I do not follow.'

'Five claimants are involved here,' he explained, 'and three of them are ladies. That is not only unusual, Golde, it is unprecedented in my experience. You can expect a wife or a daughter to lay claim to an inheritance, as the lord Nicholas's widow will do in this instance, but it is rare to have two other women hurling themselves into the fight.'

'Do they have legitimate claims?'

'So they believe.'

'Who are they?'

'One is a Saxon woman, Asa, who lives here in the city. What her relationship with the lord Nicholas is I can only guess, but she purports to have a letter from him which bequeaths those holdings to her. In other words,' he observed drily, 'she only has a claim on the property now that he is dead. While he was alive, this Asa could only sit and wait.'

'Is that what you think she did?'

'I do not know, Golde. I have not met her and may be maligning her unfairly. But let me put it no higher than this,' he said. 'The death of Nicholas Picard is highly convenient. If we find in favour of Asa, she will be a woman of property.'

'Who is the other claimant?'

'One lady Loretta, widow of Roger de Marmoutier. She

came out of the blue this morning to attest her right to that property. I can only surmise how powerful an advocate she will be, but it means that we will be hard put to sift out the truth. Three women and two men.' He gave a wry chuckle. 'There will be a fierce battle in that shire hall.'

'Who are the men?'

Ralph pulled a face. 'The abbot of Tavistock is one of them. You can always rely on the Benedictine Order to make a grab for any property that comes into dispute. Abbots have greedy fingers.'

'Do not be so irreverent.'

'Nor so prejudiced,' he said, chiding himself. 'I am sorry, my love. I condemn this prelate before I have even set eyes on him. He may yet turn out to have the strongest claim of all.'

'You said that there was a fifth contender.'

'Ignore him, Golde. He is of no account.'

'Then why does he register a claim?'

'Out of sheer folly. He will not detain us long.'

'What is his name?'

'Engelric.'

'A Saxon, then?'

'Yes,' said Ralph dismissively. 'We only hear him out of courtesy. He has a claim of sorts, but it has no real worth. The struggle will be between the abbot and the three ladies. Engelric will not figure very much.'

Golde understood why. She also realised why her husband was so reluctant to talk about the man's claim. Evidently, he was the Saxon thegn who owned the property before the Conquest and had it taken forcibly from him. Engelric's fate mirrored that of her own father. Out of concern for her feelings, Ralph did not wish to remind her of her lost status. Born into a noble family, Golde was practising her trade as a brewer when he met her in Hereford. It had been a long and painful fall from the position she once occupied. Ralph was glad that marriage to him had elevated her once more to the rank he felt she deserved.

Recollections of her past brought a more immediate memory to mind.

'I spoke with the lady Albreda today,' she said.

'Was she meek and mild or cold and supercilious?'

'Neither, Ralph. She was polite and almost friendly.'

'Almost?'

'I had the feeling that she was trying to apologise to me without quite knowing how to do it. Apology is not something which the lady Albreda has much experience of, I should imagine. But at least she did not patronise me.'

'I am relieved to hear it.'

'How she will behave in front of her husband is another matter. I am not looking forward to sitting beside her at table again.'

'You will not have to, my love. Leave it to me.'

They were alone in their chamber in the keep, enjoying the pleasure of being together again after a long day apart. Ralph reflected how much more practical and loving his marriage was than that of their hosts. After a tiring session in the shire hall, he could come back to a cordial welcome and a sympathetic ear. However weary or jaded he might be, Golde had the capacity to revive him. It was one of the things he treasured most about her. He was about to tell her so when there was a tap on the door.

'Who is it?' called Ralph.

'Me,' said Hervey de Marigny. 'With glad tidings.'

'Then bring them in.' He opened the door to admit his colleague who acknowledged Golde with a smile. 'Well, Hervey? Do not keep me in suspense. What are these glad tidings? Has Canon Hubert decided to resign his place on the commission? Was Brother Simon caught naked in a brothel? Put me out of my misery.'

'I have just come from my lord sheriff.'

'And?'

'His messenger arrived as we were talking.'

'And?' pressed Ralph. 'And? And? And?'

'They have been taken,' said de Marigny. 'Arrested by the sheriff's officers. The men who murdered Nicholas Picard will be hurled into the castle dungeons before this night is out.'

Patience did not come easily to Baldwin of Moeles. He was a man of action who chafed at idleness and loathed delay. Instead of waiting for his men to bring the prisoners to him, he took an escort and rode north to meet the returning posse. He was almost five miles away from Exeter when he heard them coming, the hooves of their horses clacking on the hard track. Baldwin reined in his horse and his escort came to a halt around him. There was enough moonlight to cast a ghostly pallor on the road ahead. Phantom figures soon came into view. The sheriff waited until they were within earshot.

'Bring them to me!' he yelled. 'Show me these foul villains!'

'Yes, my lord sheriff!' replied the captain of the posse.

They were soon drawing up in front of Baldwin. Dropping from the saddle, he went to a horse across which one of the robbers had been tied. The man was exhausted by the pummelling he had taken and was running with sweat. The sheriff grabbed his hair and lifted up the head so that he could stare into the prisoner's face.

'Do you know who I am?' he growled.

The man spoke no French but he clearly recognised the sheriff. He began to gibber with fear. Baldwin struck him across the face, drawing blood from his nose.

'Why did you kill Nicholas Picard?' he demanded.

'We found money upon them,' said the captain. 'Far more than two wretches like this should be carrying.'

'And rings?' asked Baldwin.

'Three of them, my lord sheriff. I believe we will find that they were taken from the fingers of their victim.'

'Animals!' howled the other, striking the captive again. 'Wild animals!' He strode across to the horse which bore the other robber. 'You will pay dearly for this, you rogue! I'll make you suffer so much that you will beg me to hang you and put an end to your ordeal.'

He lifted the man's head to peer into his face, but found the eyes closed tight. When he shook him violently by the shoulder, Baldwin saw that his body was limp and unresponsive. The captain shifted uneasily in his saddle.

'We obeyed your orders, my lord sheriff,' he explained, 'and travelled as fast as we could. His ropes were not secure enough. As we galloped along, he was thrown from his horse and his head hit a stone.'

Baldwin fumed. 'Dead! He has escaped my revenge?'

'It was an accident. We tried to revive him but his brains

were dashed out. That is why we slowed down. To make sure that his accomplice came back alive.'

The sheriff took out a dagger and cut the ropes which held the corpse in place. Taking him by the neck, he heaved the man off the horse and onto the ground, kicking him over with his foot so that the face was upturned. Baldwin spat contemptuously at the prostrate body.

'Leave him there,' he decreed. 'Someone from the nearest village can bury him in the morning. I want no offal coming into my castle.' He pointed to the other prisoner. 'Guard him well and bring him safely back to Exeter. I'll burn the truth out of him with a hot poker!'

It was Gervase Bret's idea. He volunteered to attend the funeral of Nicholas Picard in order to pay his respects to a man whom he had come to know well through his perusal of the Domesday returns and in the hope of learning something about those closest to the deceased. Ralph Delchard was happy to concur. The first person to be examined that day was the abbot of Tavistock and Ralph felt confident that he, Hervey de Marigny and Canon Hubert could cope without their young colleague for a morning. He anticipated resistance from Hubert, who had not been consulted about the decision to release Gervase, but he was prepared to ride out the other's displeasure in the way which had become second nature to him.

The funeral service was held at the cathedral. Osbern, bishop of Exeter, was himself officiating, a mark of Picard's status in the county. The cathedral had the ancient right to bury its citizens in its own cemetery, and Nicholas Picard was also accorded the privilege of lying within the precincts. Where he might have lain in the churchyard of the humble village church on his estates, he was instead translated to the cathedral. The hideous nature of his death provoked widespread shock and sympathy, bringing a large congregation to the funeral service. People came in from all over the county of Devon to watch the last remains of Nicholas Picard being consigned to an untimely grave.

Gervase stationed himself near the main entrance so that he could take note of visitors as they arrived. He had no difficulty in identifying the widow. She led the procession which followed the coffin. Flanked by Dean Jerome and Tetbald the Steward, she walked slowly with her head down in meditation. For all her apparent grief, Gervase did not get the impression of a woman who was disabled by her husband's murder. Her gait was steady, her manner dignified. Even in the brief glimpse he had of her, Gervase caught something of her strength of character. Directly behind her were family members and behind them came Baldwin the Sheriff with his wife.

While the procession was making its way down the nave, he slipped into the cathedral and found a place to stand at the rear. It was a moving occasion. Osbern was faultless. He made a public event seem very private, reaching out with voice and gesture to everyone in the congregation and delivering a eulogy which brought murmurs of agreement time and again. Mass was sung, then the coffin was carried out to the cemetery. The mourners filed out after it and stood around the grave in a wide circle.

Gervase was both participant and observer, touched by the solemnity of the occasion yet trying to glean something from it. He had noticed Saewin when the town reeve first appeared and he now worked his way around to him. The latter stood respectfully on the fringe of the gathering and gave him a nod of acknowledgement. Gervase waited until the coffin was lowered reverentially into the ground. He was grateful that Nicholas Picard's widow had not seen her husband at the mortuary. Simply remembering the savage injuries made his stomach turn.

'Who is that man with the widow of the deceased?' he asked.

'That is Dean Jerome.'

'On the other side of her, I meant.'

'Tetbald the Steward,' said Saewin. 'You will see a lot of him at the shire hall. He is to represent the lady Catherine. And there is someone else with whom you will become acquainted.'

Gervase followed the direction of his pointed finger and saw a tall, elegant woman accompanied by a stocky individual of middle years whose features, beard and garb confirmed his Saxon origins. They seemed an unlikely couple and Gervase decided that the man must be her servant. He was too ill favoured to occupy a more intimate station.

'Who is that?' he enquired.

'The lady Loretta, widow of Roger de Marmoutier.'

'Why is she here?'

'Everyone knew the lord Nicholas.'

'Yes,' said Gervase, 'but she knew him as the man who, allegedly, took property from her which had formerly been in the hands of her husband and then her son. I would have thought she had reason to despise Nicholas Picard.'

'She is a compassionate woman. And death can make even the vilest hatred melt away. The lady Loretta would hold no grudge against a man who had been murdered in such a terrible way.'

'Who is the man with her?'

'One of her household. Eldred by name.'

Gervase sought the identity of a dozen more people and Saewin was an obliging assistant. Work as the town reeve meant that he knew almost everyone in Exeter. From the looks and nods that his companion was collecting, Gervase could see that Saewin was greatly respected in the community. That boded well. Gervase was about to leave when he found that he himself was under surveillance. A short, slim young woman of quite striking beauty was studying him from the other side of the grave as if she was trying to weigh him up. When their eyes met, she gave him such a look of intense curiosity that he found it impossible to tear his gaze away from her.

'Who is that young lady?' he said, nodding his head towards her.

'That is someone else whom you will come to know.'

'Why?'

'She will be involved in the dispute over the lord Nicholas's property.'

Gervase was intrigued. 'Is that Asa?'

'Yes.'

What an extraordinary face! he said to himself. *Entrancing!*

He was alarmed by his reaction and lowered his eyes. Gervase had never experienced such a feeling of sudden affection at a funeral before. When he dared to look up again, Asa had vanished into the crowd.

Chapter Five

Geoffrey, abbot of Tavistock, turned out to be a peppery individual. He treated the commissioners less like royal agents to be respected than renegade monks to be brought into line by stern discipline. Attended by his prior, a cadaverous man with piercing eyes, the abbot stormed into the shire hall to advance his claim with unassailable confidence. He was a big man with a hooked nose and a domed forehead which was covered in freckles. Years of study had rounded his shoulders and left his eyes with an irritating blink. His voice seemed almost comically high for a person of his bulk but it was a potent weapon on behalf of his abbey.

'Those holdings rightly belong to me,' he asserted boldly. 'They were granted to the abbey when I replaced Sihtric as father of the house and they should have remained in our possession.'

'Why did they not do so?' asked Ralph Delchard.

'I was disseised of the property.'

'You were,' said Hervey de Marigny, 'or the abbey was?'

'The two are effectively the same.'

'Not in law,' corrected Canon Hubert. 'The property in question was, in point of fact, once held by the abbey.'

'For whom I speak, Canon Hubert.'

'Granted, Father Abbot.'

'Why, then, do you quibble so? I hold property through the abbey and on my own account as a layman. I have striven to build up the wealth of our house in Tavistock in order to do God's work the more effectively but I have been baulked along the way by certain people.' He glared along the faces ranged in front of him. 'I hope that you will not baulk me as well.'

'This case will be decided on its merits,' Ralph assured him.

'Then the land must be returned to me.'

'To the abbey, you mean,' said de Marigny.

'To both of us. At the earliest opportunity.'

'Unfortunately, that will not happen,' said Ralph. 'Four other people have lodged claims on this property and we must examine them all before we reach a final decision. What puzzles us is this. When our predecessors came to prepare the returns for this county, you did not come forward to contest these holdings. Why was that?'

'I was deliberately misinformed about the date of their visit here. By the time I reached Exeter, they had moved on to Totnes. Do you see what this means?' he said, eyes widening with anger. 'I was the victim of a conspiracy. They prevented me from fighting on behalf of Tavistock.'

'They?' repeated Ralph. 'Who might they be?'

'One of them goes to his grave today.'

'Nicholas Picard? How did he conspire against you, my lord abbot?'

'With great cunning. Look how easily he tricked your predecessors. If they had been more diligent, you would not now be here to repair all these holes in their workmanship. I hesitate to speak ill of the dead,' he continued without the slightest hesitation, 'but the lord Nicholas was unscrupulous where property was concerned.'

'Yet he did not take those holdings from you,' said de Marigny. 'That, according to your deposition, was the work of Roger de Marmoutier.'

'Another grasping baron!'

'Our evidence suggests otherwise.'

'Then your evidence is false,' retorted the abbot, eyes blinking rapidly. 'The land in question was seized illegally by the lord Roger. I protested strongly but my protests were overridden.'

Ralph glanced down at a document in front of him. 'Roger de Marmoutier had a royal charter to substantiate his claim.'

'So does the abbey of Tavistock. Mine predates his.'

'Then it is rendered invalid by the charter which succeeds it. King William is empowered to give but he is also able to take away. Those holdings were granted to the lord Roger for services rendered on the battlefield.'

The abbot spluttered. 'They were first given to me for services rendered on the much more important battlefield of missionary Christianity. When I came to Tavistock, the abbey was in a deplorable condition. Sihtric, my predecessor, had the most appalling reputation. He was a disgrace to the Benedictine Order.' He inflated his chest. 'I took a moribund house and turned it into a vigorous monastic centre.'

'This is well known, Father Abbot,' said Hubert, stepping in to cut him off before his speech became an extended sermon. 'You have been justly praised for the remarkable work you have done at Tavistock. That is not the point at issue.'

'It is, Canon Hubert.'

'I beg to differ.'

'Those holdings were granted to me by way of reward.'

'But that reward was in time transferred to Roger de Marmoutier.'

'And there is another factor to consider here,' said Ralph. 'The abbey was not cruelly stripped of that property. When it was taken from you, there was a compensatory grant of land.'

'That is irrelevant!'

'No, it is not,' said de Marigny. 'It alters the case completely. This is not an act of disseisin. Fair exchange was involved.'

'Fair exchange!' The abbot's voice soared even higher. 'Prime land was taken from us and barren land given in return. Do you call that fair exchange, my lord? There is richer soil near Exeter. As well as producing a regular harvest, the holdings under discussion also support sheep, cattle, pigs and a large herd of unbroken mares.'

'What would your monks want with unbroken mares?' asked Ralph mischievously. 'A herd of unbroken nuns would be more appropriate livestock, would it not?'

There was uproar. The prior leapt to his feet to remonstrate, Canon Hubert added his condemnation, Brother Simon gave a squeal of horror and the abbot of Tavistock howled with righteous fury, pointing a finger of doom at Ralph as if trying to excommunicate him on the spot. Hervey de Marigny burst out laughing but quickly controlled his lapse. The soldiers at the rear of the hall took longer to suppress their mirth. It was fully five minutes before peace returned to the shire hall. Ralph apologised profusely and stroked the ruffled feathers of the monks back into place.

'Now,' he said quietly. 'Let us look more deeply into this claim.'

Gervase Bret left the funeral service with a number of images jostling in his mind. Nicholas Picard's composed widow and her attentive steward, Tetbald, fought for his attention with the poised Loretta and her Saxon companion, Eldred. Bishop Osbern remained a vivid memory, as did Dean Jerome and Saewin, but it was Asa who finally put her rivals to flight and became sole occupant of the disputed territory. Gervase could not stop thinking about her. The look which they exchanged across the grave had been compounded of hope, curiosity and admiration. As he recalled the breathtaking shock of her loveliness, Gervase had to remind himself that someone equally beautiful and very trusting was waiting in Winchester for him to take her as his bride. Nothing and everything had happened during his silent communion with Asa. The encounter left him feeling guiltily exhilarated.

A figure swooped down on him as he was coming out of the cemetery. Baldwin the Sheriff moved from mourning to revenge with chilling speed.

'One moment, Gervase,' he said.

'Yes, my lord sheriff?'

'I did not expect to see you here, but I am glad that I have done so. It saves me having to enlist the services of the town reeve.'

'Saewin?'

'Only a Saxon can understand another Saxon,' he said peevishly. 'I have a man in my dungeon who will yield up nothing but gibberish even under torture. May I employ you as an interpreter?'

'Is this man one of the robbers?'

'Yes, Gervase. The only one to survive. I want the full story of how and why they murdered Nicholas Picard. I owe it to his widow and his family to beat the truth out of the prisoner's carcase. Will you help us?'

'I am at your service, my lord sheriff.'

'Let us return to the castle at once.'

It was not an assignment which Gervase accepted with any alacrity and it would keep him away from his duties in the shire hall even longer, but it was an opportunity which could not be refused. He and Ralph were not convinced that the robbers had killed Nicholas Picard before making off with their booty. Gervase hoped to learn if their doubts were justified. Baldwin's wife had already returned to the castle with an escort, and six soldiers from the garrison accompanied the sheriff and his guest there. Surrounded by the armed guard, Gervase felt as if he were under arrest.

The dungeons were situated below ground in the outer bailey. Stone steps led down to a narrow passageway with damp walls. Torches were placed in holders to throw a jagged light and further illumination came from the glowing coals in the brazier. Pokers and tongs were being heated in the fire. Gervase gulped at the realisation that his host would use the most barbaric methods of torture without compunction. When the gaoler saw them coming, he took one of the torches from its holder and used it to conduct them to a heavy oak door with an iron grille in it. Through the bars, Gervase could see a man curled up in the foetid straw.

When the door was unlocked, Baldwin pulled it open, then snatched the torch from the gaoler and went into the cell. Kicking the prisoner awake, he held the flames close to the man's face and made him recoil with horror. Gervase noted that he was fettered and that his naked torso already bore the hideous marks of whip and fire.

'Tell the truth!' ordered the sheriff, kicking the man again.

'Let him be, my lord sheriff,' said Gervase.

'Ask him why they slaughtered Nicholas Picard.'

'I could do so more easily alone.'

'I will stay here and watch.'

'He will speak more freely if you quit the cell,' said Gervase. 'He is in abject terror. I will not get a word out of him while you stand over the fellow like that. Wait outside and you will easily overhear us.'

Baldwin was unhappy with the suggestion but he agreed to it. Thrusting the torch into Gervase's hand, he lumbered out and stood in the passageway with the gaoler. The cell was small, low and noisome. No natural light penetrated. The straw was clotted with excrement and it took Gervase a moment to accustom himself to the stink. The smell of fear was also overpowering. He knelt down and spoke softly to the man.

'I need to ask you some questions,' he said.

The prisoner was surprised to hear his own language. They were the first words addressed to him in the dungeon which were not followed by a blow. He turned a wary eye on his visitor.

'Who are you?' he said gruffly.

'My name is Gervase Bret and I am in the king's service. Some days ago, a man was ambushed in a wood not far from the city. It is very important for us to find out who murdered him and why.' He held the torch nearer his own face so that the man could see he posed no threat. 'Did you and your accomplice kill him?'

'No!'

'Is that the truth?'

'Yes!' said the other with a note of pleading. 'We are robbers and not murderers. Masterless men who live by stealing. Or did live,' he added ruefully. 'They have already slain my brother Alnoth, and they will soon send me after him.'

'The lord sheriff tells me that you were found with money and rings upon you. They were taken from the dead man, Nicholas Picard.'

'I confess it freely.'

'How did they come into your possession?'

'By chance.'

'Go on.'

'Alnoth and I were heading for the wood that evening. When darkness falls, it is an ideal place for an ambush and we have found more than one fool riding home alone.' He ran a

108

tongue over parched lips to moisten them. 'As we approached, a horse came galloping out of the wood. We knew that something amiss had happened.'

'What did you do?'

'We rode into the wood with caution. We soon found him.'

'Where?'

'Beside the track and beneath an overhanging beech,' said the other, grimacing at the memory. 'His face was cut to ribbons and his throat cut. Alnoth and I could not bear to look on him.'

'Yet you stole his purse.'

'Yes.'

'And his rings?'

'He had no more use for them,' said the man truculently. 'They were pure gold. We planned to sell them but they caught us. Yes,' he said with a touch of defiance. 'We are robbers and we stole from a dead man but we did not kill him. I swear it!'

'Who did?'

'I do not know.'

'Did you see anybody else in the wood?'

'No,' said the man. 'All we heard were the hooves of a horse. When we reached the body, someone was galloping away in the direction of the city.'

'Only one horse?' asked Gervase.

'Only one.'

'Can you be certain of that?'

'My brother and I are robbers,' said the other. 'Sharp ears are a necessary part of our trade. We are used to keeping out of sight and listening. We saw the dead man's stallion leaving the wood and we heard only one other horse.'

'A solitary attacker, then?' mused Gervase. 'No accomplices.'

'All we knew was that there were rich pickings that cost us no effort. We took what we wanted and fled.'

'To Crediton, I hear?'

'We stayed at an inn. That was our mistake.'

Gervase moved in closer to study the man's face. He was still relatively young, not much above Gervase's own age, but a life on the run had ploughed deep furrows and a night at the mercy of Baldwin of Moeles had sown them with anguish. It was the ugly face of a desperate man who pursued a life of crime with his brother. Whatever he said, he knew that he would die at the hands of the sheriff. The man had nothing to lose and no reason to lie. Gervase believed his story implicitly.

'Thank you,' he said warmly.

They were the only kind words the man had heard since he arrived there.

'Thank you?' he echoed. 'For what?'

Gervase left the cell to be accosted by an impatient sheriff.

'Did you draw a confession out of him?' he asked.

'No, my lord sheriff.'

'Would he say nothing?'

'Only that they did not kill the lord Nicholas. All that he will admit is that they stole the money and rings. His story rings true. I am sorry,' said Gervase firmly, 'but you have merely caught a thief. You have not arrested the murderer.'

They rode home in silence, their horses moving at a dignified trot which suited their mood. When they reached the manor house, Catherine went straight to her chamber. Tetbald dismissed the knights who had escorted them to and from the funeral then adjourned to the kitchen. Ordering refreshment, he took it up to her in person on a wooden tray.

Catherine was seated in a chair when he let himself in. She refused the offer of food, but consented to take the cup of wine he had brought. Tetbald set the tray down. She sipped her drink reflectively.

'Did you see her?' she asked in a flat voice.

'Who, my lady?'

'Asa.'

'Yes,' he said. 'I knew that she would be there.'

'She has too much gall not to be. Gall and impertinence.'

'We could hardly prevent her, my lady.'

'Her presence did not offend me, Tetbald,' she said. 'I ceased to be offended by my husband's behaviour a long time ago. If I had not done so, I would have led a miserable existence and misery has no appeal for me. No,' she continued, 'I was interested to see Asa there. And I do believe that she came to pay her respects rather than to gloat. Besides, she thinks herself a beneficiary of Nicholas's death.'

'The commissioners will not take her claim seriously.'

'She purports to have a letter written by my husband.'

'But was it witnessed?' he said.

'I think it unlikely.'

'Then what significance will the commissioners attach to it, my lady? A letter of intent is not a legally binding document. Beside your claim as the widow, Asa's is quite derisory. She will be humiliated in the shire hall.'

'I am almost tempted to be there to watch that happen.'

'That might not be wise,' he warned.

'I will not lock myself away for ever, Tetbald.'

'People will expect you to grieve.'

'I grieved when he was alive,' she said bitterly. 'Now that he is dead, I am free of him. Free of the lies, the deception and the endless—'

Her voice broke off as kinder memories surfaced. She had married Nicholas Picard out of love and there had been true happiness at the start. In the welter of recrimination, it was easy to forget that. The cathedral where he was buried was also the place where they had married. She recalled the fragile joy of her wedding day and felt the first pang of regret at his passing.

'Children,' she whispered. 'It might all have been different had I borne him the family he craved. I let him down. Nature can be harsh at times. I prayed for children but they never came.' A harder note intruded. 'But not even a family would have held him down. A character such as his does not change. Children would simply have imprisoned me here even more strictly and left him to roam at will.'

'It is all behind you now, my lady.'

'Yes, Tetbald.'

'And the ordeal of the funeral is over.'

'It was no ordeal,' she said calmly. 'I did my duty. They all saw that. The widow of Nicholas Picard did what was expected of her. Nobody could look into my heart.'

He smiled furtively. 'I did, my lady.'

'You have been a rock, Tetbald.'

'I have tried to be.'

'Without you, I would not have borne up so well.'

'It is a privilege to be of service,' he said, moving familiarly across to take her hand. 'There is nothing I would not do for you, my lady.'

'We both know that.'

'It fills me with joy to be able to plead on your behalf in the shire hall. Those holdings are yours. The other claims are worthless.'

'The people who make them do not think so.'

'They are wasting their time,' he assured her, placing a faint kiss on her hand before releasing it. 'Have faith in me and I will bring that property back to its rightful owner.' Seeing her nod then appear to drift off into a reverie, he asked: 'Would you prefer to be left alone, my lady?'

'For a while.'

'I will come back later.'

'You will be welcome.'

'Thank you.'

'It is I who should be thanking you,' she said with a weary smile. 'You helped me through it. You were there for me.' A recollection nudged her. 'I saw you talking to the lord sheriff after the service.'

'He had good news for us. Or what he assumed would be good news.'

'What did he say?'

'The men who killed your husband were captured. One died but the other is being held in the castle dungeon. He will doubtless hang for the crime. I almost pity the wretch.'

'Did you say that to my lord sheriff?'

He gave a lazy smile. 'That would have been foolhardy.'

* * *

113

When he reached the shire hall, Gervase was plunged into the swirling waters of debate. The abbot of Tavistock was a pugnacious advocate, stating his case in uncompromising terms and responding instantly to any challenge from the commissioners. Gervase's legal expertise was in demand at once and though it was tested by the combative prelate, it was not found wanting. By the end of the session, the abbey's claim had been thoroughly scrutinised, but no verdict could be reached until the other disputants had been examined. Abbot and prior departed, leaving the commissioners to review the events of the afternoon. When their discussion was over, Canon Hubert and Brother Simon went back to the sanctuary of the cathedral. Ralph's impatience boiled over.

'What happened at the funeral, Gervase?' he said. 'I have been dying to ask you but had to listen to that garrulous abbot instead. Tell all.'

'There is more to tell than I expected, Ralph.'

'In what way?'

'The lord sheriff employed me as an interpreter. He took me to the castle dungeons to talk with the man they arrested last night.'

'What did you learn?' asked Hervey de Marigny.

Gervase gave them a faithful account of all that had transpired at the cathedral and at the castle, omitting only the effect which Asa had had on him. Ralph was intrigued by the visit to the dungeon, but de Marigny was more diverted by the names of three mourners at the funeral.

'The lady Loretta,' he observed, 'the widow of the deceased and the Saxon woman, Asa, were paying their respects to a man whose land they all covet. Three claimants at the same service. I wonder that a fourth did not find it in his heart to attend.'

'A fourth?' said Ralph.

'Geoffrey, abbot of Tavistock.'

'There was no love lost between him and Nicholas Picard.'

'Perhaps not, Ralph, but a devout Christian like the abbot should surely not have missed the chance to attend. Apart from anything else, he would have rubbed shoulders with the sheriff and the bishop, two men whose friendship he must assiduously cultivate in this shire. For such a politic being, his absence was strange.'

'Or tactful.' said Ralph thoughtfully. 'I have just recalled what I was told about Walter Baderon.'

'Who?'

'The captain of the guard at the North Gate on the night of the murder. According to the town reeve, this man saw the lord Nicholas quit the city. What interested me was the name of Walter Baderon's master.'

'The abbot of Tavistock?' guessed de Marigny.

'The same.'

'It is probably just a coincidence,' said Gervase. 'You surely are not suggesting that the abbot was party to a murder?'

'What I am suggesting,' said Ralph, 'is that one of us takes the trouble to question this Baderon when he comes on duty this evening.'

'That will be my office,' volunteered de Marigny.

'Thank you, Hervey. Meanwhile, Gervase and I will go for a ride.'

Gervase was surprised. 'Will we?'

'Let us collect our horses from the castle.'

'But where are we going?'

'Where else?' said Ralph. 'To the scene of the crime.'

Loretta had been one of the last to leave the cathedral. Bishop Osbern's eulogy brought her close to tears and she paid the tribute of a passing sigh to the widow of the deceased. Left alone in the cemetery with her servant, Eldred, she took a final look at the mound of fresh soil over the last resting place of Nicholas Picard before moving to a stone tomb in the shade of the cathedral. Both her husband and her son were buried there, giving her a double reason to make frequent visits. Her mind went back to the time when Roger de Marmoutier was alive and the master of countless acres of Devon farmland. They had enjoyed great wealth in those days and the position which went with it. Tragedy then stalked the family. She lost a husband, a son and some of their most prized holdings. It was a story of continuous loss.

As she gazed at the tomb which contained her loved ones, she vowed that she would regain the forfeited property. It was hers now. All that she had to do was to persuade the commissioners of the strength of her claim and Loretta was confident of her ability to do just that. However, it was important to know something of the men she would face before she took her turn in front of them at the shire hall.

'Eldred,' she called, raising a hand to summon him to her side. 'I will go home now. Call on the town reeve and entreat him to visit me this evening. I need Saewin's advice.'

Eldred nodded obediently then went swiftly off on his errand.

After lingering for a few more minutes, Loretta ran a pensive hand along the stone tomb then turned away in distress. A solitary figure was now standing beside the grave of Nicholas Picard, weeping quietly to herself. When Loretta saw who the woman was, she seethed with anger. Chin held high and eyes staring straight ahead, she walked past the mourner with an air of contempt.

Asa did not even notice her.

Golde was surprised to be summoned and she walked to the apartment with a mixture of curiosity and trepidation. The lady Albreda was an indifferent hostess who unsettled her guests. When she tried to be more pleasant towards them, there was a sense of effort. Before she was conducted into her presence, Golde wondered whether she would meet rebuff or apology on the other side of the carved door.

'You sent for me, my lady?' she asked quietly.

'Yes,' murmured the other. 'Please sit down.'

Albreda was reclining in a chair, her arms draped over the sides and her body slack. Her eyes were closed and her face screwed into a ball. Lowering herself onto a stool beside her, Golde studied her with alarm.

'Are you unwell, my lady?'

'No.'

'Do you need a physician?'

'There is nothing wrong with me.'

'You seem to be in pain.'

'I will be fine in a moment.'

'Is there anything that I can do?'

'Just sit quietly with me, please.'

She held out a pale hand and Golde took it between both palms. They sat in silence for a long while. Albreda slowly relaxed. The expression of suffering left her face, to be replaced by a look of regret. When she opened her eyes, they were moist with tears.

'What is wrong, my lady?' whispered Golde.

'I should not have gone to the funeral,' said the other meekly, 'but my husband insisted and I had to obey. It was harrowing, Golde. I all but fainted with the agony of it. Nicholas Picard was such a handsome man in the prime of life. My heart went out to his widow, the lady Catherine.'

'She must be destroyed with grief.'

'It is beyond bearing. To lose a husband is punishment enough. To have him cruelly murdered is a tragedy that would overwhelm anyone. I do not know how the lady Catherine maintained her calm.' She looked at Golde. 'Have you ever lost a loved one?'

'My first husband died some years ago, my lady.'

'Then you know something of grief yourself.'

'Yes,' said Golde, unable to resist a gentle reproach. 'Even though he was only a brewer. He was a good man and a loyal husband.'

'I offended you on that score,' admitted the other. 'When you told us that you carried on his trade, I was condescending. It was unpardonable. I was tense and nervous that night, Golde. I did not behave as a hostess should towards her guests.'

'Let us put all that behind us.'

'Please,' said Albreda, squeezing her hand. 'I want us to

be friends. I need you.' She gave a sad smile. 'Have you ever noticed that it is often easier to confide in a stranger than in someone you know well?'

'Yes, my lady.'

'I sensed that I could talk to you.'

'I am listening.'

There was another long pause while Albreda gathered her thoughts. Golde was glad that she had answered the summons. The awkwardness between the two women was dispelled. The gaunt and stately lady was showing signs of human frailty. Golde felt that she was in a privileged position of trust. She glanced around the apartment. It was a small room with tapestries on all four walls. An archway led to a bedchamber and it was apparent that it was not shared with the sheriff.

'I love my husband,' said Albreda defensively. 'He is a fine man who does a difficult job extremely well. Devon is a large and unruly county. It needs someone as strong and forceful as Baldwin to keep it under control. He has many virtues, Golde. I appreciate them.'

'That is as it should be.'

'Yes,' agreed the other. 'But is this?' Her gesture took in the whole chamber. 'Do you live apart from your husband, Golde?'

'No, my lady.'

'Would he be content if his wife did not share his bed?'

'He would not.'

'Does he truly care for you?'

'Oh, yes,' said Golde. 'Every day brings proof of it.'

'Then you are blessed in the lord Ralph. Cleave to him. Live under the same roof as man and wife. There is no pleasure in being a married nun.' She hunched her shoulders. 'I was jealous of you at first. You seemed to have what I had always sought and what I might once have had.'

'My lady?'

'It is all past now. I must learn to forget.'

'Forget what?'

'Past mistakes. Irremediable errors.'

'I do not understand.'

'Look at me, Golde. What do you see?'

'A handsome woman of good repute.'

'Am I not a sorry spectacle?'

'No, my lady!'

'I have heard them sniggering at me. I have seen them shooting glances in my direction. They think me a ridiculous woman, neglected and unloved. Drifting through my days in a dream.'

'That is unfair.'

'Yet it contains a grain of truth.' Albreda sat forward and grasped both of Golde's hands. She stared deep into her eyes, simultaneously appraising and appealing to her, searching for a reassurance which would allow her to proceed. 'I sense that you are discreet,' she said. 'Are you?'

'Yes, my lady.'

'Nothing of what I tell you must leave this room.'

'You have my solemn oath.'

'I am letting you see my weakness, Golde. I would not have others see it and mock it. They would not understand. You will.' She bit her lip before she continued. 'Do you begin to guess what I am saying?'

'I think so, my lady.'

'Today has been a dreadful ordeal for me. I tried to think of others but I kept feeling my own sense of loss. Do you hear me?'

'Yes, my lady. The lord Nicholas was a friend.'

'He was more than that to me, Golde.'

'I see.'

'It was not as you may think,' said Albreda seriously. 'I have been a devoted wife. I have kept my marriage vows and never looked at another man. But a little flame has always burned away inside me. Until today. When Nicholas was lowered into his grave, the flame went out for ever.'

'Did you love him so much?'

'Yes, Golde. That was the irremediable error of which I spoke.'

'What was?'

'Nicholas Picard once asked me to marry him. I declined his offer.'

Chapter Six

Ralph Delchard and Gervase Bret rode out of the city to inspect the scene of the crime. Trapped in a musty shire hall for most of the day, Ralph found the fresh air bracing, and after the grim visits to a funeral and a castle dungeon Gervase was also glad to exchange Exeter for the refreshing tranquillity of the countryside. When they reached the wood on the road north, it did not take them long to find the place where the ambush occurred. There were several beech trees but few grew alongside the meandering track and overhung it. They dismounted to examine what they felt certain was the correct spot. Dried blood still clung to the grass and there were signs of a struggle. Twigs were snapped off from a bush, wild flowers had been unceremoniously flattened and the earth was heavily scored.

Ralph knelt down to run an exploratory hand over the ground.

'This was definitely the place,' he decided. 'Ideal for an ambush.'

'Yes,' said Gervase, glancing around. 'Where would the killer have lurked? Every tree could have hidden him.'

'You are standing beneath the one that did, Gervase.'

'What do you mean?'

'Look upwards.'

Gervase raised his eyes to the overhanging bough. It was thick enough to support the weight of a man, and the abundant foliage would have provided concealment, but the branch was high above the track.

'I know what you are thinking,' said Ralph, rising to his feet. 'How did the murderer get up there?'

'Exactly.'

'There is only one way to find out, Gervase.'

'Is there?'

'You or me?'

'I do not understand.'

'One of us has to climb the tree,' said Ralph with a smile. 'Since you are younger and more agile, I accept your offer to tackle it.'

'But I did not make an offer.'

'Surely you wish to spare my old bones?'

Gervase grinned. 'No,' he said with a nudge. 'What I will promise to do is to catch you if you fall.'

'Get up there, man!'

'Is that a request or an order?'

'Common sense. I would climb up it like a bear whereas you can run up it like a squirrel. Go on, Gervase. I'll warrant you will find something of interest once you work your way out onto the bough.' He walked to the trunk and linked his hands together. 'Come, I'll help you.'

Gervase appraised the tree. It was a fully grown beech, now in full leaf and with boughs reaching out in all directions. There was an air of solidity and permanence about it. After rubbing his palms together in preparation, he steeled himself then put a foot into the cradle made by Ralph's hands. His friend hoisted him effortlessly up to the first branch. Gervase got a firm grip before swinging a leg up and hooking it over the bough. He made slow progress. Gervase was lithe enough but his work at the Chancery in Winchester gave him little opportunity to develop his tree-climbing skills. Ralph directed him from below, telling him which branch to move to next and urging him on.

Eventually, Gervase was sitting astride the bough which overhung the track. He moved himself carefully along it, making the whole branch genuflect gracefully and rustle its leaves. When he reached a point directly above the track, he was screened from view by the foliage.

'What can you see?' called Ralph.

'Everything.'

'A good view of the road from Exeter?'

'A perfect one, Ralph.'

'Could you jump onto a passing traveller from there?'

'It would be a long drop.'

'Long but not impossible.'

'Not impossible for some,' said Gervase. 'Inadvisable for me.'

'Can you see anything else up there?'

'Yes.'

Gervase looked at the marks along the bough. The bark had been scratched by sharp claws but there was also a much thicker souvenir, an inch or more in width, running, it seemed, over the whole circumference of the branch. Pale, shiny wood showed through the stripped bark. He ran a meditative finger over it.

'Are you still up there?' said Ralph impatiently.

'Yes.'

'Well?'

'I think that someone tied a rope up here and swung down. A fairly heavy man, judging by the marks he left. He may have practised a few times,' he concluded. 'That would explain why the bark is worn through.'

'Anything else?'

'Scratches made by claws.'

'What sort of claws?'

'Come up and see for yourself, Ralph,' he teased.

'No thank you.'

'You'll get a fine view.'

'I prefer the one from down here.'

'The scratches are very deep.'

'Can you guess what sort of animal put them there?'

'No,' said Gervase. 'Not a big one, I suspect.'

'There we are, then,' said Ralph with light sarcasm. 'All we need to look for is a small creature who uses his claws to climb the tree and a rope to get down from it. Would that description fit the man you saw in the castle dungeon?'

'No, Ralph. He was not the killer.'

'How can you be certain?'

'Only a determined man would take the risk of climbing up here and hurling himself on someone passing below. Two robbers would find a much easier way to stop their victim and, as we both know, they would never let his horse get away. Apart from being a valuable prize, it might return to the man's stables and alert the household.'

'Which is exactly what it did.'

'The prisoner at the castle was telling the truth.'

'So who was our woodland assassin?'

'Someone who was strong, fit and daring.'

'With claws instead of fingernails.'

'I just can't explain these scratch marks,' said Gervase. 'Unless they were made by some animal at a different time and are unrelated to the ambush. But we have established one thing, Ralph.'

'What's that?'

'How a single attacker gained the advantage over Nicholas Picard.'

'The element of surprise?'

'And the force of his descent.'

Gervase lifted a leg over the bough and hung with his arms at full stretch. Without warning, he suddenly dropped to the ground, missing Ralph by a matter of inches and sending the latter scrambling backwards in alarm. Gervase bent his knees to lessen the impact of the landing.

Ralph was indignant. 'You almost hit me!'

'That is how he did it.'

'Putting the fear of death into a friend like that?'

'No, Ralph,' said Gervase, dusting himself off. 'I think that he used that rope to swing down and knock the lord Nicholas from the saddle, then stunned him before slitting his throat.'

'How did he know that his victim would ride this way?'

'It is the only road that leads to his manor house.'

'But how could he be sure that Nicholas Picard would be alone?'

'Because he saw him enter the city,' said Gervase. 'Without an armed escort. Knowing that his victim would have to ride back through the wood on his own, he set up the ambush. We are looking for someone who is well acquainted with the lord Nicholas and his habits. This was no random attack, Ralph. Too much preparation was involved.'

'What about the claw marks up there?'

Gervase rubbed his smoothly shaven chin while he ruminated. 'They still puzzle me,' he admitted.

It was an occasion for a gentler approach. Hervey de Marigny knew that there were times when subtlety achieved far better results than threat and abuse. Those were the weapons for which Baldwin the Sheriff first reached and they were not always the most effective ones against a seasoned knight like Walter Baderon. Softer words were needed.

'Good even, friend,' said de Marigny.

'My lord.'

'You have a long night ahead of you.'

'Do not remind us!' moaned Baderon. 'While others may sleep in their beds, we have to stay on sentry duty here at the North Gate.'

'I am surprised you do not fall asleep through boredom.'

'It is an unwelcome duty.'

'Whom do you serve?'

'The abbot of Tavistock.'

'A churlish gentlemen, I hear.'

'But a good master,' said the other loyally.

'How long have you been with him?'

'Nigh on fifteen years, my lord.'

'Yet you still have to mount a guard here?' said de Marigny. 'After all that time, I would have thought you might have earned sufficient thanks from the abbot to be excused such onerous duty.'

'We all have to take our turn.'

'Is there nothing to liven up the long night hours?'

'Liven them up, my lord?'

'Come, sir,' said de Marigny with a confiding chuckle. 'I have done my share of standing on guard in the darkness. On cold nights, we had drink brought out to warm us up. In summer, we had a woman or two to help us pass the time. There is good sport to be had up against a wall.'

Walter Baderon sniggered. 'We learnt that long ago, my lord.'

'Are the ladies of Exeter obliging?'

'Very obliging.'

'And not too costly?'

'They will always do favours for a soldier.'

'Especially a captain of the guard like yourself.'

'I always have first pick.'

Hervey de Marigny laughed. He had sauntered out to the North Gate shortly after Baderon and his men relieved their predecessors on sentry duty. Before their stint even began, they looked jaded. Conversation with a visitor to the city was a pleasant relief. Walter Baderon fell into it without realising to whom he was talking.

'You have my sympathy, friend,' de Marigny went on, drawing attention once again to the common ground between the two of them.

'Why, my lord?'

'Exeter is not the most hospitable city for Normans.'

'That is true!'

'I was part of the army which besieged the place. These men of Devon are hostile and unforgiving. I would not turn my back on any of them.'

'Nor me.'

'Are you still resented and sneered at?'

'Daily.'

'We had more than harsh words hurled at us.'

'We, too, have incidents from time to time,' said Baderon, hand on the hilt of his sword. 'It is usually when some Saxon youths have drunk too much of that foul ale they brew. They taunt us to build up their courage then draw their weapons.'

'What do you do?'

'Bang their heads together and send them home.'

'No bloodshed?'

'Not unless they really annoy me.'

They chatted on amiably, both of them keeping one eye on the traffic coming in and out of the gate. There was no hurry. The commissioner took time to win the man's confidence. It would be worth it. They had been together for half an hour when de Marigny came round to the subject which brought him there.

'Have they caught the villain yet?' he asked.

'What villain?'

'The one who ambushed the lord Nicholas,' he said casually. 'I have only been in the city a few days but people talk of nothing else. They are certain that the victim was murdered by Saxons out for revenge.'

'That may be so, my lord.'

'Have any arrests been made?'

'Word has it that two men were taken. One was killed but the other is being held in the castle dungeon.'

'That is good to hear. Who was this Nicholas Picard?'

'A baron of some substance.'

'Buried here at the cathedral, I believe.'

'That is so, my lord.' His lip curled. 'I dare swear that there was much weeping among the ladies at the graveside.'

'Why so?'

'The lord Nicholas was a very popular man.'

'Indeed?'

'Ladies came running and he did not turn them away.'

'A man after my own heart!'

'And mine, too!'

'Yet struck down before his time.'

'Alas, yes.'

'When was this?'

'A few days ago, my lord,' said the other, ready to reveal his own part in the story. 'He rode out past us that evening without noticing that we were here. I hailed him but got no reply. I remember thinking how wrapped up in his own thoughts he was.' He gave a shrug. 'Twenty minutes later, he was dead.'

'Twenty minutes?'

'It could not have taken him much longer to reach that wood.'

'Unless he stopped on the way.'

'He did not do that, my lord,' said the other. 'He was riding home.'

'How can you be sure of that?'

'By the route that he took. I walked through the gate and watched him ride off until he was out of sight. From the moment he left the city, the lord Nicholas was doomed.'

'Did anyone trail him?'

'Nobody whom I saw.'

'Then someone must have been lying in wait.'

'So it seems.'

'Resentful Saxons?'

'Most like.'

'Who else could have a reason to murder him?'

Baderon checked his reply at the moment it was about to leave his mouth, resorting instead to a shake of the head, but de Marigny did not let the matter go. He lifted an artless eyebrow.

'So you recognised him when he left the city that night?'

'Yes, my lord.'

'How?'

'Everyone knows – or knew – the lord Nicholas.'

'Including the abbot of Tavistock? Did he know him?'

'Only too well!' came the rueful reply.

'Oh?'

'That is all I can tell you,' said the other brusquely. 'Except

131

that the name of Nicholas Picard was not spoken with any affection in Tavistock.'

'Abbots are famed for their generosity of spirit, are they not? Why is your master an exception to the rule?' When there was no answer, de Marigny shifted his ground slightly. 'What of the lord Nicholas's wife?' he asked. 'How did she view her husband?'

'Lovingly.'

'Yet you suggest that he was unfaithful to her.'

'The lady Catherine accepted her lot without complaint.'

'Might she not have resented her husband beneath the surface?'

'Perhaps.'

'You do not sound convinced.'

'The lady Catherine was a tolerant wife.'

'You seem to know her well.'

'Only by repute.'

'Have you never met the lady?'

A long pause. 'Once or twice.'

'What was your opinion of her?'

'It is not my place to have an opinion, my lord.'

'Every man is entitled to an opinion where a woman is concerned. Was she beautiful or ill favoured? Tall or short? Happy or long-suffering? You must have some memory of her.'

'The lady Catherine made an unfortunate marriage.'

The words slipped out quietly but they were all that Walter Baderon was prepared to say on the subject. There was no point in pressing him. He was on the defensive now. Affecting indifference, de Marigny turned to a discussion of the town's fortifications.

'Exeter was well-defended when we laid siege to it.'

'Its defences are even stronger now, my lord.'

'So I have observed. King William does not trust the men of Devon. When we took possession of the city, he not only ordered that the castle be rebuilt and extended, he made sure that the whole county was ringed with fortresses.' He gave a sympathetic smile. 'And that all of them were served by knights such as yourself.'

'It is necessary work.'

'And it has its moments of interest.'

'Interest, my lord?'

'You are a prime witness in a murder inquiry.'

'Yes,' said the other uncertainly.

'Let us face it, my friend. You were probably the last person to speak to him. I doubt that his killer had much time for conversation. By being at your post on the night in question, you were in a unique position.' He glanced at the gate. 'You say that you watched the lord Nicholas until he disappeared from sight?'

'I did.'

Hervey de Marigny smiled disarmingly. 'Why?' he asked.

When the town reeve arrived at the house, he was admitted by Eldred who gave him a nod of welcome before conducting him to the parlour. The servant remained long enough for the exchange of pleasantries between Saewin and Loretta, then withdrew silently. Loretta was seated at the little table. She waved her visitor to a stool opposite her. He perched uneasily on the edge of it, wondering why she had sent for him but feeling too abashed to ask. There was something about her which always induced a sense of exaggerated respect in him.

'I saw you at the funeral,' she began.

'Yes, my lady. It was a harrowing occasion.'

'For most of us, that is,' she observed wryly. 'The lord Nicholas's widow did not seem harrowed. When my husband died, I was on the verge of collapse. The funeral was an ordeal from start to finish. That did not appear to be the case today. The lady Catherine was a robust mourner.'

'Each of us grieves in his or her own way,' he said.

'I could not agree more, Saewin.'

'She is a noble lady and bore her affliction with dignity.'

'And what a terrible affliction it was!' she said with a sharp intake of breath. 'A dear husband, brutally murdered. It must have been a comfort to her to know that the sheriff had the culprit in his dungeon.'

'Yes, my lady,' he said evasively.

'Are you hiding something from me?'

'Not at all.'

'Then why do I get the impression that you are? At the funeral, they were all talking about the arrest of the two men responsible. I overheard the details a dozen times. Are you telling me that they are not true?'

'I know no more than you, my lady.'

'Will the man be convicted and hanged?'

'Probably.'

'Good. Only then will the lady Catherine be able to mourn properly.'

'There may be something in that.'

'Oh, there is, Saewin. There is.'

He could never understand why she made him so uncomfortable. It was not simply her extraordinary poise and natural authority. When he dared to look at her with any degree of scrutiny, he could admire her mature beauty and her immaculate attire. There was nothing accidental about the lady Loretta. She took great pains with her appearance.

'When will I be called to the shire hall?' she asked.

'Tomorrow, I believe.'

'Has the decision not yet been made?'

'It is a question of time, my lady,' he explained. 'The commissioners never know how much to allot to each person. It took them a whole day to examine the abbot of Tavistock and they are still not done with him. Tomorrow, the first claimant to be called is Engelric. Who can say how long he will keep them engaged?'

'Engelric's claim is ludicrous.'

'They feel an obligation to hear it.'

'Only to dismiss it summarily. Will I be the next to be heard?'

'No, my lady.'

'Who will precede me?' His embarrassment was an answer in itself. 'I see,' she said crisply. 'I have to give way to a person of her rank, do I?'

'It is not a question of giving way.'

'Is my claim considered to be inferior to hers?'

'No, my lady.'

'And inferior to that of Engelric?'

'There is no significance in the order,' he insisted. 'If there were, then you should feel reassured for the last person to

135

be summoned before the commissioners will be Tetbald the Steward. That would suggest that the claimants are being questioned in a sequence of rising importance.'

There was a considered pause during which she studied his face and noted the obvious tension in his body. A smile which was intended to relax him instead made him feel even more unsettled.

'How favourably did they look upon the abbot of Tavistock?' she said.

'The proceedings are held in private, my lady.'

'You saw the abbot when he left and you must have gleaned something from their manner when the commissioners dispersed. Was his claim felt to be a just one?'

'They did not confide in me, my lady.'

'You were there, Saewin. You must have some idea.'

'The abbot departed in an angry mood, that is all I know.'

'Then you have told me what I hoped to hear,' she said calmly. 'I'll wager that Engelric will be sent on his way empty-handed as well. That means there are only two of us in contention.'

'Three, my lady.'

'I do not count *her*,' she said with scorn.

'Nevertheless, Asa will be called before them.'

'Then me.'

'Then the lady Catherine's steward.'

'I have met Tetbald,' she said with a look of distaste. 'But tell me about these commissioners, Saewin. That is what I really wish to find out. What sort of men are they? Describe each one to me.'

He rubbed his palms nervously. 'I am not able to do that, I fear.'

'Why not?'

'My office rests on my discretion.'

'You are not being forced to be indiscreet,' she argued. 'I would never dream of placing you in such a position. Besides, what you tell me will go no further than these four walls.' She leant forward. 'All I seek is a few facts. If I am to face these judges, I would like to know what awaits me.'

'Decent men, well versed in their craft.'

'They are led by Ralph Delchard, I understand?'

'My lady . . .'

'It is not a secret. Who is he?' His hesitation irritated her. 'Is it such an impossible favour that I ask?' she asked. 'Perhaps you should remember some of the favours I have done you and your kind, Saewin. Who brought the message to you earlier?'

'Eldred.'

'And who admitted you to my home?'

'Eldred.'

'I took him into service when nobody else would do so. And on whose recommendation, Saewin? Who brought Eldred to me?'

He lowered his head. 'I did, my lady.'

'You sought a favour for a fellow Saxon. I granted you that favour.'

'Have you been disappointed in him?'

'No, Eldred has been a loyal servant.'

'Then I was in some sense doing you a favour, my lady.'

'Do not try to twist your way out of this,' she warned. 'There is something else that you are forgetting, Saewin. Something which involved my husband. Do I need to jog your memory about that?'

He shook his head. 'I am indebted to the lord Roger.'

'I am glad that you remember it. There were many who felt the office of town reeve would be safer in Norman hands but my husband rated you highly. He argued strongly on your behalf, Saewin.'

'I know.'

'But for him, you would not hold your position. Is that not so?'

'It is, my lady.'

'Yet you still deny me?'

'Not deliberately.'

'Then why do I feel slighted?' she said levelly. 'Why do I feel insulted at having to ask in this way? Why do you betray my husband so?'

'It is not betrayal, my lady.'

'Then what is it?'

Saewin could no longer stay in his seat. Jumping to his feet, he turned away and walked up and down for a few moments, weighing up his options and trying to compose himself. Loretta watched him closely. When he finally turned to her, she gave him an expectant smile which melted all his resistance. He capitulated with great reluctance.

'What do you wish to know, my lady?' he asked.

When they returned to the castle, Baldwin was in the outer bailey, issuing orders to one of his men. Dismounting from their horses, Ralph and Gervase walked across to meet him. The sheriff's greeting was polite but lacked any real warmth. His eyes kindled with suspicion.

'Where have you been?' he said.

'For a ride,' replied Ralph.

'In which direction?'

'I forget, my lord sheriff. We simply wanted to get out of the city to breathe some clean air. Devon is a pretty county. We are sorry that we will not get to see much of it.'

'Did you go to the wood?'

'We may have done.'

'What were you hoping to find there?'

'Peace and quiet.'

'Why waste your time?' said Baldwin. 'A man was murdered but his killer is now in custody. That is the end of the matter.'

'Only if your prisoner is indeed the culprit,' Gervase pointed out. 'And I do not believe that he is, my lord sheriff.'

'We have a confession from him.'

'Oh?'

'He lied to you but was forced to yield up the truth to us.'

Gervase did not wish to know any of the details. Under torture, the prisoner would have confessed to anything. He felt sorry for the man and was grateful that he had spoken with him before his spirit was broken. There was no point in arguing that he was innocent. Only the arrest of the real murderer would convince Baldwin that his prisoner did not kill Nicholas Picard, and they had little evidence on which to act so far. Gervase and Ralph were working on instinct but it had always served them well in the past. They had to bide their time.

'I hear that you crossed swords with the abbot of Tavistock,' said the sheriff with a grim chuckle. 'He is a bellicose man when roused. I have had a few skirmishes with him myself.'

'We still have bruises from our encounter with him,' said Ralph. 'He is a pugnacious Christian and no mistake!'

'He presented his case well,' said Gervase.

'To what effect?' asked Baldwin.

'We will have to see, my lord sheriff. Four other claimants have to be heard before the abbot's deposition can be weighed in the balance. This dispute will take some time to resolve.'

'Surely not. The widow must inherit.'

'It is not as straightforward as that.'

'No,' added Ralph. 'We have three ladies, a battling abbot and a Saxon thegn in contention here. The property in question was problematical enough while the lord Nicholas was alive. His death has introduced even more complications. What surprises us,' he continued, 'is why such a wealthy and important man took so little account of his personal safety. To ride home alone at dusk was very foolhardy.'

'He was a fearless man.'

'Fear might have kept him alive.'

'He was not to know that robbers lurked in the wood.'

'It is a place where ambush is always a threat to a lone traveller. What had he been doing in Exeter that made him so careless?'

'I can answer that,' said a voice behind them. 'Dipping his pen in the ink of life, then signing his death warrant.'

They turned to see Berold the Jester. He had crept up behind them to eavesdrop on their conversation. Wearing a hauberk that was far too big for him, he was holding a sword that was absurdly short and garlanded with coloured ribbons. His eyes twinkled merrily either side of the iron nasal of his helm.

'Have you been here so long and learnt so little?' he mocked.

'About what?' said Ralph.

'The lascivious lord Nicholas. The wonder is that he was out of a woman's arms long enough to get himself killed. Three women fight over his property but it was promised to thirty or more in the bedchamber.'

'Do not listen to him,' said Baldwin indulgently.

'Nicholas Picard was led by the pizzle,' said Berold, performing an obscene mime with the sword. 'His brains were in his balls.'

'Peace!' warned his master.

'He fooled many a husband in Exeter.'

'Enough, I say!'

'He was better at fooling than I am.'

'Berold!'

'Look to the ladies! That is my counsel.'

'Leave us!'

'The secret lies between a woman's thighs. Remember that. Nicholas Picard kept his prick hard.'

Before the sheriff could cuff him into silence, Berold jumped back, thumbed his nose at him, sheathed his sword then cartwheeled round the courtyard. Baldwin watched him with amusement.

'Berold pops up when you least expect him.'

'Is it true about the lord Nicholas?' asked Ralph. 'Was he such an amorous friend to the ladies?'

'He was a handsome man, Ralph. Many favours came his way. Who would not take advantage of such bounty?'

'Gervase would not. He is betrothed.'

'Nicholas Picard was married. That did not restrain him.'

'Did his wife tolerate his wanderings?'

'I think she was grateful for them,' said Baldwin darkly. 'But ignore what Berold told you. He always exaggerates. It goes with his trade. If he did not make me laugh so much, I would have thrown him out years ago.' He turned on his heel and marched off towards the keep.

'What do you make of that, Gervase?' asked Ralph.

'I think that the fool speaks more wisdom than his master.'

'So do I. Nicholas Picard loved a sport which probably cost him his life.' He grinned broadly. 'When the good Bishop Osbern delivered his eulogy at the funeral, did he make mention of any of this?'

'No, Ralph.'

'I wonder why.' He guffawed loudly as they strolled across the courtyard.

By the light of the candle, Asa stared at the letter but saw only the man who had written it. She ran the parchment softly against her cheek to savour his memory. Her tears had stopped now to be replaced by a dry-eyed nostalgia that was in turn buttressed by a quiet determination. Her letter was not only a treasured memento. It was a weapon with which to fight for her rights. An heirloom.

Asa had not stirred from her bedchamber since she returned from the funeral. Food and drink lay untouched on a tray beside her. She was deaf to the entreaties of her servant. The service at the cathedral had been a trial, but she endured it willingly for his sake. In an almost exclusively Norman gathering, Asa was an obvious outsider, a Saxon interloper who was made to feel the lowliness of her position, hurt by remarks, wounded by glances, insulted by gestures, disdained by all. It was worth it. The letter wiped away all memory of the slights she had suffered. She kissed it softly then caressed his signature.

Footsteps ascended the stairs then there was a tap on the door.

'Yes?' she called.

Goda entered and shut the door behind her. 'You have a visitor.'

'Who is it?'

'Can you not guess?'

Her heart sank. 'Oh, I see.'

'What shall I tell him?'

'That you found me asleep.'

'He will have heard our voices.'

'Then tell him that I am unwell.'

'Will you not even speak with him?'

'No, Goda. Send him away.'

'But he is anxious to see you.'

'Another time.'

'He will not be pleased.'

'I will live with his displeasure,' said Asa with sudden anger. 'Who does he think he is? I am not at his beck and call any time of the day. Has he forgotten where I was this morning? At a funeral service. I wish to mourn in private, Goda. I need to be alone.'

'Shall I tell him to come back?'

'Simply get him out of my house.'

'It is not wise to offend him,' warned the servant. 'He can be helpful.'

Asa pursed her lips and nodded. 'That is true, alas. My whole life turns on men who can be helpful to me. Say that I am unable to see him now,' she continued. 'Give him my apologies.'

'When is he to call again?'

A sense of power coursed through Asa and made her smile.

'When I send for him,' she said airily.

Chapter Seven

Bishop Osbern was a generous host, attentive to the needs of his guests and somehow finding time in a busy day to spend with them. Canon Hubert and Brother Simon were invited to his lodging that evening. Dean Jerome was also in attendance. All four of them sat round an oak table and talked at leisure. The whole room was filled with a wonderful sense of Christian fellowship. While Hubert basked in it, Simon positively glowed. They were happy to be on consecrated ground again.

'It has been a testing day for you, I hear,' said Osbern softly.

'Yes, Your Grace,' sighed Hubert. 'The debate was interminable.'

'So I understand from Geoffrey, abbot of Tavistock. He, too, is a welcome guest here but I thought it more politic to keep you apart from him. If you are locked in legal argument with each other, it is perhaps best to confine your meetings to the shire hall.'

'A sensible course of action.'

'Yes,' added Simon. 'Thank you for yet another kindness, Your Grace.'

'My concern was not only for you,' admitted Osbern. 'A selfish motive was involved as well. Geoffrey has many fine qualities but he can be combative. And inordinately loud. Had we brought him face-to-face with you then the peace of this house would assuredly have been broken.'

'Your decision was wise, Your Grace,' said Jerome from behind his lugubrious mask. 'When Geoffrey raises his voice in Exeter, he is heard by his monks in Tavistock. But,' he said, quick to absolve himself of the charge of prejudice against a guest, 'there is no more effective abbot in the whole of Devon. His career has been an inspiration to others and we are delighted to have him beneath our roof once more.'

'In other circumstances,' said Hubert pompously, 'I am sure that we would enjoy each other's company, but I fear that my position as a royal commissioner makes that impossible at the moment.'

'Quite so,' agreed the bishop.

Osbern looked tired and frail. The network of blue veins seemed to be more prominent and there were deep, dark bags of skin beneath his eyes. Simon felt that they were imposing on the bishop when he was clearly exhausted, but Hubert paid no heed to the signs of fatigue. While he had the ear of the bishop, he was determined to make the most of it.

'You were chaplain to King Edward,' he recalled.

'That is so, Canon Hubert.'

'Was he as devout as report has it?'

'More so,' said the bishop fondly. 'He was a zealous student of the Scriptures and could discuss them knowledgeably. It was a delight to be part of such a Christian household.'

'Do you imply that King William's household is not Christian?'

'Heaven forfend! That would be a gross slander. The king is a devout man in his own way, less given to meditation than King Edward, perhaps, but no less dedicated to building a strong Church which can provide spiritual guidance to the nation.' Osbern sat back in his chair. 'I was honoured to be chosen as chaplain to two kings, a Saxon and a Norman.'

'You are the only man alive who can say that, Your Grace,' said Jerome with a ghoulish smile. 'You provide the bridge between the two reigns.'

'Over the chasm that was Earl Harold,' said Hubert.

'*King* Harold,' corrected Osbern.

'We do not recognise him as an anointed king.'

'His people did and so do I. We should give every man his due. Earl Harold seized the crown at Edward's death and wore it proudly until it was knocked from his head at Hastings. They do not think of him as a mere earl in this county,' he said. 'To the men of Devon, he was and will always be King Harold. With good reason.'

'What reason is that, Your Grace?' asked Simon.

'His father's family held considerable property in the West Country. King Harold himself owned Topsham, which is barely four miles away, and held fifteen other manors in Devon. That is why there was so much resistance here. The sons of King Harold chose to stir up rebellion in Exeter because they could rely on local support for their cause. This city was once under siege.'

'The lord Hervey de Marigny has told us all about it, Your Grace,' said Hubert. 'He took part in that siege and praises the bravery of Devonians.'

'He is right to do so. They are courageous men.'

'But a conquered people all the same.'

'Not in their hearts, Hubert. There the flame of freedom still flickers.'

'Does it?'

'Baldwin the Sheriff rules here but only because he has a garrison at his back. After all this time, the old resentments remain. Well,' said the bishop, 'look at the funeral we had this morning. I took care not to say this in my eulogy because I did not want to incite anger at such a solemn ceremony, but it does seem likely to me that the lord Nicholas was murdered because he was a symbol of what is perceived as Norman oppression.'

'Nobody could be less oppressive than you, Your Grace,' said Simon.

'A cathedral with a Norman bishop can be just as potent an image as a castle with a Norman garrison. Church and State are viewed together by the Saxons. Blame attaches to us all.'

'I have not been aware of undue resentment,' said Hubert.

'That is because you have not so far been exposed to it,' explained the bishop. 'But it is there below the surface. Is it not, Jerome?'

'Yes, Your Grace,' agreed the dean. 'Saxons have long memories.'

'And indomitable spirits. Even a man as fearsome as Baldwin of Moeles is unable to quell them completely.' He turned to

Simon. 'But you have not yet met the sheriff, I understand?'

'No,' said the other. 'Nor do I wish to, Your Grace.'

'Why not?'

'Simon flees from boisterous company,' said Hubert paternally. 'He is still shaken by the encounter we had with one of the lord sheriff's men.'

'Oh?' said Osbern. 'Who was that?'

'Berold the Jester.'

The bishop grinned. 'A humorous fellow!'

'Only if you find humour in blasphemy, Your Grace,' said Hubert as he worked up some indignation. 'We were shocked and disgusted by his antics. Had the man stayed longer, I would have upbraided him in the strongest terms.'

'Why?'

'Berold the Jester – mark this, Your Grace – had the gall to appear before us in a Benedictine cowl.'

'That sounds like him!' sighed Jerome.

'He is a law unto himself,' said Osbern easily. 'He will stop at nothing.'

Hubert was not appeased. 'Register a protest on our behalf.'

'To whom?'

'The sheriff.'

'There is not much point in that,' said Jerome gloomily. 'Berold is a licensed fool and the sheriff encourages his outrageous behaviour. The marvel is that he only came to you in the guise of a monk. He has worn the mitre of a bishop before now.'

'There is no real harm in the fellow,' said Osbern.

'I disagree, Your Grace.'

'Do not take it personally, Canon Hubert. Ignore the jester.'

'What if he comes to taunt us again?'

A smiling Osbern spread his arms in a gesture of tolerance. 'Turn the other cheek,' he suggested.

It was late when they retired to their apartment and Ralph Delchard had to suppress a yawn. Grateful for time alone with him at last, Golde took the opportunity to hurl questions at him.

'Why was the sheriff in such a jovial mood tonight?' she said.

'Because he thinks that he has solved the crime.'

'Has he?'

'No, Golde.'

'Have you told him so?'

'Gervase did that office for me, but Baldwin would not listen to him. He prefers to believe that he has Nicholas Picard's killer languishing in one of the dungeons.'

'What will happen to the man?'

'He will be convicted and hanged.'

'Even though he is innocent?'

'Innocent of the murder, my love,' said Ralph, 'but guilty of a hundred other crimes. Weep no tears for him. He has robbed and beaten travellers for years. When he found the murder victim lying in the wood, he even stripped him of his rings. What kind of villain thieves from the dead? No,' he continued, raising a palm to hide another yawn, 'he is not worth a heartbeat of sympathy. He deserves to hang.'

'Will nobody speak on his behalf?'

'Baldwin is resolved. The man must die.'

'Is there no way to save him?'

'Not from the sheriff's wrath,' he said. 'What we are hoping to do is to find the real killer. That will at least spare the prisoner the ignominy of going to his grave for a murder he did not commit. He has crimes enough to fill his coffin without that unjust charge.'

'Do you have any suspects in mind?'

'One or two.'

'Who are they?'

'The first is a certain Walter Baderon.'

'Who is he?'

'A knight in the service of the abbot of Tavistock. Captain of the guard at the North Gate when Nicholas Picard rode through it for the last time. Hervey talked to the man this evening. He told me of their conversation over our meal tonight. We both think Baderon merits investigation.'

'Why should he wish to kill the lord Nicholas?'

'That is what we need to find out.'

'Surely the abbot is in no way involved?'

'Stranger things have happened, Golde.'

'Who else is under suspicion?'

'You *are* a torrent of questions tonight.'

'I am interested, Ralph.'

'And I am weary, my love. Interrogate me in the morning.'

'But you will leave at first light.'

'Then you must wake me up in the middle of the night to examine me more closely.' He embraced her gently. 'I will give you all the answers you require in the dark. That is a promise. In any case,' he said, releasing her, 'I have questions of my own to put.'

'To me?'

'Who else?'

'I am at your disposal, my lord,' she said with a mock curtsey.

'When was the rift healed?' he asked.

'Rift?'

'With the lady Albreda. You and she were talking away as if the pair of you were old friends. Your tongues were wagging so much, I wonder that you had time to put any food in your mouths.'

'We had much to discuss.'

'That was not the case on our first night here.'

'Things have changed.'

'How?'

'We got closer.'

'When?'

'Who is a torrent of questions now?' she teased him.

'The lady Albreda is a lump of ice. How did you manage to melt her?'

'She offered the hand of friendship.'

'Why?'

'Because I am a woman. She felt that she could confide in me.'

'And did she?'

'Yes, Ralph.'

'I love scandal,' he said, rubbing his hands. 'Tell me all.'

'No.'

'But I am your husband.'

'That makes no difference.'

'Golde!'

'I am sworn to secrecy.'

'You can trust me.'

'I can,' she said, 'but the lady Albreda cannot. Besides, there was no scandal. She simply wanted to unburden her soul. And apologise for her coldness towards me.'

'There must be something you can tell me.'

'There is, Ralph.' She kissed him. 'I love you.'

'Something about Baldwin's wife, I mean.'

'I can tell you that she is unhappy, but you guessed that for yourself.'

'He has the look of an unruly husband.'

'So does Ralph Delchard.' They shared a laugh. 'I am not holding anything back in order to annoy you. I gave her my word, Ralph.'

'I understand.'

'You always respect a confidence. So must I.'

'No more questions, then,' he decided. 'Except perhaps a last one.'

'Well?'

'Did the lady Albreda speak fondly of Nicholas Picard?'

Golde was caught unawares and her expression betrayed her. Ralph was content. Giving her a kiss of gratitude, he swept her up in his arms and whirled her round. Golde was soon laughing.

'I thought that you said you were tired, Ralph.'

He gave a chortle. 'I soon will be, my love.'

It was well after midnight when he got there. Tethering his horse, he made his way on foot towards the manor house. A crescent moon was shedding enough light to guide him but retaining enough shadows to give him ample cover. He crouched in the bushes to study the building. Though he had never been inside it, he had a clear idea of what he would find there. He also knew about the hazard which he had to overcome in order to reach the house in the first place. Waiting until a cloud drifted across the moon, he made his way round the property in a wide circle so that he could view it from all directions and consider every avenue of escape. It was an hour before he was ready to move in.

The dogs were waiting for him. Four of them were on patrol, mastiffs with keen ears and strong jaws. Two were asleep but the others remained alert, padding up and down outside the front of the house. When one of them heard a sound, it gave a warning bark which brought the sleepers awake in an instant. They raced to join the other guard dogs and all four of them went sniffing off into the darkness. He was ready. Instead of trying to avoid them, he knelt down and guided them towards him with a humming noise. They bounded forward through the undergrowth, sensing an intruder and growling with pleasure at the prospect of action.

Then the miracle happened. When they reached him, four dogs who could have torn him apart did nothing of the kind. They sniffed all around him, stopped growling and wagged their tails. One even gave him an affectionate lick. The man continued to hum to them until all four animals were lying happily at his feet. After patting each in turn, he made his way towards the house.

Tetbald the Steward was poring over a document when she came into the room. Her sudden entry made him look up in astonishment. She was disturbed and dishevelled. He rose to his feet at once.

'Is something amiss, my lady?'

'What are you doing, Tetbald?'

'Preparing for my visit to the shire hall,' he said, indicating the pile of charters on the table. 'I need to know the wording of every document. I did not expect you to rise so early. That is why I am working in here.'

She looked anxiously around. 'Do you have the box with you?'

'What box?'

'The wooden box which belonged to my husband.'

'No, my lady.'

'Then where is it?'

'I have no idea.'

'It was kept in his bedchamber.'

'Then it should still be there.'

'It is not, Tetbald. I have just checked.'

'One of the servants must have moved it.'

'I gave clear orders that it was not to be touched,' she said sharply. 'My husband kept valuable items in that box. I have been searching for the key to open it.'

'The box must be in the house somewhere,' he insisted.

'Well, it is not in his chamber.'

'Let me see.'

It was past dawn but Tetbald still needed the candle to guide them up the dark staircase. When they entered the bedchamber, he held the flame over the table on which the box had formerly stood. There was no sign of it.

The lady Catherine became increasingly nervous. 'We must find it,' she said, biting her lip. 'It was the place where he locked important material away for safety. My husband was always opening and shutting that box. I could hear him from my own chamber.'

'It has to be here,' he said, conducting a search. 'One of the servants may have moved it in error and forgotten to replace it on the table.'

'It is not here! I feel it!'

'Do not upset yourself, my lady.'

'Who took it, Tetbald?'

'I do not know,' he said, holding the candle in the darkest recesses of the room. 'What made you want it?'

'I had a dream that it was being stolen.'

'There is no question of that. Nobody could get into this house.'

'But someone could get out,' she argued. 'What if one of the servants made off with the box?'

'They would never get past the dogs, my lady.'

'In my dream, the box was taken by a man.'

'Then your imagination was playing tricks on you. Who would want to take a box when there are things of much greater value to steal? Let me rouse the servants, my lady. One of them will know where it is.'

He was about to move away when a gust of wind rapped hard on the shutters before pulling one wide open. It flapped to and fro in the wind. The lady Catherine's anxiety turned to panic. She ran to the shutters and saw that the catch had been broken. Tetbald quickly reached the same conclusion. He looked out through the window.

'We have had an intruder, my lady.'

'He stole that box!'

'Why?'

'I saw him!' she said with a shiver. 'I saw him in my dream.'

'But how did he reach the house?' wondered Tetbald. 'The dogs are trained to attack. One of them must have heard him. Why did they not bark?' Another thought struck him. 'What *else* did he steal?'

Engelric defied their expectations. When they took their places behind the table at the shire hall, the commissioners felt certain that the first witness that morning would be yet another dispossessed Saxon who wished to roar in anger at them. The old man who limped in through the door was anything but bellicose, giving them a cheerful wave of greeting as if they were friends from whom he had been long parted. Short, wizened and white-bearded, Engelric supported himself on a stick. His face was mobile, his mouth almost toothless. Accompanied by a younger man, he made his way to the bench at the front and sat down.

Since he could only speak his native tongue, Engelric had to be examined by Gervase Bret who translated the old man's answers for the benefit of his colleagues. Married to a Saxon, Ralph Delchard had by now picked up enough of the language to be able to understand it fairly well but he lacked Gervase's speed and fluency. Hervey de Marigny was fascinated by the old man but Canon Hubert would soon grow impatient at the plodding pace that was imposed upon them by the use of an interpreter. Trying to estimate the witness's age, Brother Simon wondered how many reigns he must have lived through.

After introducing himself and his colleagues, Gervase administered the oath then began his examination, speaking slowly and with deliberation.

'What is your name?'

'Engelric, son of Wulfgar.'

'Please state your claim.'

'It is simple,' said the other with a shrug. 'The holdings at Upton Pyne belong to me. They were granted by royal charter at the time of King Edward, who held me in high regard.' He nudged his companion who produced a document from the satchel on his lap. 'Here is the charter in question. You will recognise the seal of King Edward of blessed memory.'

The document was passed to the commissioners for inspection and Engelric's opening words were translated by Gervase. After scrutinising the charter, Hubert passed it on to Ralph.

'It seems genuine enough,' said Hubert, 'but completely worthless. That land was granted to the abbot of Tavistock by a charter which renders this one invalid. Later documents supersede the abbot's claim.'

When Gervase translated, the old man was ready with his reply.

'Those holdings were not taken from me to be given to the abbot,' he said. 'They were exchanged for property that was already owned by the abbey but further afield and less profitable to farm. I yielded up my land in the firm belief that the abbey would give me theirs, but they refused to do so. That is why I am here today. To ask for the return of land which was unfairly taken from me.' A second nudge brought another document out of the satchel. 'Here is the deed of exchange.'

The document produced far more interest as there had been no mention of it during the debate with the abbot of Tavistock himself. Offering himself as an injured party, the abbot was, it seemed, guilty of inflicting an injury himself by reneging on a transaction. Engelric had produced the king's writ to prove that an exchange should have taken place. The commissioners were impressed. Having studied the returns for the whole county, they knew that over a thousand estates were surveyed in Devon yet barely a tenth remained in the hands of the men who held them before the Conquest. The fact that Engelric was one of the chosen few showed how much respect he had earned from his new overlords.

'This man was cheated out of his land by the abbey,' said de Marigny.

'I suspect that he was not the only one,' said Ralph. 'I will enjoy asking our choleric abbot why he forgot all about this exchange and remembers only the slights inflicted on him.'

'Let us not get diverted by this,' warned Hubert, holding the second document. 'Though this, too, has the feel of authenticity, it does not alter the situation. By diverse means, the holdings at Upton Pyne came into the possession of Nicholas Picard. This old man and the abbot of Tavistock are locking horns in a tussle that neither can win. Later grants make theirs null and void.'

'Not necessarily, Canon Hubert,' said Gervase. 'We do not yet know the substance of the other claims. If they turn out to be fraudulent then the property could still revert to the abbey.'

'Or to Engelric,' said Ralph. 'We must find a just solution.'

'Ask him why he was allowed to keep his manor,' suggested de Marigny, eyeing their witness with admiration. 'He must have been a man of some distinction in his day.'

'He still is,' said Gervase.

He spent an hour questioning the old man and extracted a wealth of information from him about the disposition of land before and after the Conquest. In spite of his age, Engelric had a fierce memory for detail. What was most startling was the total lack of bitterness which he displayed. There were no wild accusations, no cries of defiance and no acrimonious recriminations. All that Engelric asked for was land which he once lawfully possessed. Gervase had to curb his natural sympathy for the Saxons and de Marigny had to remind himself that sentiment played no part in judicial decisions, but it was Ralph who was most deeply affected by the evidence that was given.

Engelric's story was that of Golde's father. They shared the common fate of so many proud thegns. In listening to the old man's history, Ralph realised that he might be hearing words from the mouth of his dead father-in-law and it gave him a new insight into the predicament which his wife faced as a young girl in Herefordshire. Canon Hubert was not persuaded that the witness had a legitimate claim but he was quick to plunder the old man's memory of details relating to other property in the vicinity. Though he might not have advanced his own cause, Engelric had been an immense help to the commissioners.

When it was time to leave, he used the stick to lever himself up again.

'What will happen now, young man?' he asked Gervase.

'Your claim will be considered alongside the others and we will reach a judgement. You will be informed of that decision immediately.'

'What of my documents?'

'You may have those back but we may need to see them again.'

Engelric nodded then bestowed an appreciative grin on the table.

'Thank you for hearing my plea,' he said politely. 'I do not have long to live and I would like to have my land restored before I die.' He looked around warily. 'A word of warning, friends,' he hissed. 'Do not trust the abbot of Tavistock. He takes without giving in exchange. Do not enter into any transactions with him. He could shame the Devil!'

Gervase smiled, Ralph chuckled and de Marigny asked what the joke was. Gervase's translation provoked a bout of blustering from Hubert, but the canon soon calmed down. Engelric had been a revelation to them. He was a sure-footed guide through the marshes of property ownership in the county and his insights were invaluable to them. They were sorry to see the old man limp out of the shire hall on his stick.

Saewin hurried through the streets of Exeter to deliver his summons. Uncomfortable memories of his last visit to the house surfaced, but he tried to push them to the back of his mind. This time, at least, he might earn some gratitude. Eldred saw him coming and went into the house to fetch his mistress. The two of them were waiting on the threshold when the reeve came up.

'Well?' asked Loretta. 'Am I summoned?'

'You soon will be, my lady,' said Saewin. 'I came to give you fair warning. The first witness has been examined and sent on his way. The second is now before the commissioners.'

'Then I am next.'

'Yes.'

'Thank you, Saewin. I appreciate your coming in person instead of sending a servant with the message. I will remember this kindness.'

'That pleases me, my lady.'

'Engelric has departed, then?'

'He has,' he said defensively. 'But do not ask me what transpired in the shire hall because I am unable to tell you. I take no part in the judicial process. I merely summon the witnesses.'

Loretta smiled. 'You have already told me what I wished to know.'

'In confidence.'

'Yes, Saewin. In confidence.'

She smiled at him again and he felt discomfited. Loretta looked more stately than ever and she was supremely assured. Saewin had forgotten exactly what he had told her about the commissioners, but it seemed to have added a new optimism. He shifted his feet and tried to excuse himself.

'How long will it be?' she enquired.

'It is impossible to say.'

A studied contempt. '*She* will not detain them for long, surely?'

'Asa is entitled to advance her claim.'

'What claim? She has never owned property in her entire life.'

'The commissioners agreed to hear her.'

'They might just as well listen to Berold the Jester.'

Saewin winced inwardly. He tried to sound as impartial as he could.

'Asa has a right to speak,' he said calmly. 'They would not have summoned her otherwise. Her claim is somewhat unusual but it is no less valid for that. Your turn will soon come, my lady. It is Asa who is facing the commissioners now.'

* * *

162

'How do we know that the letter is not a forgery?' asked Ralph Delchard.

'I will swear that it is not,' she said.

'We need more proof than your word.'

'Then I will show you another letter from the lord Nicholas. You can compare the handwriting and see that both were written by him.'

'Or forged by the same hand.'

'There was no forgery, my lord.'

'Do you really claim that Nicholas Picard wrote this?' he said, holding up the document. 'What would make a man in his position consider such a strange commitment?'

'Have you never given a gift to someone you loved, my lord?'

'Of course. But nothing of this size.'

'He was generous whereas you are mean.'

Even Hubert smiled at her rebuff. Asa was in no way intimidated by the commissioners. Her manner was composed, her answers clear and unequivocal. Fearing that they might have to use Gervase once more as an interpreter, they were pleasantly surprised to learn that Asa had a good command of Norman French. It made possible a livelier dialogue.

'Let us go through it again,' said Hervey de Marigny as he ran an approving eye over her. 'We are not trying to catch you out. We simply ask for confirmation that this letter was written by the lord Nicholas.'

'Then show it to his wife.'

'That is a preposterous suggestion!' protested Hubert.

'Why?' she said.

'The lady Catherine would be outraged.'

'If you believe that, you do not know the lady Catherine. After all those years of marriage, she had the measure of her husband.' Asa pointed to the letter. 'She will read it without a tremor. And she will confirm that her husband wrote it.'

'In spite of its extraordinary contents?' said Hubert.

'The lady Catherine is an honourable woman. She would not lie in order to discredit me. On the other hand,' she added, 'the letter is my private property and I would not willingly let anyone but yourselves view it. There must be several documents at the house which bear the lord Nicholas's hand. Ask to see one and place it beside my letter.'

The commissioners held a silent conference. They were in no doubt that Asa was speaking the truth. The letter was clearly genuine and its underlying affection was quite moving. It was not difficult to see what attracted Nicholas Picard to Asa. She had a pert beauty that was enhanced by her poise and her forthrightness. There was a sense of independence about Asa which somehow made her more appealing.

'How long did you know the lord Nicholas?' asked Gervase.

'For two years or more.'

'And did you . . . were you . . . during that time . . . is it fair to say . . . ?'

Ralph came to his rescue. 'What my colleague wishes to ask is how close the relationship actually was. The lord Nicholas was clearly somewhat more than a casual acquaintance.'

'You have read his letter, my lord. We were lovers.'

'In the carnal sense?'

'What other sense is there?'

Ralph grinned, de Marigny chuckled, Gervase looked

away, Hubert stared at her in sheer disgust and Brother Simon put his hands over his ears in alarm. Asa was unperturbed at their reactions.

'You are men of the world,' she said brightly. 'Well, some of you are. I am sure that you understand. Love does not only exist within marriage.'

'It should!' boomed Hubert. 'It was ordained for lawful procreation.'

Asa almost giggled. 'That is not what we called it.'

Gervase made an effort to control his embarrassment. 'We are moving away from the crucial question,' he argued, taking the letter from Ralph. 'What we must ask is whether this is a binding document or merely a letter of intent.'

'A letter of intent,' decided Ralph.

'It is a form of will, my lord,' she insisted.

'Yet it is not dated or witnessed.'

'He wanted me to have that land.'

'Then he should have left it to you in his last will and testament.'

'Do we know that he has not?' she asked.

The question threw them all into disarray. It was minutes before they disentangled themselves sufficiently to continue their examination. Asa remained alert and responsive throughout and gave an honest account of her relationship with her benefactor. What value they could place on the letter they did not know, but it could not be dismissed until they had sight of the last will and testament of the deceased. Having assumed that it would favour the widow, they were now forced to speculate that it might contain some alarming surprises for her.

Before she left, Asa took the opportunity to ask them a number of pertinent questions and she seemed satisfied with their answers. Hubert and Simon had exuded censure, but the other commissioners had been objective judges. Reclaiming her letter, she glided serenely out.

Gervase was entranced. 'What a remarkable young woman!'

'With a good fighting spirit,' observed de Marigny.

'She clearly loved the lord Nicholas. And he loved her.'

'At a price, Gervase.'

'What do you mean?'

'Did you not see what was right in front of your eyes?'

'I saw a self-possessed woman who stood up for herself.'

Ralph exchanged a knowing glance with Hervey de Marigny.

'It is easy to see that you were never a soldier,' he said, slipping an arm round Gervase. 'Asa is a comely girl and I have seen her kind in many towns. That sweetness did not disguise her occupation. If she can charm those holdings out of Nicholas Picard, she must be a remarkable young woman.' He whispered in his friend's ear, 'But she is also a prostitute.'

Gervase felt the hot blush rising swiftly up his face.

Chapter Eight

Tetbald the Steward was thorough. He organised a complete search of the house itself and sent men out in all directions to make a wide sweep of the property. When the lady Catherine joined him, she had recovered her composure but had an air of resignation about her.

'Has the box been found?' she asked.

'No, my lady.'

'Where have you searched?'

'Everywhere.'

'Including the undercroft?'

'The undercroft, the outbuildings, even the stables. There is no sign of the box, my lady.' He gave a reassuring smile. 'But nothing else seems to have been taken. That is some consolation.'

'Is it?'

'The thief might have stolen your jewellery, my lady.'

'He might also have murdered me in my own bed,' she said with a quiet shudder. 'That is what frightens me. A man was able to get into my house and enter the bedchamber next to mine in order to take that box. What if I had awakened while he was there? What if I had gone into my husband's chamber to investigate?'

'It is as well that you did not.'

'I will never feel safe in that bed again.'

'You will, my lady,' he said firmly. 'I give you my word on that.'

Catherine nodded and touched his arm in a gesture of affection. They were in the parlour and the shutters were wide open. Dogs could be heard barking excitedly some distance away. Tetbald looked in the direction from which the sound came.

'Why could they not bark like that during the night?' he said.

'Perhaps they did and nobody heard them.'

'They are schooled to attack any intruders, my lady. No man could hold off four of them. The last time someone wandered onto the property at night, he was all but eaten alive.'

'How, then, did the thief elude them?'

'I do not know, my lady,' he admitted. 'Unless he fed the dogs some meat that was seasoned with a potion to make them drowsy. Yet the animals seem alert and healthy this morning. We found nothing wrong with them. It is all very puzzling.'

'Puzzling and disturbing.'

'I will get to the bottom of it somehow,' he promised.

'I hope so, Tetbald. This has shaken me.'

'What was in the box that would make it such a target?'

'I do not know. My husband kept it locked.'

'And you have no key?'

'I have been searching for it ever since . . .' Her voice faded away.

'Ever since his death.'

'Yes, Tetbald,' she murmured. 'Ever since then.'

'It was not in his bedchamber,' he said. 'I looked there myself. The lord Nicholas must have hidden it well. And that means the box must have contained items that he wanted nobody else to see.'

'Not even his wife,' she said dully.

'Especially not you, my lady.'

He was about to reach out to her when the barking of the dogs grew louder. Looking through the window, he saw two men walking towards the house and carrying a wooden box between them. The dogs were scampering at their heels.

'They have found it!' he said.

Saewin the Reeve made sure that Asa left the shire hall before Loretta was summoned. He was anxious to avoid a confrontation between the two women and did not relish the idea of being caught in the middle of it. The delay gave the commissioners time to take refreshment and to reflect on the evidence they had so far taken that morning, and to compare it with the deposition from the abbot of Tavistock. Of the three witnesses, Canon Hubert leant in favour of the prelate, airily dismissing the claims by the two Saxons as annoying irrelevancies. Hervey de Marigny was more impressed by Engelric than his colleague had been, suspecting that the old man might well have borne arms during the siege of Exeter and that he deserved the respect due to a worthy enemy. Ralph Delchard was at once amused and interested by Asa's contribution to the debate and it was she who occupied Gervase Bret's mind as well.

While the others were nibbling their food, he took Ralph aside. 'Were you speaking in jest?' he asked.

'About whom?'

'Asa. Is she really . . . what you said she was?'

'Yes, Gervase,' he said with a grin. 'To me she is not a prostitute of the common sort. My guess is that she has very few clients and selects them with great care. Nicholas Picard was one of them.'

'How do you know?'

'Because of the terms in which his letter was couched. Some men pay her in money, some in other ways. The lord Nicholas chose to reward her with the gift of some land.'

'But she only stood to get that in the event of his death.'

Ralph grew serious. 'That point was not lost on me, Gervase. She is a charming creature, but I think it would benefit us to take a closer look at Asa. It would be intriguing to learn who else enjoys her favours – and at what cost. Asa was a delight,' he said, recalling her performance before them. 'The lord Nicholas was fortunate in his choice. Asa knows how to pleasure a man.'

'How can you tell?'

'I only have to look at her.'

'Why did I not see what you saw?'

Ralph chuckled. 'Wait until you have been married to Alys for a month,' he said, digging an elbow into his ribs. 'Your eyes will be opened to the wonders of the world, Gervase. You will be able to appraise a woman properly.'

Saewin entered to tell them that the next claimant had arrived.

Resuming their seats, they signalled to the reeve and Loretta was soon brought in. The contrast with Asa could not have been more striking. As she sailed towards them, Loretta bore herself with great dignity and settled herself down on the bench before the commissioners with an almost regal air. Eldred followed her in, bearing a leather satchel. Though he sat beside her, he somehow seemed invisible. All attention was concentrated on Loretta.

When the preliminaries were dealt with, Ralph began his examination. 'Why have you come before us, my lady?'

'To attest my right to certain holdings in Upton Pyne.'

'You could have done that when our predecessors visited Exeter,' he reminded her. 'Yet no claim was lodged on your behalf. Why did you not seek redress from the first commissioners?'

'I was absent from the city during their visit.'

'Were you not given notice of their arrival?'

'Yes, my lord,' she said, 'but I was already in Normandy when it was sent. By the time I returned, your predecessors had completed their business here and moved on. I was too late.'

'Could nobody have spoken up on your behalf?'

'No one was authorised to do so,' she said with a hint of arrogance. 'I have learnt to manage my own affairs.'

'That does you credit,' he said with a smile of admiration.

Loretta ignored it. 'May I proceed with my claim?'

'Of course.'

Taking his cue, Eldred extracted some documents from his satchel and handed them over to Ralph before taking his seat once more. Loretta delivered her speech as if it had been carefully rehearsed.

'When you have had time to peruse the documents,' she

said levelly, 'you will appreciate the strength of my claim. My husband was Roger de Marmoutier, a name that will not be unknown to you, my lord. He fought at Hastings, as you did yourself, and was rewarded with holdings in three counties, the bulk of his property being here in Devon, held under the honour of Bramford. He retained his estates in Normandy where he used his wealth to build two churches and to endow the abbey at Bec, where,' she said, turning to Hubert, 'I believe you were once sub-prior. My husband held the abbey in the highest esteem. But that is not germane to this discussion,' she continued. 'All that I am concerned to establish are the credentials of my late husband who was granted the holdings in Upton Pyne for services rendered to the king. His writ lies before you and you will observe that one of the signatories is Bishop Osbern.'

Ralph glanced at the document before passing it to Gervase. 'Nobody doubts the legitimacy of this grant,' he said, 'apart from the abbot of Tavistock, that is. What concerns us is not how your husband came to acquire that land but how your son came to lose it.'

'By an act of treachery, my lord.'

'Treachery?'

'There is no other word for it,' she said. 'William, my late son, was tricked out of that part of his inheritance.'

'By whom?'

'Nicholas Picard.'

'That is a serious allegation,' warned Hubert.

'It can be substantiated.'

'Take care, my lady. It is easy to slander the dead. The lord Nicholas is not here to defend himself.'

'Nor is my son,' Loretta said bitterly. She paused briefly to gather her thoughts. 'Forgive me,' she continued. 'The events which I must describe are still vivid in my mind and cause me much distress. It is difficult for me to speak of them before strangers.'

'We understand, my lady,' said de Marigny with sympathy. 'Take your time. There is no hurry.'

'Thank you, my lord.'

'We are sorry that you have to dwell on such sad events. The loss of a husband and a son in such a short time must have been a shattering blow to you. But the facts must be heard.'

'They will be,' she said, bracing herself. 'Thus it stands. When my husband died of a fever, he bequeathed the holdings in question, along with other property, to our son, William. The land at Upton Pyne was very dear to my husband, but it had always been coveted by the lord Nicholas.'

'Why, my lady?' said Gervase.

'Because it has rich soil and good grazing. It is also adjacent to the estates held by lord Nicholas. That proximity, alas, was fatal.'

'In what way?'

Loretta gave a little sigh. 'I loved my son,' she said, 'but I will not hide his defects from you. Where his father was conscientious, William was lazy. He was also impetuous at times, given to drink and to gambling. We tried to correct his faults but he was too wilful to be schooled. Do not get the impression that he was a complete wastrel,' she added swiftly. 'My son was kind and considerate at heart. He adored his parents and was always stricken with guilt when he upset us, but he was too easily led astray. The lord Nicholas was quick to see that.'

'What did he do?'

'Befriended my son and made much of him. Took him hunting, showed him favour, bestowed gifts upon him. You must remember that William was young and impressionable. He looked up to the lord Nicholas. When the wager was suggested, he took it without a second thought.'

'Wager?' said Ralph.

'That is how the land was forfeited.'

'What were the terms of the wager?'

'They were to have a passage of arms. Sword and lance in single combat. When one was forced to submit, the other took the prize.'

'And what was at stake?'

'The holdings in Upton Pyne.'

Hubert was shocked. 'William de Marmoutier risked all that land on a single engagement?' he said.

'Earl Harold did the same at Hastings,' noted de Marigny wryly.

'I told you that my son could be headstrong,' said Loretta. 'And he stood to gain an equivalent number of acres from the lord Nicholas if he vanquished him, as he fully expected to do. But he reckoned without his opponent's greater experience and guile. Wine was served before the contest. I am told that William drank too much too fast. It was not a fair fight in any way. My son was duped.'

'So the holdings were won by Nicholas Picard?' said Ralph.

'That is what he alleged, my lord, though no formal transfer took place. A couple of days after the contest, my son was out hunting when he was gored by a stag. He bled to death before they found him.' She hunched her shoulders. 'You can imagine my grief. While I was in mourning, the lord Nicholas took possession of the land at Upton Pyne. There was nothing that I could do until now.'

'You could have appealed to the sheriff.'

'He upheld the lord Nicholas's right to the property.'

'Could you not have pleaded with the lord Nicholas himself?'

Loretta lifted her chin. 'That would have been demeaning, my lord. I will beg from no man. I wanted to secure those holdings by legal means and not by grovelling. William was cheated out of that land. I have come here to demand its return.'

'We do not respond to demands,' said Hubert fussily. 'Our task is to consider the worth of each claim before arriving at a judgement. Besides, there are certain things I would like to know about this alleged act of treachery. Can independent witnesses be called who will support your version of events? Do you have any written proof of this wager? Why did the sheriff ratify the lord Nicholas's possession of those holdings?'

Loretta's replies were short and direct. When other questions were directed at her by each of the commissioners, she answered them with ringing confidence. She withstood their interrogation for over two hours without showing any sign of strain or discomfort. They were impressed but they were also slightly disconcerted. Loretta seemed to know a great deal about each one of them and slipped in remarks which sometimes brought them to a halt. It was almost as if she was examining them.

When her documents had been inspected, they were returned to Eldred who led the way out of the hall. As Loretta disappeared, Ralph sat back in his chair with a sigh of approval. 'The most convincing claimant so far,' he decided.

'Too convincing in some ways,' said Hubert. 'She seemed to know exactly what we would ask her.'

'She was a highly intelligent woman,' said Gervase admiringly. 'And a very beautiful one. It was difficult to believe that she could have a son of that age. She must have been very young when she married.'

'Like you,' said Ralph. 'Young and innocent. Now, Gervase, which way do you incline? Do you still favour Asa's claim or has she been displaced in your affections by the lady Loretta?'

'Affection does not come into it, Ralph.'

'Which one of them would you choose?'

'Neither,' said Gervase. 'I favour Engelric.'

Golde had been in Exeter for some days without ever leaving the confines of the castle. When she was invited by the lady Albreda to explore the city beyond its walls, she accepted the offer at once. Horses were ready for them at the stables and so was their guide. Golde was surprised to see that it was Berold the Jester. He wore loose-fitting Saxon apparel with cross-gartered trousers and a floppy cap.

'Good day, ladies!' he said, doffing the cap to bow low. 'Let us mount up and dazzle the city with our beauty.'

'Where will you take us?' asked Golde.

'There and back.'

'Where and back?'

'Hither and thither, my lady.'

'You talk in riddles.'

'Yes,' he said cheerily. 'We will go there as well.'

'Where?'

'From the end to the beginning.'

'Lead on, Berold,' said Albreda. 'We will follow.'

When they were perched on their saddles, the jester mounted his own horse and turned it towards the main gate. Four armed soldiers acted as an escort to the ladies. The seven of them came out of the castle and headed first for the cathedral precincts. People quickly made way for them in the crowded streets. Berold acknowledged passers-by with an imperious wave of the hand, pulling faces at children to make them laugh and beating mischievously on any shutters that came within reach. He was a voluble guide, at once distracting and delighting them with his nonsensical comments. The four soldiers were soon chuckling aloud.

'Take no notice of the names,' advised Berold. 'They are put there to deceive you. South Street runs north, Broad Street is narrow, Fore Street lies aft, Friernhay Street contains neither friars nor hay and High Street is the lowliest place in Christendom.'

'What of Bartholomew Street?' asked Albreda.

'He fled from the city years ago.'

When they turned into the precinct, Berold made jesting reference to the two churches on their left and St Petroc's on their right, but Golde did not hear him. Her gaze had settled on the minster church itself, climbing into the sky on its way to heaven. Glimpsed from her apartment at the castle it was striking enough, but she now felt the full impact of its size and ambition. When she lived close to Hereford Cathedral, she had taken its magnificence for granted and rarely tossed it more than a glance. The novelty of Exeter made her stare and wonder. It was only when she had carried out a detailed inventory that she looked away from the edifice to find that Albreda and Berold were no longer with her.

They had ridden across to the cemetery. Berold was surveying the gravestones as if they were soldiers on parade but Albreda was staring sadly at one particular spot. Ravens were pecking at the mound of earth which marked the last resting place of Nicholas Picard. She tore herself away to rejoin Golde and offer an apology. Berold trotted up behind her.

'What would you like to see now, my lady?' he asked Golde.

'Waterbeer Street,' she said without hesitation.

'A foul-smelling lane.'

'Not to me, Berold.'

'I would like to see it as well,' said Albreda. 'I scorned your interest in brewing because I knew nothing about it. You can educate me, Golde.'

'With pleasure, my lady.'

'What is the difference between ale and beer?'

Berold cackled. 'The difference between poison and piss.'

'Hold your foul tongue, Berold,' scolded Albreda playfully. 'I want Golde to answer. Well, is there a difference?'

'Oh, yes,' said Golde. 'All the difference in the world.'

It was a pleasant afternoon. They wandered in and out of the streets until they had seen almost the whole city. Golde's curiosity was unlimited and Berold's jests were ceaseless. Hours slipped happily by. When the party was ready to return to the castle, Golde remembered something.

'There is one last place I wish to visit.'

Berold pretended to lift a skirt and the men sniggered at him.

'Where is that?' asked Albreda.

'I would like to take a closer look at the tunnel that was built under the wall,' said Golde. 'The lord Hervey told us about it and we saw it on our approach. It was built during the siege but abandoned when the city finally surrendered. Could we go there, please?'

'I would rather adjourn to the castle,' said Albreda, 'but there is nothing to stop you from finding this tunnel. Berold will escort you.'

'Thank you, my lady.'

While the others trotted off towards the castle, Golde followed the jester on a twisting route. He did not seem happy with the assignment to act as her guide and fell unusually silent. When they left the city, he wheeled his horse to the right until they reached a cavernous opening in the earth. Berold stopped well short of it and pointed a finger.

'There it lies, my lady. The entrance to Hell.'

'Why do you say that?'

'Men belong above ground, not tunnelling away like moles.'

'How deep is it?' she wondered.

'I do not know, my lady. I think it has been filled up.'

'Let us see,' she said, nudging her horse forward to the very edge of the tunnel. 'It looks like a cave. Does it go all the way under the wall?'

Before she could get a reply, her horse suddenly shied with fright, rearing up on its hind legs and dislodging her from the saddle. Golde hit the ground with a thud and rolled over. Berold was beside her in a flash.

'Are you hurt, my lady?' he said with concern.

* * *

It had been a long but productive day in the shire hall. Three witnesses were examined and the evidence of a fourth, the abbot of Tavistock, was set against their claims. Only one more person remained to be seen and they decided to postpone his appearance until the morrow. Word was sent to Tetbald the Steward, informing him that he must be at the shire hall before the Terce bell sounded to represent the widow of Nicholas Picard. Relevant documents would be required. Canon Hubert excused himself and took Brother Simon off to the more curative ambience of the cathedral. Exposure to two potent women, Asa and Loretta, had taken its toll of the scribe. He needed solitude.

Ralph and his companions gathered up their satchels. 'We have learnt a lot today,' he said with satisfaction.

'But not the most important thing,' remarked Gervase.

'What is that?'

'Whether or not the murder is directly connected to this dispute.'

'It must be, Gervase.'

'We have not established a clear link.'

'Do not forget Walter Baderon,' said de Marigny. 'There is something odd about that fellow. He was on duty at the North Gate when the lord Nicholas left that night. Baderon could easily have pursued him.'

'At whose behest?' asked Gervase. 'The abbot's?'

'He might have had his own reasons for killing the lord Nicholas.'

'They *all* have their own reasons,' complained Ralph. 'The abbot, that old Saxon, Engelric, the lovely Asa, the haughty Loretta and even the widow. Yes,' he added with a smile, 'the lady Catherine might have the best reason of all to kill her husband. She had to endure one betrayal after another. Five names to go on our list and there will be other suspects before we are done.'

'This case must not be allowed to drag on,' said Gervase.

'Have no fears. We will get you to the altar in time.'

'Not if we proceed at this pace with every dispute.'

'Justice cannot be rushed, Gervase. A lawyer should know that.'

'I do know it.'

'Then stop hurrying us.' He ran a finger across his chin. 'Hubert was right about the lady Loretta. She was too well informed about us and our methods of questioning. I will have a word with Saewin about her. I feel there is still much to discover about the lady Loretta.'

'And about Asa,' said Gervase.

'She will be your quarry.'

'Wait! I am not the right person to chase her.'

'You are exactly the right person, Gervase, because you are young enough to attract her but innocent enough to be immune from her charms. Hervey and I have neither of those virtues.'

Gervase was alarmed. 'What must I do?'

'Pry and probe. Find out all you can about Asa.'

'How?'

'I leave that to you, Gervase. We have every faith in you.'

'We do,' said de Marigny jocularly. 'And while you pursue the ladies, I will address myself to the men. I will learn more about this Engelric and take a second look at Walter Baderon. I still think that he is holding something back about the abbot of Tavistock.'

'That only leaves the grieving widow,' said Ralph. 'And her steward, of course. Tetbald. I will be interested to see what sort of figure he cuts before us. And I will be fascinated to see the last will and testament of Nicholas Picard.' He lifted an eyebrow. 'If such a thing exists.'

Catherine used a palm to smooth out the parchment before reading through the document again. She knew it almost by heart now, but she still enjoyed the thrill and reassurance it imparted. She did not hear Tetbald come into the parlour behind her.

'I will need to take that with me, my lady,' he said.

'When?'

'Tomorrow. Word has just come from the commissioners. I am to present myself at the shire hall before Terce. They will want to see all the appropriate documents.'

'Including the will?'

'Especially that, my lady.'

She let her gaze fall on the document again, then she picked it up.

'This is what he was after, Tetbald,' she said.

'Who?'

'The thief. If the will were destroyed, my claim would be more difficult to substantiate. That was why he came in search of it.'

'I am not so sure, my lady.'

'Why not?'

'You are the widow of the deceased. If he dies intestate, then the laws of inheritance still favour you. Even without that will, your position would be far too strong to be challenged. No, my lady, I believe that the intruder came only for the box which he took away.'

'He must have been a powerful man. That box was heavy.'

'Yes,' he agreed. 'And it was found some distance from the house. If he carried it all that way, he was a brawny fellow.'

Catherine trembled slightly. 'Thank heaven I did not wake!'

'You might have frightened him away.'

'If he was bold enough to break into my house, he would be willing enough to silence me. I had a fortunate escape, Tetbald. Has the crime been reported to the sheriff?'

'I sent a messenger to him this morning, my lady.'

'Good. He may have an idea of the likely identity of the thief.'

'We know some things about him ourselves.'

'Do we?'

'Yes, my lady,' he said, checking off the points on his fingers. 'We know that he is a strong man. Wily enough to evade our dogs. Familiar with the interior of the house. Practised at his craft. Aware of what was inside that box. One more thing. He had a key to the box.'

'How on earth did he get that?'

'I can only guess. When they found the box, it was open and empty. The lock had not been forced. It must have been opened with a key.'

'No wonder we could not find it in the house.'

'Your husband must have kept it on him, my lady.'

As a thought seized her, Catherine rose angrily to her feet. 'Yes, Tetbald,' she hissed. 'And who would have known that?'

Ralph Delchard shifted at random between anxiety and reproach. 'Why did you not send for me, Golde?'

'You were busy at the shire hall.'

'An injury to my wife takes precedence over that.'

'It is not a serious injury, Ralph.'

'It might have been,' he argued. 'You were thrown from your horse and stunned in the fall. You might have broken an arm or a leg.'

'My ankle has been badly sprained, that is all.'

'You poor darling,' he said, kissing her cheek. 'Does it hurt?'

'Not really. There is a dull ache.'

'I will leave more than a dull ache when I find the ostler who gave you that mettlesome horse. I'll beat the villain black and blue!'

'It was not his fault, Ralph.'

'The animal unsaddled you.'

'Only because it was frightened.'

'By what?'

'I have no idea,' said Golde. 'To be honest, I am trying to forget the whole incident. I felt so silly when I found myself lying on the ground like that. It was humiliating.'

Ralph stood up. 'Berold was to blame,' he decided. 'It was his fooling which made your horse rear up like that. Wait until I see him. I'll play a jest or two on him for a change.'

'This was nothing to do with Berold,' she insisted. 'He was nowhere near me. And when I fell, he came to my aid at once. Berold was kindness itself. You should be thanking him for taking such good care of me.'

'*I* will take care of you now, my love.'

'Then do so more calmly, Ralph.'

He gave an apologetic smile and knelt down beside her

again. They were in their apartment and Golde was lying on the bed, her shoes removed and one ankle swathed in bandaging. Her sleeve was torn and muddied by its sudden contact with the ground and her apparel bore other signs of the accident, but she was in good spirits.

'They have looked after me very well, Ralph.'

'That is my office.'

'Berold raised the alarm,' she recalled, 'and they carried me back to the castle. Joscelin the Steward took charge. He sent for the doctor and had me brought up here. His wife sat with me until you got back. And look,' she said, indicating the tray of food. 'Joscelin had this prepared in the kitchen and sent up to me. I am treated like a queen.'

'You *are* a queen.'

'All that I need is a few days of rest.'

'Then you will have it, my love.'

'Not if you are so tense and anxious,' she said. 'It is all over, Ralph. I am not badly hurt. Try to relax. How can I rest when my husband is in such a restless state?'

'I feel guilty that I was not there to save you.'

'That is what the lady Albreda said, but what could either of you have done? When a horse rears up like that, it does not give you forewarning.' She reached out to take his hand. 'Forget about me. I am fine now. Tell me about your day. Has it been as boring as you feared?'

'No,' he said. 'It was quite intriguing in its own way. We started with a wizened old Saxon and ended with a dignified Norman widow. In between them came a young woman who threw Gervase into complete disarray.'

'Why?'

'You will have to ask him.'

'Who was this woman?'

'Asa. Unusually beautiful for a Saxon woman.' He dodged the punch which she aimed at him. 'I said that to test you, Golde. If you can still strike out at me, then you are not as bad as I thought.' He slipped an arm round her. 'I hate to see you like this. I'll be an attentive nurse.'

'I would prefer a husband who settles down.'

He beamed at her. 'Then you have one.'

'Tell me more about your session at the shire hall,' she urged. 'How is the lord Hervey settling in? You, Gervase and Canon Hubert are veterans but he has never sat in judgement before. Is he enjoying it?'

'Very much, Golde.'

'He is shrewd and sensible.'

'And as tenacious as any of us,' said Ralph. 'When Hervey starts to question a witness, he does not let them off the hook for a second. Yes, we are blessed in our new commissioner. Hervey de Marigny is a great asset to us.'

'How much longer must you do this disagreeable chore, my friend?'

'A few weeks more.'

'You will be glad to shake the dust of Exeter from your feet.'

'Yes.'

'And then what? Back to your manor?'

'Yes, my lord.'

'Have you seen much of the abbot while you have been here?'

'No.'

'He is staying as a guest of Bishop Osbern, I hear.'

'That is so.'

'What brought him here in the first place?'

A studied pause. 'You know that better than I, my lord.'

Walter Baderon was far less forthcoming this time. Hervey de Marigny tried to strike up a conversation with him at the North Gate but to no avail. Baderon was suspicious and reserved. He had clearly found out who the other man was. The commissioner gave up. Since there was little to be gained from further questioning, de Marigny elected to take a walk in the evening air.

After a valedictory exchange with the captain of the guard, he sauntered out through the North Gate then turned east in the shadow of the wall. The very fact that he had met with such resistance from the knight gave him food for thought. He was certain that his earlier conversation must have been reported to the abbot of Tavistock. There would no doubt be repercussions from the volatile prelate.

Hervey de Marigny paused to look up at a wall which had once kept him and a large Norman army at bay for so long. Memories flooded back. He recalled the sight of the audacious Saxon who stood on the ramparts and bared himself to break wind at them as an act of defiance. It brought a ripe chuckle out of him. Lost in his reminiscences, he strolled slowly on towards the East Gate. He was relaxed and off guard. It never occurred to him that he was being watched.

Chapter Nine

His opportunity to meet her came much sooner than he expected and in the most unlikely place. Gervase Bret stole away from the noise and bustle of the castle that evening to spend some time in prayer at the cathedral. Since the time when he and Ralph had been caught in the mortuary like naughty children, he did not feel comfortable in the castle chapel and sought instead the anonymity of the minster church of St Peter. Its chill atmosphere was like a warm embrace to him, its cavernous interior a haven of privacy. He stayed on his knees for a long time but felt no pain or discomfort when he rose to go, only a sense of relief that was tinged with quiet pleasure. Alys had featured largely in his prayers.

Others were using the cathedral for silent meditation before

Compline. He did not disturb them as he went quietly out, but his departure was noted. He had gone no more than twenty paces from the building when he heard footsteps hurrying after him. Gervase turned to see Asa coming towards him, her face bright with a mixture of hope and apprehension. She stood before him with a deferential smile.

'I saw you leaving and wished to speak to you,' she said.

Gervase was embarrassed. 'This may not be the ideal time,' he said.

'I will not detain you long.'

'They will expect me back at the castle.'

'Please stay,' she said, putting a hand on his arm. 'There is something I must tell you that I was unable to say in the shire hall. It is important for you to understand. Will you hear me?'

'Very well,' he consented, gently detaching his arm. 'What is it?'

'I know what you must think of me,' she began, 'and I do not blame you. In your position, I would think the same. You see me as nothing more than the mistress of a Norman baron, a welcome diversion for him from an uncaring wife. For that is what she is, I do assure you. I did not lure Nicholas away from her. He came of his own accord.'

'I can well believe it, Asa.'

'Can you also believe that I loved him?'

'Yes.'

'That is what my claim is all about: the love I was privileged to share with the lord Nicholas, who was my lord in every sense but one. Let me be frank. In a city like Exeter, I am not short of suitors. Several men have found their way to my door, but none,' she said with a nostalgic smile, 'was quite like him. He was unique.'

'So we have gathered.'

'No,' she said hotly. 'What you have gathered is a false portrait of him.'

'Indeed?'

'He always aroused gossip. Handsome men usually do.'

'That is true.'

'But most of the rumours were cruel and inaccurate,' she said with vehemence. 'You were no doubt told that he was a slave to lust, that he kept a dozen or more women to satisfy his appetite.'

Gervase gave a little cough. 'His fondness for women was remarked upon,' he said uneasily.

'Does that make him some kind of monster?'

'No, no.'

'Are you not also fond of women?'

'Well, yes,' he said awkwardly. 'I suppose that I am.'

'So are your colleagues, the lord Ralph and the lord Hervey. I saw it in their eyes. They are real men – like Nicholas Picard.' She searched his face for a sign of approval before continuing. 'I was the only one, Master Bret. He chose me above all others. You saw that letter from him. What other man would be so generous towards a lover?'

'Very few, I suspect.'

'All of them make promises. The lord Nicholas stood by his.'

'I must take your word for it.'

She pouted with disappointment. 'You think I am lying.'

'No, Asa.'

'You think I am trying to influence you in some way.'

'Not at all,' he said. 'I am glad that you have spoken out like this. It has clarified things. The more we understand, the better are we able to reach a considered judgement.'

'I want what is rightfully mine.'

'We appreciate that.'

'But you do not,' she challenged. 'You think that I somehow tricked that letter out of him. You see it as some sort of payment for my favours. I know the way that men's minds work.' She put her head to one side and studied him quizzically. 'I do not get the feeling that you are married, Master Bret. Are you?'

'No.'

'Betrothed?'

'Yes.'

'For how long?'

'Too long.'

'Do you miss her?'

'Very much.'

'Did you pray for her in the cathedral?' He nodded. 'Then you, too, have felt the strange power of love. You know what it is like to worship another human being so completely that you will do anything for them and cannot bear to be apart from them. Is that how it is with you?'

'It is,' he murmured.

'What is her name?'

'Alys.'

'She is very fortunate.'

'Thank you.'

'And so were we,' she emphasised. 'Neither of us were innocents when we met. Both of us had a past to regret. But those mistakes helped us to recognise true love when it finally came. I would have *died* for that man!'

Someone walked past and looked hard at her. Asa became aware of how public a place it was for her confession. It made her self-conscious. Lowering her voice, she gabbled the rest of what she wanted to tell him.

'I never sought any gift from him,' she insisted. 'He was a gift in himself. The lord Nicholas offered those holdings to me as a proof of his devotion. He wrote that letter in my house and swore that I would be named in his will. I believed him.' Her head drooped. 'Of course, I never thought for a moment that the time would come so soon when that letter would take on real meaning. I would far sooner have him alive than claim my inheritance. He was everything to me and I to him. If anything had happened to his wife, I swear that he would have asked me to marry him.' Her eyes were moist. 'Since he died, I have been distraught.'

'I saw you at the funeral,' he said.

'They did not want me there.'

'They?'

'Respectable people. His widow, his family, his friends.'

'Why did you come?'

'I had to, Master Bret,' she said simply. 'I loved him.'

She touched his arm again and this time he did not remove it.

Disquiet did not set in until the next morning. When they parted, Ralph Delchard had confirmed their usual arrangement to meet for breakfast so that they could discuss with Gervase what lay ahead for them at the shire hall. When his colleague failed to appear, Ralph was not at first disturbed. Hervey de Marigny was usually the last to haul himself out of his bed. In any case, Ralph's mind was still on the injury sustained by his wife, and, when Gervase joined him at the table there was a new subject to preoccupy him. Ralph listened with rapt attention to the account of his friend's meeting with Asa at the cathedral, but took a more sceptical view of it.

'It was no chance encounter, Gervase.'

'What do you mean?'

'She probably followed you there,' said Ralph. 'Asa must have spotted you heading for the cathedral and seized her opportunity.'

'For what?'

'Working on your sympathy.'

'That is not what she did, Ralph.'

'Then she is more cunning than I thought. Asa had you so entranced that you did not even notice how subtly she was influencing you.'

'She merely wished me to understand her situation.'

'So that you would recruit the rest of us to her cause.'

'No!'

'Asa took advantage of your soft heart, Gervase.'

'It is not that soft,' said the other firmly. 'Nor am I so easily led astray by a pretty face. I am not blind, Ralph. I can see when someone is trying to use me. Asa did not ask me to help her in any way. She simply wanted to correct the impression I had of her.'

'And did she?'

'To some extent.'

'Did she sound no false notes at all?'

'Oh, yes,' he said. 'There were a few things which did not ring true. Asa spoke of being distraught at the lord Nicholas's death but she seemed robust enough at the shire hall yesterday. She also claimed that he would have married her if his wife had died. I was not at all sure about that. It is unlikely.'

'Impossible!' said Ralph scornfully. 'Men do not marry women like Asa. She was deceiving herself – or trying to deceive you. What else aroused your suspicion?'

'Asa was eager to make me believe that the two of them had drifted together by accident.'

'That woman does nothing by accident.'

'Quite so. I think she deliberately chose the lord Nicholas and then surprised herself by falling in love with him.' He saw the look of disbelief on his companion's face and became defensive. 'It can happen, Ralph. There was genuine affection between them. She was never his harlot, I am certain of that. They were lovers. He *cared* for her.'

'Do you?'

Gervase reddened and Ralph burst out laughing. They finished their breakfast in silence before they became acutely aware of de Marigny's absence. A servant was summoned at once and sent off to rouse the commissioner from his bed, but the man soon returned with the news that the bedchamber was empty. Ralph began to feel alarmed.

'Where can he be?' he said.

'I have not seen him since yesterday evening.'

'Nor I, Gervase. I never stirred from Golde's side.'

'Perhaps he went for a walk in the city.'

'This early in the day? He values his sleep too much.'

'Then he may be with the sheriff. Or somewhere else in the castle.'

'We shall see,' said Ralph, getting up. 'It is not like Hervey to miss a meeting. And it is most unlike him to forgo a meal.'

He sent for Joscelin and the steward appeared within minutes. When he was told the problem, he took charge at once, dispatching a number of servants on a search of the castle while assuring the visitors that there was no need for concern. Joscelin felt sure that Hervey de Marigny would soon be found and brought to the hall. Ralph was unconvinced and Gervase shared his anxiety. The pattern which the three commissioners had set each morning at the castle had been broken.

The servants returned one by one but none had located the missing man. He had last been seen leaving the castle the previous evening. None of the guards remembered his coming back. Joscelin did his best to calm the apprehension that was now spreading.

'Let me organise a more methodical search,' he volunteered.

'We will be part of it,' said Ralph.

'I will find more men. The castle is large with many places to hide.'

'Hervey de Marigny is not given to playing games.'

'What was the last thing he said to you, Ralph?' asked Gervase.

'I cannot recall.'

'Did he not talk about seeking out Walter Baderon?'

'He did, Gervase,' said the other. 'But he can hardly have been talking to the captain of the guard at the North Gate all night! I sense trouble.'

'There is one other possibility,' said Joscelin tactfully.

'Is there?' said Ralph.

'Some of your men have been visiting houses of resort in the city.'

'They are soldiers, Joscelin. Entitled to their pleasures.'

'I accept that, my lord,' said the steward. 'And it is, in any case, none of my business. Could not the lord Hervey have gone in search of like entertainment and stayed there all night?'

Ralph pondered. 'He could have,' he said at length, 'but I am certain that he did not. Hervey de Marigny is conscientious. He knew how important it was to meet over breakfast this morning for a discussion. Something is seriously amiss here.' He headed for the door. 'Bring everyone you can, Joscelin. I will round up our own men. We will find him if we have to turn this castle inside out.'

Tetbald was annoyed. Having ridden all the way to Exeter in a steady drizzle, he was peeved to be kept waiting in an anteroom at the shire hall long after the echoes of the Terce bell had died away. He took out his anger on the town reeve.

'What is going on, Saewin?' he demanded.

'There has been a delay.'

'I can see that, man. What is the cause of the delay?'

'I do not know.'

'You do not know or you will not tell me?'

Saewin's face was impassive. 'There is a delay,' he said calmly. 'That is all I have been instructed to say.'

'I have been cooling my heels here for an eternity!'

'So have I, Tetbald.'

'Are none of the commissioners here?'

'Not yet.'

'Then where are they?'

'I believe that they are still at the castle.'

'Do they always summon people long before they are needed?'

'No, Tetbald. They have been very punctual until today.'

'Then why am I the one to suffer?'

'Be patient.'

'How can I be patient when I am wet and hungry? Do you know what time I left in order to be here before Terce?' He stamped a foot in irritation. 'Send word to the commissioners that I am here.'

'They already know of your arrival.'

'Then urge them to begin their proceedings.'

'I could not do that if the lady Catherine herself were here to appear before them,' said Saewin, asserting his authority with quiet force. 'So I will certainly not do so for her steward. If the commissioners choose to keep you waiting here all day, it is within their rights to do so. Nothing will be gained by trying to browbeat me, Tetbald. You merely blame a messenger who brings you bad tidings, and that is unjust.'

Tetbald was checked. Controlling his temper, he saw the folly of upsetting the one man who might be able to explain what was happening. Saewin clearly knew more than he was prepared to say. He would also be aware of the developments which had so far taken place in the dispute. Tetbald decided that it was time to adopt a more persuasive approach towards the reeve.

'I am sorry,' he said with a shrug. 'You are right to rebuke me, Saewin. You are simply doing your office – as, indeed, am I. This is a time of trial for us and it has put us under severe strain. The lord Nicholas's death was a blow which has left us dazed.'

'I appreciate that.'

'The foul murder has been followed by another crime.'

'Oh?'

'A robbery at the manor house.'

'What was stolen?'

'That is beside the point,' he said evasively. 'It is the fact of the crime which has wounded the lady Catherine. An intruder somehow entered the house at night. That is very disturbing, Saewin.'

'I can see that.'

'The lady Catherine was appalled. She is grieving over her husband and in no fit state to suffer another cruel shock. It has made her very nervous.' He pulled himself up to his full height. 'I see it as my duty to protect her from any further unpleasantness. Not only has her husband been killed and her house broken into, the lady Catherine has to suffer the indignity of seeing her property fought over by vultures who have swooped on the dead body of the lord Nicholas. I hoped that I could quickly resolve this dispute in her favour and be able to take some good news to her for a change.'

'That may yet happen, Tetbald.'

'If and when the commissioners get here.'

'Yes.'

'So what is holding them up?'

'I am not at liberty to tell you.'

'Why not? Is it so secret?' He produced an oleaginous smile. 'Come, sir. Let us not quarrel. All I seek is an explanation. Is this delay related to one of the claimants? The abbot of Tavistock, perhaps? Or the lady Loretta? Or has some new vulture come to peck at the corpse?'

'There has been an unfortunate delay. Accept that fact.'

'I will if you tell me what lies behind it.'

'The commissioners do not have to justify their decisions.'

'What exactly did they tell you?'

He put a hand on the reeve's shoulder and smiled at him again, but Saewin said nothing. Tetbald eventually gave up. Removing his hand, he scowled darkly and was about to issue another stream of protests when they were interrupted. A figure appeared at the door and gestured to Saewin. The reeve seemed slightly embarrassed. He turned to Tetbald.

'I must go,' he said.

Then he followed Engelric out.

The debate which raged at the castle was far more heated than anything which had taken place at the shire hall. Ralph Delchard was on his feet, gesticulating wildly, Canon Hubert, jowls shaking, was at his most determined, Gervase Bret was unusually agitated and even Brother Simon, normally a mute witness on such occasions, felt obliged to add his comments. Their clamour reverberated around the hall.

'The proceedings must be suspended forthwith!' insisted Ralph.

'That would be madness!' yelled Hubert.

'Hervey de Marigny is missing. The commission cannot possibly sit without him.'

'Why not, my lord? We have done so before on many occasions.'

'I can vouch for that,' said Simon gently. 'The three of you have coped with many disputes on your own and could do so again.'

'Devon presents us with more work than most counties,' observed Gervase from his seat at the table. 'That is why the lord

Hervey joined us and he has been as able a judge as any of us.'

'Able and upright!' endorsed Ralph.

'On the other hand,' resumed Gervase, 'I am not convinced that we have to bring our deliberations to a halt until he has been found.'

'We must, Gervase!' said Ralph.

'We must not!' countered Hubert.

Ralph waved his arms. 'He is our colleague and friend. We must lead the search for him.'

'That is the sheriff's duty,' said Hubert.

'Do you not *care* what has happened to the lord Hervey?'

'Deeply,' said the canon, 'but I also care for the important work with which we have been entrusted. It must not be set aside, my lord. While the sheriff does his duty, let us continue to do ours.'

'We have a duty to Hervey de Marigny!' urged Ralph.

Hubert was adamant. 'Our first commitment is to the king's will.'

'Would you really sit idly by in the shire hall while a friend is lost and possibly in danger?' Ralph swung round to Gervase. 'Help me out here. Let me hear at least one sane voice.'

'I am wondering what the lord Hervey himself would wish,' said Gervase thoughtfully. 'What has befallen him I do not know, and I hope for news of his whereabouts very soon. But I suspect that he would not want us to abandon our work on his account.'

'Exactly!' said Hubert.

Ralph was perplexed. 'You are against me, Gervase?'

'Of course not. I share your fears.'

'Then do something about them and join the search.'

'That is what I am suggesting,' argued Gervase. 'But that search must not only be undertaken in the nooks and crannies of Exeter. Besides, we are strangers to the city and would not know where to start looking. No, Ralph,' he said earnestly, 'the place for us to conduct our search is in the shire hall. We always felt that the lord Nicholas's death was directly related to this dispute and so is the lord Hervey's disappearance. I am certain of it. Solve the dispute,' he advocated, 'and we solve both mysteries.'

'Sage counsel,' said Simon.

Hubert smiled grimly. 'Our three votes outweigh you, my lord.'

'I am the leader of this commission,' Ralph reminded him.

'But our judgements rest on majority decision.'

'Only in the shire hall, Hubert!'

'And that is where we should be, my lord.'

'But it seems so heartless,' said Ralph with passion. 'Heavens above, man! If you went astray, would you want your colleagues to proceed calmly on as if nothing had happened?'

'Yes, my lord,' said Hubert.

'It is indecent!'

'It is a necessity.'

'I agree with Canon Hubert,' said Gervase.

'You simply wish to discharge our duties here so that you can gallop back to Winchester and get married!' Ralph was hurt. 'Really, Gervase. I expected support from you at least. The lord Hervey is a Norman baron in a city which is full of resentful Saxons. Anything might have happened to him. Can you really turn your back on him like this?'

'I am not turning my back on him, Ralph.'

'You are putting your own selfish needs first.'

'No!'

'Then what are you doing?'

'Directing my energies to resolving this dispute. Until we do that, we will never know the full truth. You must see that, Ralph.'

'All I can see are three men deserting a friend in need.'

'I resent that accusation, my lord,' said Hubert.

'So do I,' added Simon.

'We are not deserting him, Ralph,' said Gervase. 'We are simply seeking to find him by other means.'

Ralph snorted. 'Ah! I see. Hervey is hiding in the shire hall. If we take our seats there, he will pop up from under the table to surprise us.' His tone was contemptuous. 'This is lunatic reasoning. There is only one way to find him and that is by joining the sheriff in his search.' He looked round the table. 'It is shameful that anyone should think otherwise.'

There was a bruised silence. It was eventually broken by Simon. 'May I speak?' he asked tentatively.

'No!' snarled Ralph.

'Brother Simon is entitled to express an opinion,' said Hubert.

'He is a scribe and not a commissioner.'

'I think we should still hear him, Ralph,' said Gervase.

'So do I,' said Hubert. 'Proceed, Brother Simon.'

The scribe glanced nervously around at the others before speaking. 'I would ask you to call to mind what happened in York,' he said querulously. 'There, too, we were burdened with an immense number of disputes and there, too, we were granted the services of an additional commissioner to help to bear the onerous load.'

'Tanchelm of Ghent,' recalled Gervase.

'A shrewd judge,' continued Simon. 'While he and Canon Hubert heard one set of disputes, you, my lord,' he said, smiling at Ralph, 'were able to deal with other cases in consort with Gervase. By dividing the work, you were able to speed up the pace of your judgements.'

'Until the lord Tanchelm was murdered,' said Ralph with a reminiscent glare. 'Did we sit in session during the hunt for the killer? Did we forget about our colleague and carry on with our work? No, we did not!' he stressed, slapping the table. 'We suspended everything until the murder was solved. We showed respect for the dead. Thank you, Simon,' he said with a nod at the scribe. 'You have given us a timely reminder of how to behave. We must do as we did in York and put our work aside.'

'But that is not what I am proposing, my lord,' said Simon.

'No?'

'The cases are similar but not identical. To begin with, the lord Hervey is simply missing. He may well be found alive and unharmed. The point which I was striving to make was this. Two commissioners were able to take responsibility in York.' He trembled under Ralph's glare but forced the words out. 'Could not two also do likewise in Exeter?'

'What do you mean?' growled Ralph.

'Simply this, my lord. I am suggesting a compromise. You wish to join the search party and must be allowed to do so.'

Ralph was determined. 'No man on earth will stop me!'

'We respect your decision,' said Simon. 'But while you join

the sheriff, Canon Hubert and Gervase can continue the work at the shire hall. This answers all needs, my lord. Does it not?'

Dean Jerome liked to preserve an atmosphere of peace and harmony but that was not always possible when Geoffrey, abbot of Tavistock chose to visit Exeter. A pious man and a renowned scholar, the abbot was also liable to outbursts which could be distressing to men of contemplative inclination. His exalted position made him difficult to criticise, let alone to control. The dean searched for a means to hurry him on his way.

'How long will you be staying with us?' he said mournfully.

'Why do you ask?' said the abbot. 'Have I outstayed my welcome?'

'Not at all, my lord abbot.'

'Bishop Osbern encouraged me to remain here.'

'And so do I,' lied the other. 'So do I. Our community is enriched by your presence. It is always a pleasure to see you in Exeter.'

'It was not pleasure which brought me here, Jerome.'

'I know.'

'I came to rectify a dreadful wrong,' said the abbot. 'Until I have done that, I will not stir from the city. If you wish to know how long I will stay, ask the commissioners. It lies in their hands to return to my abbey that land which was seized illegally from it. Our cause is just.'

'I never doubted that, my lord abbot.'

'Then speak to the commissioners on my behalf. Canon Hubert resides here with you,' he said, 'though I have somehow been prevented from meeting him within these walls. I am

204

sure that both you and Bishop Osbern wish to see the property restored to my abbey. Help to bring that desired end about.'

'It might be looked upon as interference.'

'Not by me.'

'By the commissioners.'

'With whom does your loyalty lie, Jerome?'

The dean was saved from the embarrassment of having to answer the question. A novice brought news that the abbot had a visitor. When he was told who it was, Geoffrey excused himself and scurried off at once. Ralph Delchard was waiting for him in the parlour. The abbot's urgency swept pleasantries aside.

'Have you arrived at a judgement?' he demanded.

'Not yet, my lord abbot.'

'But my case is unanswerable.'

'That is a matter of opinion.'

'What is holding you up?'

'A number of things,' said Ralph. 'One of which has brought me here this morning. We are beset by a serious problem.'

'The only problem you have is an inability to make up your minds. The abbey of Tavistock held those holdings in Upton Pyne until they were taken from us. Restore them and the matter is settled.'

'Only to your satisfaction.'

'And to yours if you value justice.'

'What I value is the safety of my fellows,' said Ralph with asperity. 'One of them may be imperilled and just now his fate concerns me far more than some land to the north of here. I need to speak with one of your knights.'

'Why?'

'I have reason to believe that he may be able to help me.'

'In what way?'

'That remains to be seen, my lord abbot.'

'Who is the man?'

'Walter Baderon.'

'Ah!'

'He was the captain of the guard at the North Gate last night.'

'I am aware of that, my lord, but I still have no idea whatsoever why you have come bursting in here in search of him. What is this all about? Which of your fellows may be imperilled?'

'Hervey de Marigny.'

'I remember him.'

'He is missing.'

'How does that concern Walter Baderon?'

'The lord Hervey spoke with him the other evening.'

'Yes,' said the other sharply. 'I know. And I would like to register the strongest objection. I will not have my men interrogated behind my back. It was a shabby device, my lord.'

'I disagree.'

'Then you set yourself a low standard of conduct.'

Ralph held back a tart reply. 'All that interests me at the moment is finding the lord Hervey,' he said. 'He talked of speaking with Walter Baderon again and left the castle to do so. I need to know what passed between the two of them.'

'Nothing, my lord.'

'Why do you say that?'

'Because I warned all my men to be wary of the lord Hervey. They were ordered to say as little as possible to him.

I reprimanded Walter Baderon for being so careless when he was first questioned. He would not have been deceived by the lord Hervey again.'

'I still have to speak to Baderon.'

'Then you will have a long ride, my lord.'

'Why?'

The abbot looked him in the eye and gave an enigmatic smile. 'I sent him back to Tavistock at first light.'

Brother Simon's suggested compromise was willingly accepted. Gervase Bret and Canon Hubert accompanied him to the shire hall and began their examination of the last claimant. Tetbald was a clever advocate. Having scrutinised the relevant documents with care, he was able to argue cogently on behalf of the lady Catherine. A note of ingratiation sometimes crept in, but it was offset by an occasional lapse into arrogance. He held up under even the most hostile questioning.

'Was the lord Nicholas prone to seize land illegally?' asked Hubert.

'No,' said the steward.

'Our evidence suggests otherwise.'

'Then your evidence is wrong.'

'Our predecessors found several irregularities relating to the lord Nicholas's estate. Why was that, do you think?'

'You will have to ask them.'

'The returns for this county make sorry reading,' said Hubert. 'We studied them at the Exchequer in Winchester. The name of Nicholas Picard occurs time and again.'

'The lord Nicholas is dead, alas,' said Tetbald smoothly. 'He cannot be called to account for any supposed irregularities. I am here to represent his widow, the lady Catherine, and shield her from further distress. The will lies before you. As you can see, all property and worldly goods of the lord Nicholas have been bequeathed to his widow.' He became almost cocky. 'That document, along with all the others I have produced, surely seals the dispute in our favour.'

'No,' said Gervase.

'Why not?'

'Because those holdings may not have been his to give. Our task is to establish whether or not the lord Nicholas acquired that land by just means or by seizure. If the latter is the case,' he cautioned, 'then the portion of the will relating to Upton Pyne is rendered invalid.'

Tetbald protested and the argument rumbled on for another hour. The commissioners dismissed him but told him that he would be summoned before them again. The steward stalked out. Hoping for a final decision, he was disappointed to be sent away without one and he was now regretting the boasts with which he had left the manor house. On his return to the lady Catherine, he would be forced to show more humility.

Hubert was at once impressed and vexed by the man.

'He spoke well enough,' he said, 'and knows every detail of the lord Nicholas's tenure, but I found his manner irritating at times.'

'Yes,' agreed Gervase. 'He was far too unctuous for my liking.'

'It was that proprietorial tone which irked me. The fellow is only the steward yet there were moments when he sounded like the beneficiary.'

'Perhaps he is.'

The thought was intriguing. Not for the first time, Hubert provided an insight which set up a whole train of new possibilities. Gervase's mind was racing. One of the images which kept returning was that of Nicholas Picard's funeral where Tetbald escorted the widow of the deceased as if he were one of the chief mourners.

It was time to break for refreshment before recalling one of the other witnesses for the second time. Gervase was about to rise from his seat when one of the sentries came into the hall. He bore a small packet in his hand and offered it to Gervase.

'This bears your name, Master Bret,' he said.

'Who gave it to you?'

'I do not know. It was tossed out of the crowd at us as we stood outside the hall. We have no idea who threw it or what it contains.'

Gervase thanked him, sent him on his way, then inspected the package. It was a bundle of letters, bound together by a ribbon. His name had been scrawled across the back of one missive. Watched by the others, he undid the ribbon and spread the letters out on the table. Then he opened one of them. Gervase read no more than a few lines before his jaw dropped.

Chapter Ten

Golde became increasingly restive. When she heard about the mysterious disappearance of Hervey de Marigny, her first instinct was to join the search, but she heaved herself off the bed only to find that her ankle would not support her weight. Confined to her chamber, all that she could do was wait, pray and ponder. It was frustrating. The longer she lay there, the more anxious she became about the commissioner's safety and the more she chafed at her isolation.

When she heard footsteps ascending the stairs outside, she hoped that it would be her husband with reassuring news about their missing friend, but the man who knocked on the door before putting his head round it was Joscelin the Steward. He gave her an apologetic smile.

'I am sorry to disturb you, my lady,' he said.

'Is there any news of the lord Hervey?'

'Not yet, I fear.'

'When there is,' she asked, 'please bring it to me.'

'I will, my lady. But I have brought something else now.'

'Oh?'

'You have a visitor.'

Golde was pleased. 'That will break the tedium. Who is it?'

'Bishop Osbern.'

Pleasure turned to consternation and Golde plucked at her chemise, worrying that she was not properly dressed to receive such an illustrious visitor and feeling at a severe disadvantage. Osbern immediately put her at ease. Stepping into the room, he thanked Joscelin with a smile, then turned his attention to Golde, who was struggling to rise.

'Rest, my lady,' he said softly. 'Do not get up for me.'

'This is an honour, Your Grace.'

'For me also.'

'Your arrival has caught me rather unawares.'

'It is good to know that the Church can still spring an occasional surprise.' He dismissed Joscelin with a nod, then moved to the stool. 'May I sit down, my lady?'

'Please do.'

'The stairs are steep and my legs are no longer young.' He lowered himself onto the stool and appraised her with sympathy. 'How do you feel now?'

'Much better, Your Grace.'

'You were thrown from your horse, I hear. They are unreliable animals at times. I can see why Canon Hubert prefers a donkey,' he said with a wry grin. 'A small creature like that would be quite unable to dislodge such a portly rider. But I am pleased to see you looking so well, my lady. You have colour in your cheeks and are patently in good spirits.'

'I was until I heard the sad tidings.'

His face clouded. 'Ah, yes. The missing commissioner. It is very disturbing. I have only just heard,' he explained. 'I came to the castle for an appointment with the sheriff but discovered that he was out leading a search party. It was his wife who told me of your accident. When the lady Albreda mentioned that you hailed from Hereford, I felt that I had to make your acquaintance and enquire after your health.'

'That was very kind of you, Your Grace.'

'I was happy to turn my visit into an errand of mercy.'

'I feel overwhelmed.'

Golde was touched by his concern for her. Though she was still in awe of her visitor, she found his a gentle presence and was able to relax to the point where she could begin to enjoy their conversation. Bishop Osbern smiled benignly and seemed completely at home in the chamber.

'Tell me about Hereford,' he said.

'I have not lived there for some time, Your Grace.'

'When did you last visit the town?'

'Some months ago,' she said. 'When my husband travelled to Chester with the other commissioners, I took the opportunity to stop at Hereford on the way in order to see my sister. It was good to be back there again. The town holds happy memories for me.'

'It does for me as well, my lady. If you spent your

childhood there, you will no doubt remember my brother, who was earl of Hereford.'

'Oh, yes, Your Grace. We all knew Earl William.'

'It was always a delight to visit him in such a beautiful town. He was so proud to be given the responsibility of mounting guard on the Welsh border. I am a man of God myself and abhor violence in all its forms, but we do, unfortunately, need brave warriors like my brother to maintain the peace and make our mission possible.' He heaved a sigh of regret. 'His son, alas, was cut from different cloth. His rashness made me ashamed to call him nephew. It has left a stain on our family.'

'The people of Hereford were shocked.'

'As well they might be, my lady. My nephew inherited an earldom from his father, then promptly joined a rebellion against the king. It was a disastrous escapade and not without its embarrassment for me. The rebellion was easily quashed but it made the king understandably wary of creating another earl of Hereford.' He waved a dismissive hand. 'But let us put all that behind us. I did not come here to bore you with a sermon on the political ills of your town. What do you think of Exeter?'

'It is a charming city.'

'How much of it have you seen?'

'A great deal,' she said with enthusiasm. 'The lady Albreda conducted me around it yesterday with Berold the Jester.'

'A lively companion.'

'He made me laugh.'

'That is his art, my lady, though his fooling sometimes has a sharp edge. Canon Hubert was shaken when Berold appeared before him in a Benedictine habit.'

'Canon Hubert is very sensitive to any ridicule.'

'I know. He urged me to complain to the sheriff but it would have been pointless.' He smiled tolerantly. You cannot have a disciplined jester. It is a contradiction in terms. But tell me about yourself.'

Golde was flattered by his attention. Osbern was genuinely interested in what she had to say and it encouraged her to talk freely about her life and work in Hereford. He was fascinated to hear that she had been a brewer of some distinction in the town and listened attentively to her account of how she met Ralph Delchard.

'It is good to know that someone in Hereford drew benefit from the visit of the royal commissioners,' he observed. 'Your husband's work will never make him popular, important as it is. He must meet with a great deal of resentment.'

'Ralph has grown accustomed to that.'

'Taxes always arouse hostility and sometimes, I fear, it can spill over into violence. I dearly hope that is not the case here.'

'Here?'

'The lord Hervey's disappearance.'

'You think he may have been attacked?' she said in alarm.

'It is, alas, a possibility,' said Osbern sadly, 'and one that the sheriff has evidently considered. Hence the size and urgency of this search party. This city has a long history of resistance to authority. The lord Hervey would not be the first man to suffer because of the office he holds.' He saw the anxiety on her face. 'Will you join me in a prayer for his safety?'

'Yes, Your Grace,' she said. 'Gladly.'

* * *

Gervase Bret was in a quandary. The letters which had been delivered to the shire hall by an anonymous hand caused him great discomfort and forced him into the anomalous position of having to deceive Canon Hubert and Brother Simon. When he glanced through them, he could see that the letters had a bearing on the dispute before them, but they were of so intimate a nature that he felt he was intruding into someone's privacy and he drew back from divulging their contents to his colleagues, deciding instead to act independently even though he saw the danger involved. Gervase knew why the letters had been addressed to him. Of the commissioners, he was the only one who could understand the language in which they were written.

Noting his embarrassment, Hubert became intensely curious.

'Are we to know what those letters contain?' he asked.

'No, Canon Hubert,' said Gervase, putting them into his satchel. 'They concern a personal matter.'

'Why were they delivered in such a strange manner?'

'I do not know.'

'It seems odd that they were brought to the shire hall.'

'Odd?'

'If it is personal correspondence, it would surely have been sent to you at the castle. Since they came here, I am bound to wonder if they pertain in any way to our deliberations.'

'No, Canon Hubert.'

Gervase's denial was firm enough to convince but it left him feeling profoundly guilty. He was glad when they recalled the first claimant to the hall. The verbal tempest created by the abbot of Tavistock diverted attention from him and gave Hubert the chance to take a leading role in the debate,

215

responding vigorously to the prelate's wilder accusations and making it clear that his own black cowl should not be taken as an indication of prejudice in favour of the abbey. Brother Simon watched in open-mouthed wonder, alternately cowed by the abbot's vituperation and inspired by Hubert's authoritative rebuttals. Gervase asked a few pertinent questions about the wording of the documents which were offered in support of the abbey, but the real battle lay between the claimant and the canon.

When the session finally ended, the abbot of Tavistock crept away to lick his wounds like an injured lion. Encouraged by what he perceived as Hubert's sympathetic treatment of him at their first encounter, he had come with high hopes, but he went away feeling battered and betrayed. Gervase was the first to congratulate his colleague on his steadfast performance.

'That was masterly, Canon Hubert.'

'I had to defend the integrity of this commission.'

'You did so superbly.'

'Thank you, Gervase,' said the other, preening himself. 'You might mention it to the lord Ralph.'

'Most certainly.'

'We have been able to manage perfectly well without him.'

'And without the lord Hervey,' added Simon.

All three of them were brought to a sharp halt. In the cut and thrust of debate, they had forgotten all about the missing commissioner. No news had been brought of Hervey de Marigny, which meant that he had still not been found. Their apprehension grew. Much as he had relished his position of command, Hubert would willingly have sacrificed it for the safe return of a respected colleague. They were in a more subdued mood when the last witness of the day was shown into the hall.

Loretta looked as poised and elegant as ever. She was accompanied by Eldred as before though he did no more than sit there in melancholy silence. Loretta expressed surprise that only two commissioners were there to examine her but Hubert assured her that he and Gervase were fully authorised to put her claim under scrutiny again.

'Does that mean you will reach a conclusion today?' she asked.

'That is highly unlikely, my lady,' said Gervase.

'Why?'

'Because we are still not satisfied that we have all the facts before us.'

'I have given you the only facts which matter,' she said blandly. 'The holdings in Upton Pyne belonged to my late son, William, and should be restored to me immediately.'

'This property seems to hold a special significance for you, my lady,' said Hubert. 'Is that a fair comment to make?'

'A very fair comment, Canon Hubert.'

'Do these holdings have some peculiarly attractive features?'

'No.'

'Then why are you so anxious to recover them?'

'It is a matter of honour,' she said.

'This dispute is very distressing to the lord Nicholas's widow.'

'I have every sympathy for her, Canon Hubert, but I will not let this opportunity pass by without asserting my entitlement. May I remind you that it was while I myself was in mourning that this property was taken from me in the first place?'

Canon Hubert backed off and left the bulk of the questioning to Gervase. Searching enquiries were put to her but Loretta was equal to each one of them and the legitimacy of her claim could not be doubted. She conducted herself with far more dignity than the abbot of Tavistock and her arguments were correspondingly more effective. Even Canon Hubert began to be swayed by her. When they had exhausted their questions, she had some of her own for them.

'Will I be called before you again?' she asked.

'It is possible,' said Gervase.

'What more can I tell you?'

'We may need to test your reaction to evidence which is given by the other claimants. They, too, may be examined again.'

'To what end?'

'The pursuit of the truth,' said Hubert.

'But it lies in the documents I have already shown you,' she said, indicating the satchel carried by Eldred. 'Study them again if you are not convinced. I have waited a long time to regain this property and my patience is not unlimited. Why waste your time listening to claims that are patently fraudulent?'

'There is nothing fraudulent about the lady Catherine's claim,' said Gervase. 'Her husband's will bequeaths those holdings to her. And the others involved in this dispute must also be heard.'

'Heard then dismissed as impudent.'

Hubert bridled. 'That is for us to decide.'

'Can you take the claim of Engelric seriously?' she said with a muted contempt. 'Or that of the abbot? They fight a battle whose outcome was settled long ago. As for the other extraordinary claimant—'

'We cannot discuss any of the contestants with you, my lady,' said Gervase firmly. 'None of them have sought to pour scorn on you. It will not help your cause to be critical of them.'

'I apologise, Master Bret,' she said quickly. 'You are right. I am letting my impatience get the better of me. You are the judges here and I am a mere supplicant. I bow to your authority.'

'You have no choice but to do so,' warned Hubert.

'I accept that.' She rose to leave. 'I bid you farewell.'

'One last thing, my lady,' said Gervase.

'Yes?'

'How do you come to know so much about the rival claimants?'

'It is in my interests to do so,' she said with a quiet smile.

Ralph Delchard's concern served to deepen his irritation. He rode beside the sheriff and helped to supervise an exhaustive search of the city. It produced no results. Premises were searched and people questioned endlessly, but Hervey de Marigny's whereabouts were not revealed. As the afternoon shaded into evening, Ralph slapped his thigh in exasperation.

'God's tits!' he exclaimed. 'He must be somewhere!'

'Not in the city,' said Baldwin.

'We have not searched hard enough.'

'Over sixty men have combed every street and building in Exeter, my lord. They even went into the crypt of the cathedral. The lord Hervey is nowhere to be found. Is there not a chance that he may have ridden out of the city without telling you?'

'No,' said Ralph. 'Besides, his horse is in the stable.'

'He may have procured another.'

'For what purpose? Hervey de Marigny came here on royal business and he would not willingly have left until it was discharged. There is only one explanation here, my lord sheriff,' he said grimly. 'Foul play.'

'Let us not fear the worst.'

'We have to face the facts.'

'He may yet be found in good health.'

'I do not share your optimism. Search more thoroughly.'

'My men have left no stone unturned,' said Baldwin, 'and your own men have been equally diligent. If the lord Hervey was in Exeter, we would surely have tracked him down by now. I will widen the search outside the city. It is the only thing left to do.'

'Not quite, my lord sheriff.'

'What is your advice?'

'Arrest the abbot of Tavistock.'

Baldwin blinked in amazement. 'On what possible grounds?'

'Concealment of evidence.'

'Can you be serious, my lord? Do you really imagine that the abbot is involved in the disappearance of the lord Hervey?'

'Indirectly, yes.'

'What evidence do you have?'

'That of my own eyes and ears. The lord Hervey told us that he would speak to Walter Baderon again when he came on duty at the North Gate.'

'None of the sentries remembers seeing them together.'

'None of the sentries *admits* to it,' corrected Ralph, 'but only because their master has told them to keep silent. Why did the abbot send this Baderon back to Tavistock if not to evade our enquiries? He is the key to this whole business, I feel sure.' He became peremptory. 'Put the abbot under lock and key while I ride to Tavistock to arrest Walter Baderon.'

'I will do nothing of the kind, my lord.'

'Then you are slack in your duties.'

'Do you dare to insult me?'

'No, my lord sheriff,' said Ralph with a note of apology. 'You have acted promptly and put your men at our disposal. I am grateful for that. But I would be even more grateful if you would at least interrogate the abbot. I am certain that he is hiding something.'

'I do not share that certainty.'

'Why was the captain of his guard sent home?'

'It might just be a coincidence, my lord.'

'I beg to differ.'

'The abbot is not responsible.'

'He *knows* something,' insisted Ralph. 'I saw it in his eyes.'

Baldwin was unmoved. 'I have no cause to interrogate him, still less to issue a warrant of arrest. Have you any idea what complications would follow? I'd have the Church itself around my ears.'

'An abbot is not above the law.'

'The law requires proof of guilt, my lord, and you have none.'

'Very well,' said Ralph. 'I'll tackle the abbot myself.'

'No,' ordered the sheriff. 'I will lead this search. The lord Hervey told you that he would talk to this Walter Baderon but it is far from certain that he did so. The last reports we have of him come from my own sentries who saw him leave the castle. Something may have happened to him before he got anywhere near the North Gate. Be ruled by me, my lord. I will not condone intemperate action.'

Ralph looked around him, his howl a mixture of anger and despair. 'Where *is* he?'

Gervase was troubled by severe misgivings. He walked up and down the street three times before he dared to approach the house. In answer to his tentative knock, Goda opened the door. She eyed him with suspicion. He stammered an enquiry but the servant did not have time to answer. Hearing his voice, Asa came swiftly out of the parlour.

'Master Bret!' she said with delight.

'I was hoping to find you at home.'

'You have brought me good news? My claim has been upheld?'

'We have not yet reached a decision,' he said, 'and your claim may be in jeopardy. That is why I came.'

She invited him in and closed the door of the parlour after them. 'What is wrong?' she asked.

'You have not been telling me the truth, Asa.'

'Yes, I have!'

'You deliberately misled me.'

'What makes you think that?'

'These letters,' he said, taking the packet from his satchel and handing it to her. 'Do you recognise them?'

She winced visibly. 'No, I do not,' she said.

'They bear your name.'

'Then someone forged my signature.'

'They could not have forged the contents, Asa,' he said. 'I have read the letters through and I know that only you could have written them.'

A long pause. 'Where did you get them?' she asked finally.

'They were delivered to me at the shire hall.'

'By whom?'

'I have no idea.'

'By her!' she sneered. 'By the precious lady Catherine! Except that she would not deign to bring them herself. That creeping Tetbald would have been given the office.'

He fixed her with a stare. 'Did you write those letters, Asa?'

'Yes,' she confessed. 'But only under duress.'

'Duress?'

'The lord Nicholas made me write them.'

'Why?'

'He said that he wanted proof of my love,' she sighed, 'though he had ample proof of that in my bedchamber. He told me that he needed some token from me to help him endure the pain of being apart. These were private letters, Master Bret,' she chided, 'and you had no business to read them. I am disappointed in you.'

'They touch on the dispute and can be construed as evidence.'

'Evidence of my love for him. I freely acknowledge that.'

'But there are other things you did not freely acknowledge,' said Gervase sharply. 'You gave me the impression that the lord Nicholas promised you those holdings as a spontaneous gesture of affection.'

'And so he did!'

'Then why does one of your letters demand written proof that you will be his beneficiary? You threatened to withdraw your favours unless he gave you a more visible sign of commitment. In other words,' continued Gervase, watching her closely, 'the letter which you produced before the tribunal was not the gift of a grateful man to a lover. It was a price exacted from him by you.'

'No!' she cried.

'You sought to deceive us.'

'That is not true.'

'It was the lord Nicholas who wrote a letter under duress.'

Asa burst into tears and hurled the letters away. In spite of himself, Gervase felt sorry for her and wanted to console her in some way, but he did not dare to reach out to her. He waited until her sobbing eased.

'Why did you write in your own language?' he asked.

'It came easier to me. I could express myself more clearly.'

'Did the lord Nicholas understand it?'

'Yes,' she whispered. 'When he saw how well I could speak his tongue, he insisted on learning mine. We spent hours on end playing with words and phrases. He wanted to be close to me and that meant learning my language, difficult as it was for him. If that does not convince you that he loved me, then nothing will.'

'The lord Nicholas loved you deeply, Asa. I am certain of it.'

'Then why torment me like this?'

'Because you exploited that love,' said Gervase. 'It is there in your letters. Every one of them contains some demand. He may not have paid for your favours with money but you still set a high price on them.'

'I was worth it!' she said with defiance.

Gervase was suddenly alarmed. He wondered what he was doing there and how he could best extricate himself. If his colleagues discovered where he had been, he was not sure that he could adequately explain himself. Asa sensed his confusion. She took a step closer to him.

'I thought you were a friend,' she said. 'I hoped that you would help.'

'I have helped you, Asa.'

'How? By reading my letters?'

'By bringing them to you in person instead of showing them to my colleagues. You spoke to us on oath in the shire hall. Those letters show that you committed perjury and make your claim worthless.'

'No!' she cried. 'I *earned* that property.'

'Not in any legal way.'

'I meant more to the lord Nicholas than any woman alive.'

'Then why did you have to wrest gifts from him?'

'It was a game we played. He liked it that way.'

'Don't lie to me, Asa.'

'He wanted me to have that property.'

'After his death,' he reminded her, 'and that must have seemed a long way hence when you forced him to write that letter of intent. Or did you think that the lord Nicholas might not have long to live?'

Gervase himself was surprised by the force and directness of his question. It struck her like a whiplash and she flinched in pain. When she regained her composure, she looked at him with a hatred that was tempered with curiosity. Gervase could

225

not tear his eyes away from hers. After a long pause, Asa reached out to take his hand in hers. He did not resist.

'What really brought you to my house?' she asked softly.

The passage of time did not still her anger. Hours after her steward had returned from the shire hall, Catherine was seething. She preserved a dignified calm in front of the rest of the household, but Tetbald was allowed to see her true feelings. When they were alone again in the parlour, she rounded on him with her eyes blazing.

'You swore to me that the matter would be decided today,' she said.

'I had every reason to believe that it would.'

'You failed me, Tetbald.'

'No, my lady.'

'All those promises, all those proud boasts.'

'You will still inherit the entire estate,' he assured her.

'That is what you said when you rode off this morning.'

'There were problems at the shire hall, my lady. A long delay. Saewin would not tell me what caused it but two of the commissioners did not even turn up to examine me.'

'Did you convince those who were there?'

'Not completely,' he confessed.

'You had my husband's will in your hands.'

'Even that was not conclusive, my lady. They haggled interminably. They are not yet sure if the holdings in Upton Pyne are a legitimate part of the inheritance.'

'They have to be,' she asserted. 'I want *everything*.'

'You shall have it.'

'Not if I have to rely on you, Tetbald. Perhaps I need another advocate.'

'It is too late to decide that now,' he said with a scowl. 'Before you blame me for things which were no fault of mine, you might remember what I have done for you so far. I have given good service.'

'True,' she conceded.

'The lord Nicholas employed me but my first loyalty was towards you.'

'I have not forgotten that.'

'Then do not treat me so harshly, my lady.'

'You displease me.'

'Their judgement has been postponed a little, that is all.'

'If it is postponed,' she said angrily, 'it means that it is no longer certain to be in my favour. There are doubts in the commissioners' minds. And you must have put them there, Tetbald.' She walked away from him and was lost in her thoughts for some time. Tetbald smarted in silence. He had never seen her so angry before and it troubled him. When she swung back to him, her jaw was set. 'I will go there myself next time.'

'That would be folly.'

'The folly lay in delegating it to you.'

'I am used to such legal wrangling, my lady. You are not.'

'My presence at the shire hall will be a weapon in itself.'

'A weapon that can be turned against you,' he argued. 'It is only days since the funeral. His widow is expected to mourn in private, to be so overcome with grief that she will not stir from her chamber. You agreed that it would be unseemly for you to be involved directly in this dispute.'

'Only because I trusted you to act on my behalf.'

'And that is what I am doing, my lady.'

'Not to my satisfaction.'

She walked to the window and gazed out at the surrounding land. Stung by her criticism, Tetbald was anxious to win back her favour. He moved across to stand directly behind her. Catherine's ire seemed slowly to abate. He could see that she was more relaxed. When he ventured to put a hand on her hip, however, she tensed immediately.

'I am sorry, my lady,' he said, swiftly withdrawing his hand. 'But I implore you to reconsider. Your appearance at the shire hall will contradict everything that I said about you. It could prove ruinous.'

'I will take that chance.'

'Would you throw it all away now when we have come so far?'

She turned to face him. 'We?' she said coldly.

'You could not have done it without me.'

'That may be so, Tetbald, but I rule in this house now. I make my own decisions and do not look to you for approval. I will go to the shire hall. If a man's whore is allowed to assert her claim,' she said bitterly, 'then his wife ought at least to have the same entitlement.'

Before he could stop her, she swept out of the room and ascended the stairs. Tetbald heard the door of her bedchamber being shut and bolted.

Ralph Delchard was still locked in argument with the sheriff when the messenger brought the news. They abandoned their quarrel at once and followed the man-at-arms as he cantered through the streets towards the South Gate. Leaving the city, they followed the river for almost half a mile downstream until they came to a small crowd of people being held back from the bank by soldiers from the castle garrison. Ralph dropped down from the saddle and pushed his way past the onlookers. Baldwin lumbered after him.

The body of Hervey de Marigny had been hauled from the water and laid on the bank. A soldier was bending over him to shield the horror from the gaze of the people behind him. When Ralph first saw his friend, he felt as if he had taken a violent blow between the eyes. He reeled back and needed a moment to steady himself. The sheriff, too, was appalled by the sight. Hervey de Marigny was almost unrecognisable. His face was hideously scored with lacerations and his throat was comprehensively cut. His lower lip had been bitten off. The body was sodden and limp, the limbs stretched at an unnatural angle. Water had washed most of the blood away, making the jagged wound on his neck look raw and livid. Ralph could still see the agony in his sightless eyes.

'Who found him?' he asked, kneeling beside the soldier.

'I did, my lord,' said the man.

'Like this?'

'No, he was half in the water. I pulled him out.'

'Had he drifted downstream?'

'I think not, my lord. It looks as if the body was dumped here. There was no attempt to weight it so that it would sink. It was almost as if the killer wanted it to be found.'

'As a warning!' said Baldwin, standing over them.

'To whom?' said Ralph.

'All of us. This is some Saxon outrage.'

'The killer will pay dearly, I know that.'

'We will hunt him down, my lord. Have no fear.'

'But I do, my lord sheriff,' said Ralph, standing up. 'I will track down the villain myself because I cannot trust you to do it.'

The sheriff bristled. 'What do you mean?'

'Look at his injuries. They are similar to those found on the body of Nicholas Picard. I believe that he and Hervey de Marigny were butchered by the same man.'

'You may well be right,' conceded the other.

'Then you will understand why I have no faith in your ability to catch the man. A prisoner lies in your dungeon, charged with the murder of Nicholas Picard. Answer me this, my lord sheriff,' said Ralph with sarcasm. 'How did he get out in order to kill his second victim?'

Chapter Eleven

The murder of Hervey de Marigny threw the whole castle into turmoil. Soldiers were put on the alert and extra guards placed at the gate and on the battlements. Patrols were mounted in the city. The show of strength was impressive, but achieved little beyond the intimidation of the citizenry. Golde was horrified at the news and insisted on struggling down to the chapel with the aid of a stick in order to pray for the soul of the dead man. Gervase Bret was rocked and it gave him no consolation that his own judgement of the imprisoned robber had therefore been vindicated. Someone had slaughtered both Picard and the commissioner in the most savage way. The culprit was still at liberty.

That thought sent Brother Simon and Canon Hubert into a state of shock. While the former fled to the cathedral for sanctuary, the latter made his way to the castle to find out what he could about the murder and to have the immediate comfort of stout fortifications all round him. Overcoming his profound shock at the discovery of the body, Ralph Delchard was impelled by a quiet rage. When the three commissioners met in the hall, he let Gervase and Hubert do most of the talking, preferring instead to brood and speculate. A veteran soldier with shared memories of combat, Hervey de Marigny had been much closer to him than to any of the others. Ralph did not relish the task of having to send word of the murder to his widow.

'This is dreadful!' said a quivering Hubert. 'We are all at risk!'

'I think not,' said Gervase.

'The lord Hervey was a royal commissioner. Now that he is dead, which one of us will be the next target?'

'I am not sure that he was a target, Canon Hubert.'

'You've seen his corpse in the mortuary.'

'Yes,' said Gervase, 'and I viewed that of Nicholas Picard as well. Both are clearly victims of one man, but there is a substantial difference in the way that they died.'

'Each was patently killed by the same means.'

'But not necessarily from the same motives.'

'I do not follow you, Gervase.'

'The lord Nicholas was ambushed,' said the other. 'Someone knew exactly where and when to attack him. Premeditation was involved. That was not the case with the lord Hervey.

He is barely known in the city and his movements follow no definite pattern. It would be impossible to lay an ambush for him. No,' he affirmed, 'I think that he went to his death almost by accident.'

'Accident!' gulped Hubert.

'Yes. He may unwittingly have stumbled on something or someone and paid the ultimate penalty. This was a crime of opportunity.'

'It still robs the world of a fine man,' said Ralph solemnly.

'And an able judge,' added Hubert. 'I had my doubts about the lord Hervey at first but they were ill founded. One thing is now obvious. We must suspend our proceedings until after the funeral. And until after this dangerous man is caught.'

'That will not be long,' vowed Ralph. 'I will find him.'

'How, my lord?'

'Leave it to me, Hubert.'

'Take care. You are dealing with a fiend.'

'That is why he needs to be caught quickly,' said Gervase. 'The sheriff seems to think that it is the work of a vengeful Saxon and that suspicion has soured relations with the city. There have been a few brawls already, I hear, and the lord Hervey's own men are threatening to wreak some havoc in Exeter by way of reprisal.'

'They answer to me now,' said Ralph curtly. 'There will be no reprisals against the city itself. We are searching for one man.'

'Unless he has confederates,' said Hubert. 'The lord Hervey would not have been easily killed by a solitary attacker. What puzzles me is why he was walking by the river so far from the city.'

'He was not,' said Ralph.

'How do you know, my lord?'

'Because there was no sign of a struggle at the spot where he was found. I believe that he was killed elsewhere and carried downriver so that it would take time for us to find the body.' He sighed ruefully. 'What a hazardous county this is! We have been in Devon barely a week and there have already been two murders. Not to mention a robbery.'

'Robbery?' said Hubert.

'You mean the two men who stole from the lord Nicholas as he lay in the wood?' said Gervase.

'No,' said Ralph, 'though that was another crime to record. The robbery I talk of is one that was reported to the sheriff by that oily steward, Tetbald. Apparently, an intruder broke in during the night and stole a box belonging to the lord Nicholas.'

Gervase started. 'What was in the box, Ralph?'

'They did not know. It was locked. When it was later found on the estate, the lid was open and the box was empty. The crime has unsettled them. The lady Catherine was deeply upset at the thought of someone creeping around her house in the dark while she was in bed.'

'She has cause to be alarmed,' said Hubert.

'Was anything else taken?' asked Gervase.

'Just the box,' said Ralph.

'So the thief knew exactly what he was looking for?'

'Yes, Gervase. And exactly where to find it. He must have been in the house before. Tetbald wonders if it might have been someone who once worked there as a servant.'

'Or lived there,' said Hubert.

'Lived there?'

'Yes, my lord. Many years ago.'

'You sound as if you have someone in mind.'

'I do. One of our claimants once owned that manor house.'

'Who was that?'

'Engelric.'

When Saewin arrived at the imposing house once more, he was shown straight into the parlour. Loretta looked calmly up from the book she was reading.

'I received your message, my lady,' he said.

'Why has it taken you so long to respond to it?'

'I was held up at the castle. There has been another murder.'

'Murder!' she exclaimed. 'Who was the victim?'

'One of the commissioners. The lord Hervey.'

'This is hideous news.'

'They found his body down by the river.'

'Poor man!' she said, putting a hand to her throat. 'It is a terrible tragedy. How could it have happened? Well,' she added quietly, 'it does at least explain why he was not at the shire hall this afternoon.'

'They were searching for him all day, my lady.'

'Has anyone been arrested for the crime?'

'Not yet.'

'Do they have any suspects?'

'The sheriff did not confide in me. I was summoned to the castle by the lord Ralph. He has asked me to tell you, and the others involved in this dispute, that the commissioners have set aside their work until further notice.'

'Is that necessary, Saewin?'

'It is what they have decided.'

'But they cannot abandon an important case like this,' she said with irritation. 'I can see that they must be deeply upset by the murder of their colleague and a small delay is inevitable, but they should not let this dispute drag on when it is so easy to resolve.'

'They do not find it easy.'

'Only because they insist on being diverted by absurd claims.'

'It is their responsibility to look at all the options, my lady.'

'Their major responsibility is to sit in judgement in the shire hall. You would do well to remind them of that, Saewin.'

'Not unless I want to bring the lord Ralph's ire down upon me,' he said. 'He is in no mood to hear complaints from us. Tracking down the killer is the only thing which interests him at the moment.'

'Then why cannot Canon Hubert and Master Bret deputise for him?' she urged. 'They did so this afternoon. Let them do so again.'

Saewin was blunt. 'I take orders, my lady. Not give them.'

Loretta set down her book and rose from her chair. Crossing to the table, she picked up the jug and poured wine into two cups, handing one to her visitor before picking up her own. Saewin was at once flattered and surprised by her hospitality. On other occasions when he called at the house, he was kept very much in his place. Loretta resumed her seat and sipped her wine.

'It was wrong of me to badger you,' she said. 'It is not your fault if the commissioners see fit to suspend their activities.

You are a good man, Saewin. You discharge your duties well.'

'Thank you, my lady.'

'My husband was right to recommend you as town reeve.'

'I was most grateful to him.'

She took another sip. 'Who else was called today?'

He shifted his feet. 'I would rather not say, my lady.'

'Why not?'

'Because I must be seen to be impartial.'

'You are,' she said with a smile. 'Everyone respects you for it. But everyone is not here, Saewin. I am. And I asked a simple question. Will it harm you to answer it as an act of friendship?'

'Probably not.'

'Then why this reluctance?'

'I am not your spy, my lady!'

As soon as he blurted out the words, he regretted them. Loretta was plainly offended by the suggestion and looked away from him, exuding a disdain that made him feel completely rebuffed. He gulped some wine down, then adopted a more conciliatory tone.

'That remark was unjust, my lady,' he said deferentially. 'What you ask is quite reasonable and I am happy to tell you. The lady Catherine's steward was the first to be called. He was an impatient man, I must say. Then came the abbot of Tavistock and the last to be examined again was yourself.'

'What about Asa?'

'She was not called.'

'Engelric?'

'Nor was he.'

'Good. That sounds encouraging.'

'Do not read too much into it, my lady.'

'I will not. What sort of impact did the steward have?'

'I do not know.'

'Find out for me.'

He hesitated. 'I am not sure that I can.'

'Will you refuse me again, Saewin?' she said levelly.

'No, my lady. Of course not.'

'Then do as I ask. The lady Catherine's claim is the only one which can offer a serious challenge to mine. I would be grateful to hear how it was presented and how received at the shire hall. Is that understood?' He assented with a nod. 'Be discreet in your enquiries.'

'I will.'

'Thank you, Saewin,' she said baldly. 'You may leave now.'

She picked up her book and started reading it again. Eldred came into the room, took the cup from the reeve's hand, then escorted him to the front door. Saewin went out into the street with a sense of indignation. Having served his purpose, he had been summarily evicted.

The murder changed everything. It not only deprived them of a jovial companion and made them grieve at their loss, it also extended the time they would have to spend in Devon. Gervase Bret's chances of getting back to Winchester in time for his wedding now looked rather slim, but he tried to put personal considerations aside and concentrate on helping to find Hervey de Marigny's killer. Ralph Delchard had ridden out of the city with his men but Gervase felt that the vital clues lay under their noses and were somehow connected with the dispute at the shire hall. Alone in his chamber, he reflected on the possibilities.

Canon Hubert and Ralph were too preoccupied with the murder to pay much attention to the reported robbery at lady Catherine's manor house. It held more significance for Gervase. He began to wonder if the stolen box had contained the compromising letters from Asa which had been delivered to him. Nicholas Picard would have kept them locked away somewhere in the house. Asa believed it was the lady Catherine who sent the letters in order to embarrass her rival but Gervase doubted if Picard's widow would be able to understand the missives even if she managed to find them. He came round to the view that someone else knew of the existence of the letters and stole them in order to strike at Asa.

The only person who could suggest the identity of the thief was Asa herself, but Gervase was very reluctant to go to her house again. During his earlier visit, he was prey to ambivalent feelings which he did not wholly comprehend and he was glad that he had finally torn himself away. To go back would be to risk further awkwardness, but he came to see that it was a necessity. Gervase was convinced that the robbery was in some way linked to the two murders. Finding the name of a possible thief was a big step towards identifying the killer himself. He steeled himself and set off to call on Asa again.

Leaving the castle, he walked swiftly through the city. Asa's house occupied a prime position in a row of small but costly dwellings with fresh thatch on the roofs and neat gardens at their rear. He had wondered on his earlier visit how she could afford such a comfortable abode. This time Gervase got no further than the end of her street. Light was now fading but he had a good view of the man who was moving furtively towards Asa's house. The visitor knocked on the door and was admitted by the servant. Gervase was shocked. The last person he had expected to see in such a place was Saewin the Reeve.

Walter Baderon was in bed with his wife when he was awakened by the thunderous pounding on his door. A servant went to open the door and a loud voice began to make demands. Baderon groped his way out of bed and stumbled downstairs to investigate. Ralph Delchard was standing in the hall with six of his men, their angry faces illumined by the flame of the servant's candle. Baderon was inhospitable.

'What is the meaning of this intrusion?' he demanded.

'Walter Baderon?' said Ralph.

'That is my name.'

'Then you should know mine because it is one that you will remember. I am Ralph Delchard, one of the royal commissioners on business here in Devon. You are aware of our work, I think.'

'What do you want with me?'

'Answers,' said Ralph. 'Honest answers.'

'About what, my lord?'

'The murder of my colleague, Hervey de Marigny.'

Baderon licked his lips but said nothing. His eyes darted. A frightened voice was heard from the top of the staircase. 'What is it, Walter?'

'Nothing, my love.'

'Who are those men?'

'I will deal with it,' he said. 'Go back to bed.'

'What do they want?'

'Go back to bed!' he snapped.

His wife withdrew nervously. Baderon took the candle and conducted the visitors to the parlour. More candles were quickly lit by the servant, who then scurried away. Baderon could see the faces of his unexpected guests more clearly. They were grim and determined.

'We have ridden through the night to reach Tavistock,' said Ralph, 'and we will not leave until you tell us what we wish to know.'

'I have nothing to tell, my lord.'

'Yes, you do. Let us start with the coincidence.'

'Coincidence?'

'When Nicholas Picard rode out of Exeter to be killed in an ambush, the last person to speak to him was Walter Baderon, captain of the guard at the North Gate. You were also the last person to speak to the lord Hervey when he left the city last evening to meet his death. Do you deny these charges?'

'Yes, my lord.'

'Then you are lying.'

'I spoke to the lord Nicholas,' admitted the other. 'I gave evidence to that effect to the sheriff. And I did meet the lord Hervey some two days ago, though he concealed both his name and his purpose from me. He was trying to trick information out of me. But that was the only time he and I spoke. I swear it, my lord.'

'He came in search of you last night.'

'Then he did not find me.'

'The lord Hervey knew his way to the North Gate.'

'He did not reach it last night, my lord. Ask the other sentries.'

'I have,' said Ralph. 'They all sing the same tune. The abbot of Tavistock is a cunning choirmaster. He has taught them well. And he sent you home from Exeter so that you would be out of the way when the body was found.'

'That is not so!' protested the other.

'Then why did you quit the city?'

'I asked to leave. My wife is unwell.'

'Another coincidence.'

'What is going on here, my lord?' said Baderon angrily. 'You have no right to barge into my home and interrogate me like this. Do you have the sheriff's writ?'

'No,' said Ralph. 'I answer to a higher authority. A royal commissioner has been slain. If the killer is not found and arrested, the king himself is likely to come riding into Exeter to know the reason why. Would you rather meet his displeasure? As for your wife,' he said with a glance upwards, 'she did not sound unwell when she spoke. Upset, perhaps, as well she might be in view of what could happen to her husband.'

'I have done nothing wrong!'

'Then why do you insult me with this pack of lies?'

'They are not lies.'

'We shall see.' He turned to one of his men. 'Fetch his wife. We will enquire after her health. Then we will let her remain to witness the rest of our interrogation. It is high time she learnt what a lying rogue she has for a husband.'

242

The man-at-arms moved away but was stopped by Baderon's shout.

'No!' he cried. 'Leave my wife out of this!'

'Is she too ill to witness your humiliation?' taunted Ralph.

'She is well enough,' confessed the other with a scowl.

'So one lie has been exposed. Let us examine the others. Did you or did you not talk to the lord Hervey last night?'

'No, my lord.'

'Did you see him anywhere near the North Gate?'

'No, my lord.'

'Then where did you see him?'

'Nowhere. Ask the other sentries. They will vouch for me.'

Ralph's patience snapped. His forearm caught Baderon full in the face and knocked him to the floor. Blood streamed from the man's nose and he began to curse volubly. Two of the men hauled him back to his feet. When Ralph threatened another blow, Baderon fell silent. He tried to wipe the blood away with the back of his hand.

'We have ridden too far to endure these fairy tales,' said Ralph. 'I will try once again. One more lie and we will drag you all the way back to Exeter in your nightshirt. Is that what you want?'

'No, my lord.'

'Then forget what the abbot told you. Speak the truth. I will ask this for the last time so take care how you answer.' He put his face in close. 'Did you see the lord Hervey at the North Gate last night?'

'Yes,' grunted the other.

'Did you talk with him?'

'Only briefly.'

'Then why did you try to deceive us?'

'On the abbot's advice, my lord,' said Baderon. 'When I told him that someone had been asking me about the lord Nicholas, he asked me to describe the man and identified him as the lord Hervey. I was ordered to tell him nothing further if he sought me out again.'

'Why?'

'The abbot did not want his name linked with the murder inquiry. He is appearing before you in a dispute. He felt that there would be undue prejudice against him if any taint of suspicion touched him or one of his men. That is why he sent me home,' he continued. 'To be safe from further questioning about the death of the lord Nicholas.'

'Or the death of Hervey de Marigny.'

'I did not even know of it until you came here tonight.'

'Is that the truth?' said Ralph, grabbing him by the throat.

'On my word of honour!'

'That is worthless. A few minutes ago, you swore that you only spoke with the lord Hervey once. That was your first mistake. Make another and I'll beat you to a pulp to get at the truth. Now,' said Ralph as he tightened his grip. 'What happened last night?'

'I was on duty at the North Gate,' said Baderon, the words pouring out in a terrified stream. 'The lord Hervey fell into conversation with me and tried to ask me about the night when the lord Nicholas died. I did as the abbot advised and said almost nothing to him. When the lord Hervey realised that I knew who he was, he gave up and walked away.'

'Where did he go?'

'Out through the gate.'

'With you on his tail?'

'No, my lord!'

'Some of your men, then.'

'We remained at our post,' insisted the other. 'The last I saw of the lord Hervey was when he walked through the North Gate. My men were witnesses. They will tell you the same.'

'All they have told me is the lie you agreed upon.'

'Now you know what really did happen, my lord.'

'Do I?'

'Yes!' vowed the other. 'It is God's own truth.'

'God's own truth?' said Ralph with irony. 'Or the abbot of Tavistock's own truth? I fancy that there is a huge difference between the two. Let us go back to the night when the lord Nicholas died. You were on duty at the North Gate. That was the exit he would have taken from the city. What did you do when he rode past you? Did you mount your horse and follow him?'

The lady Albreda was coming out of the chapel when Berold accosted her. Having prayed for the soul of the departed, she was in no mood for jesting and was relieved that he himself was solemn for once. He slipped something into her hand.

'What is this, Berold?'

'I was asked to give it to you, my lady.'

'By whom?'

'A man at the castle gate.'

'What sort of man?'

245

'I have never seen him before.'

'Did he not have a name?'

'He did not stay long enough to give it, my lady,' said the other. 'He thrust the letter into my hand, bade me deliver it, then ran away.'

'Strange behaviour!' she said. 'Thank you, Berold.'

He gave a nod, then slipped past her into the chapel. Albreda glanced down at the letter with curiosity. Before she even opened it, she had a sense of impending disaster.

The ecclesiastical community was stunned by the murder of Hervey de Marigny. Bishop Osbern was horrified and a wave of quiet terror spread outwards from the cathedral to wash over the city's many churches. It was felt that a murderer was stalking the city. Two leading barons had already fallen victim to him. A third attack was only a matter of time. Fear kept many on their knees in prayer or safely hidden behind locked doors. Only when the killer was caught would the shadow of death be lifted from the city of Exeter.

'We feel as if we are being held hostage,' said Dean Jerome gloomily.

Canon Hubert sighed. 'It is a time of tribulation for us all,' he said. 'The lord Hervey took such pride in his appointment as a commissioner. Nobody could have expected his career would end so suddenly and so brutally.'

'The sheriff will not rest until the murderer is brought to justice.'

'The lord Ralph has set his own inquiry in motion.'

'Let us hope that, between them, they bring success.'

They were standing outside the cathedral with the wind plucking at their cowls. The dean looked more morose than ever and the canon was unusually subdued. Accustomed to a ready acceptance of God's will, they yet found there were times when they dared to question divine dispensation and this was one of them. When they searched for meaning in the death of Hervey de Marigny, they found it elusive.

'Why?' mused Hubert. 'Why, why, why?'

'I wish that I had the answer.'

'Is it merely a demonstration of the mutability of human existence? Or are we looking at a warning from the Devil rather than a sign from God? The lord Hervey had only been in the city a matter of days. He had no enemies here. Who could possibly wish to kill him?'

'The same man who struck down the lord Nicholas.'

'For what purpose?'

'Who can say, Canon Hubert?'

'I can make no sense of it.'

They were still struggling with their bewilderment when a man came walking towards the main entrance to the cathedral. Carrying a sack and a length of rope, he gave the dean a submissive nod and went on into the building. Hubert recognised the newcomer at once from his two appearances at the shire hall.

'That was the lady Loretta's servant, was it not?'

'Yes, Canon Hubert. She has kindly loaned him to us.'

'For what reason?'

'Eldred has to go up into the tower from time to time.'

'Does he tend the bells?'

'No,' said Dean Jerome, 'but he performs a great service for us.'

'In what way?'

'We have a problem which you no doubt have encountered at Salisbury Cathedral as well. It is one which we share with some of our churches and we are lucky to have Eldred to call on. He helps to get rid of them, Canon Hubert.'

'Get rid of what?'

'Bats.'

Golde's sprained ankle was no longer so tender. She still suffered an occasional twinge of pain but could now hobble around without the aid of a stick. When she was summoned to the lady Albreda, she managed to walk to the latter's apartment with relative ease, but she was grateful to be able to sit down once more. Albreda seemed tense and drawn.

'How are you this morning?' she enquired.

'Much better, my lady.'

'Good.'

'I would never dare to admit this to Ralph,' said Golde, 'but it was more comfortable in bed last night when he was not there. He was not able to kick my ankle again in his sleep.'

'Where, then, did he spend the night?'

'I do not know, my lady. He rode to Tavistock on an errand.'

'An important one if he spurned your bed to go there.'

'Ralph went to make enquiries in connection with the lord Hervey's death. That is all he would tell me. He and his men have not yet returned from Tavistock.'

'I see.'

There was a long pause. Albreda seemed to be wrestling with her thoughts and Golde waited with a patient smile. At length, her companion bit her lip and gave a nervous laugh.

'You said a moment ago that you would not dare to admit something to your husband. Is that true, Golde?'

'It was said in fun.'

'But there are things you hold back from him?'

'Not as a rule.'

'What if they threatened your happiness?'

'I do not understand.'

Albreda held up the letter in her hand. 'This was given to me earlier this morning,' she explained. 'And by Berold, of all people! There is a cruel irony in that, for this is anything but a jest.'

'What is it, my lady?'

'A letter which I wrote some years ago to the lord Nicholas. A fond and very private letter, Golde. It was intended for his eyes alone.'

'How did it come into Berold's possession?'

'A stranger thrust it into his hands at the castle gate.'

'Why?'

'So that I would not know who sent it.'

'But is that not obvious?' suggested Golde.

'Obvious?'

'If the letter was kept by the lord Nicholas, his widow must have found it after his death. She decided to return it to you.'

'The lady Catherine would not have done that, Golde. She would have been far more likely to burn it in anger than send it back out of consideration to me. The problem is,' she said, lowering her head, 'that it was not the only declaration of love I sent to her husband. If he kept this letter, he may well have kept the others. They are much more damaging to me.'

'Damaging?'

'My husband would be enraged if he read them.'

'But there is no chance of that, is there?'

'There is every chance, Golde. Why else should this letter be given to me in such a mysterious manner if not as a warning? Someone has got hold of my correspondence. They are in a position to cause me intense embarrassment and to create a rift with my husband that might never be healed. I am in peril here, Golde.' Albreda gave a sudden shiver. 'What am I to do? What would you do in my place?'

'Show the letter to my husband.'

'That would be madness!'

'Not if he loves and trusts you.'

'I would sacrifice both love and trust if he saw this.'

'Why?'

'It was written after I was married.'

'Oh!'

'Do not misunderstand,' said the other hurriedly. 'I have not been unfaithful to my husband. From the time that I married him, I never saw the lord Nicholas alone, but . . . I was still attracted to him and we remained friends. Baldwin was away a great deal. I was bored and alone. On impulse, I wrote this letter to the lord Nicholas but regretted it the moment it left my hand.'

'How did he respond?'

'Very warmly. He encouraged me to write again.'

'And you did.'

'Yes,' confessed Albreda. 'I was young and foolish, Golde. I did not know what I was doing. I was excited by the idea of a secret love which sustained me but which brought no harm to anyone else. And that is how it was for a while until I saw the folly of it all and stopped writing.'

'Did you realise that he would keep your letters?'

'No, Golde. I begged him to destroy them and he swore that he did.'

'What of his letters to you?'

'I burnt them as soon as I had read them.'

'But their contents stayed with you.'

'Yes,' she said softly. 'I remember every word that he wrote to me.'

'The important words are the ones you wrote to him,' Golde pointed out. 'They have the power to hurt you. I still believe that you should go to your husband and tell him the truth.'

'I could never do that.'

'After this length of time together, he surely cannot doubt you?'

'I fear that he may.'

'Be honest with him.'

'I dare not, Golde. He has such a vile temper and this letter will spark it off. There is no telling what he would do. I am frightened of him. The person who has my letters knows that only too well.'

'But why should they strike at you, my lady?'

'That will soon become apparent.'

'What do you mean?'

'This was sent to me as proof of intent,' she said, glancing down at the letter once more. 'Though they were written in all innocence, the other letters are more incriminating than this. That is why I implored the lord Nicholas to destroy them once they had been read. He did not and they have come back to haunt me. I am being blackmailed, Golde.'

'By whom?'

'I wish I knew.'

'You must have some idea.'

'None whatsoever,' said Albreda with a note of despair. 'When this letter was put into my hand by Berold, I flew into a panic. That is why I turned to you for help. Only another woman could understand the position that I find myself in.'

'My counsel remains the same. Tell your husband.'

'No, Golde!'

'Then you will for ever be at the mercy of the blackmailer.'

'Not if I can buy my letters back.'

'Is that what has been suggested?'

'No, but it is clearly implied. He will want something from me and will no doubt set a high price on his demand. When the moment comes, I will need someone to act as my go-between.' A look of pleading came into her eyes. 'Will you do that office for me, Golde?'

'It is not one that I take on with any willingness.'

'But you will do it?'

'I am not sure, my lady,' said Golde. 'I am touched that you were able to confide in me and I will support you all I can, but I loathe the idea of giving in to blackmail. It is a despicable crime.'

'I have no choice.'

'You do, my lady.'

'Please do not tell me to go to my husband again.'

'I was not going to do that.'

'Then what else can you advise?'

'Find the person who sent you that letter.'

Chapter Twelve

Tetbald worked hard to restore himself to her favour. Having got so close to the lady Catherine, he found it galling to be thrust away so abruptly. He was submissive and obedient, quick to anticipate her needs and ready to satisfy them at once, never critical, never complaining and never again making the mistake of issuing a veiled threat. The steward's behaviour slowly won back her approval and Catherine allowed him minor concessions and even an occasional indication of affection. Tetbald was encouraged. His obsequious manner gradually evanesced into a renewed confidence. It put a spring into his step and he moved about with something of his earlier sense of possession.

The barking of the dogs alerted him to the arrival of a visitor and he was astonished to see that it was Gervase Bret. Escorted by four of the knights from Hervey de Marigny's retinue, the young commissioner had ridden out to the manor house to continue his own investigations, firmly believing that the clue to both murders lay in the dispute in which both victims had been involved. Tetbald answered the door himself and invited the visitor in. The escort dismounted but remained outside.

'Why have you come, Master Bret?' asked Tetbald.

'I needed to ask some questions of you,' said Gervase.

'But the proceedings at the shire hall have been postponed. That was the message that came from the town reeve. Or has that decision been revoked?' He rubbed his hands unctuously. 'It would be pleasing to hear that you had already arrived at a judgement in our favour. That is the kindest news I could bear to the lady Catherine.'

'You will have to wait a while before you can do so, Tetbald. 'My enquiries concern the murder of the lord de Marigny.'

'Yes,' said the steward, composing his features into a token sympathy. 'We heard about that from Saewin's messenger. It was a great shock to us. Who would dare to kill a royal commissioner?'

'The same person who dared to kill the lord Nicholas.'

'Do you think so, Master Bret?'

'I am certain of it.'

'There was no mention of this when the message came.'

'It has still to be proved,' admitted Gervase. 'But I did not only come here to visit you this morning. I was hoping for a word with the lady Catherine herself.'

'That is out of the question. The lady Catherine is in mourning and will see no visitors.'

'She might if she knew the gravity of the situation.'

'She has her own grief,' said Tetbald firmly. 'I am sorry, but I cannot allow you to disturb her. Any questions you may wish to put to the lady Catherine, you may put to me. I speak for her.'

'Not when I am here to speak for myself,' she said crisply.

They turned to see her slowly descending the stairs. Gervase studied her carefully. She was wearing sober attire and an expression of distant pain but he did not feel that she was consumed with grief. As at the funeral, he sensed that her sorrow was not as deep as might be expected from the widow of a murdered husband. Catherine led him into the solar and beckoned for Tetbald to follow. Annoyed that he had been overruled by her, the steward was mollified by the fact that he was to be included in the discussion with Gervase. It was a sign that she knew how much she could rely on him.

When the others sat down, however, he remained standing. Catherine was very keen that he should be seen solely as her steward. Gervase noted the glance which passed between them and remembered the familiarity with which Tetbald had spoken of her at the shire hall.

'I was sorry to hear of the death of your colleague,' she began, hands folded in her lap. 'It is an appalling misfortune.'

'Yes, my lady,' said Gervase.

'Where was he killed?'

'We do not know. The body was found in the river, some half a mile away from the city, but we feel that it was not the scene of the crime.'

'I overheard you say to my steward that there might well be a link with my husband's murder.'

'That is what has brought me out here, my lady.'

'I would rather not know the details,' she said, averting her gaze.

'You will not need to, my lady. Suffice it to say that there are striking similarities between the two crimes except that the one seems to have been planned and the other random.'

'I hope that the sheriff will soon solve both murders.'

'He has many officers involved in the enquiries,' explained Gervase, 'and is leading them with the utmost urgency. But it is another crime which interests me. I believe that you reported a robbery to the sheriff?'

'I instructed my steward to do so.'

'That is correct,' said Tetbald, glad of the opportunity to speak. 'I made the sheriff aware of the robbery when I came into the city yesterday to appear before you at the shire hall.'

'A box was stolen, I understand.'

'Yes,' said Catherine. 'It belonged to my husband.'

'It was stolen and later found empty,' added Tetbald.

'I will answer on my own account,' she said with a hint of reproach. 'The theft was of my property and from my home.'

'Yes, my lady,' said Tetbald, smarting under the rebuff.

'What was in the box?' asked Gervase.

'I do not know,' she said. 'My husband kept personal items in there and I could not find a key to open it. And it could not easily be broken into. I imagine that it may have contained important documents or even gold, for he used it like a strongbox.'

'Yet it did not hold his will or any of the charters relating to his property.'

'No, Master Bret. Those were kept together in a cupboard.'

Gervase began to fish. 'It seems strange that a wife does not know what a husband keeps locked away in a box,' he said casually. 'Is there anyone who would know what it contained?'

'No,' she asserted.

'How can you be so sure?'

'Because my husband was very secretive. He confided in nobody.'

'Not even you?'

'I respected his right to lock his possessions away,' she said easily. 'I have a strongbox of my own in which I keep things of special value.'

'Jewellery, perhaps?'

'Amongst other things.'

'Yet that was not taken?'

'No, Master Bret.'

'Why was the other box taken in preference to yours?'

'I have no notion.'

'Could it be that the thief knew what he would find?'

'No, Master Bret. I think he stole it by chance.'

Gervase glanced around. 'When there are so many other things of value in the house to steal, several in this room, for instance? Where was the box kept?'

A moment's hesitation. 'Upstairs,' she said.

'In your bedchamber?'

'Close by it.'

'So the thief might well have disturbed you.'

'Happily, he did not,' said Tetbald.

'But the possibility was there,' said Gervase. 'Why take the risk of going upstairs at all when he could have taken many valuable items from the ground floor? It is puzzling, my lady. Has the house been broken into before?'

'No, Master Bret.'

'We have dogs to guard it,' said Tetbald.

'Why did they not alert you to the presence of an intruder? They barked loud enough when we rode up. Were they not on guard on the night of the burglary?'

'They were,' she admitted, 'but they did not raise the alarm.'

'Is that not strange?'

'Very strange and very worrying.'

'Have you any idea who the intruder could be?'

'None.'

'What about you, Tetbald?'

'I am baffled.'

'Yet this is a very singular thief,' said Gervase. 'There are guard dogs here and somehow he evades them. He finds his way around the house in the dark. And he takes only one item, even though it is in a room close to that of the lady Catherine. There can be very few men who fit that description.' He looked from one to the other. 'Has Engelric ever visited this house?'

'Not since we took possession of it from him,' said Catherine.

'Did he protest when you did so?'

'Strongly.'

'The lord Nicholas had to threaten him in order to keep him off the property,' added Tetbald. 'Engelric was somewhat younger then. He has mellowed a great deal since that time.'

'Yet he still resents the loss of this manor house?'

Catherine was cold. 'That is his problem.'

'Does Engelric have sons?' asked Gervase.

'Two of them.'

'Did they have cause to come here at any time?'

'Not to my knowledge.'

'But the family were your husband's sub-tenants. There were surely times when they came to pay rent or to transact business with the lord Nicholas? On such occasions, is it possible that your husband had that box with him and opened it in their presence?'

'It is possible,' she conceded.

'But highly unlikely,' said Tetbald quickly. 'Rents were usually paid by Engelric and his sons to the estate reeve. He brought the money here and the lord Nicholas locked it away.'

'In the box that was stolen?'

'Perhaps.'

'But you are not certain?'

'We never saw that box open,' said Catherine evenly. 'As I told you, my husband was an intensely private man. He did not involve me in the running of his estate in any way.'

Gervase heard a slight rancour in her voice. He also noticed that the steward had moved a step or two closer to her. There was a more overtly protective air about him now even though Catherine, calm and assured, did not seem in need of his defence.

'On the day that he was killed,' said Gervase softly, 'your husband was returning from Exeter. Do you know why he went there?'

'On business,' said Catherine.

'What was the nature of that business?'

'He did not tell me.'

'But I believe that he intended to call on Saewin,' volunteered Tetbald. 'He wanted to know when you and the other commissioners were due to arrive in the city.'

'Could he not have sent a servant on such an errand?'

'He could have, Master Bret. But he did not.'

'He must have had other business to transact in the city?' probed Gervase. 'The lord Nicholas would hardly ride all that way to spend a few minutes with the town reeve. Whom else would he normally visit when he went to Exeter?'

'I do not know,' said Catherine.

'Did you never ask him?'

'It was not my place to do so.'

'But you were his wife.'

'A wife is not her husband's keeper.'

'He went to Exeter alone that day. Without an escort. Was that usual?'

Tetbald leapt in. 'These questions are distressing the lady Catherine,' he said warningly. 'They show a grave lack of consideration on your part, Master Bret.'

'I am sorry. I did not mean to cause offence.'

'The lord Nicholas did sometimes ride into the city alone. He was careless of danger. The wood through which he had to ride has harboured robbers in the past but he ignored the threat. If that is all you wish to know,' he said, trying to ease their guest on his way, 'I am sure that the lady Catherine would appreciate being left alone now. It is still only a matter of days since the lord Nicholas was killed. You must surely see that you are trespassing on her grief.'

'Let me be the judge of that,' she said with a reproving glance.

'The doctor advised rest, my lady.'

'I know what the doctor advised, Tetbald. But I am the only person who knows how I feel. Master Bret will not leave until he has asked the main question which brought him here. And so I will answer it honestly,' she said, turning back to Gervase. 'Well?'

'Does the name Asa mean anything to you?'

'It does.'

'Were you aware of her friendship with your husband?'

'Of course.'

'Did you ever see any letters which she may have written to him?'

'No,' she said with a sneer, 'but I would be surprised if the woman was able to write. I understand that her talents lie elsewhere.'

'When he rode into Exeter for the last time,' said Gervase, choosing his words with care, 'is it at all possible that the lord Nicholas might have wished to visit her?'

'Yes,' she snapped. 'It is. But now that you have forced me to confess that, you are welcome to leave my house. Or is it your intention to inflict further humiliation upon me, Master Bret?'

When Ralph Delchard and his men finally reached the castle, they were hungry and fatigued. The journey from Tavistock was taxing. Ralph was not pleased to find Canon Hubert waiting for him inside the gate.

'What news, my lord?' he said eagerly.

'We are weary from travel, Hubert. That is the news.'

'Was no arrest made?'

'None was necessary.' Ralph dismounted and let one of his men lead the horse away to the stables. 'Walter Baderon was not involved in the murder of the lord Hervey.'

'But you told me that you believed he was.'

'I was wrong.'

'So the journey was a waste of time?'

'Not at all, Hubert. I was sure that Baderon had valuable information to give us. And so he did – when I persuaded him to part with it. After such a long ride, I was in no mood to be baulked.'

'What did he tell you?'

'That will become clear in time.'

'But I wish to know now,' said Hubert. 'I want to be able to take some comfort back to the cathedral. Bishop Osbern is disturbed, Dean Jerome is frankly alarmed and Brother Simon is in fear of his life. The whole community is in need of reassurance. May I give it to them?'

'Not yet, Hubert.'

'There must be something that you can tell me.'

'There is.'

'What is it?'

'Whoever else is in danger, it is not Brother Simon.'

'What . . . ?'

'Just convey the good tidings to him,' said Ralph with a yawn. 'You will have to excuse me now. I must go to my wife. Golde will have been worried by my long absence.'

'But you have told me nothing to console me.'

'That was not the purpose of my visit to Tavistock.'

Ralph left him mouthing protestations and lurched wearily across the courtyard. When he reached the keep, he needed to put a steadying hand against the wall as he ascended the stairs. He opened the door of his apartment and gave his wife a tired smile.

'Ralph,' she said, struggling to get up from the bed.

'Rest, my love. Think of your ankle.'

'It is fine now. I can walk on it again.'

She threw herself into his arms and kissed him warmly. After a long embrace, she led him across the chamber so that he could sit down. Ralph slumped heavily into the oak chair.

'You look exhausted,' she said solicitously.

'Then my looks do not belie my condition.'

'Was the journey worthwhile?'

'I believe so.'

'What happened?'

'I will explain at another time,' he said. 'When I have strength enough to do so. First, tell me what has been going on here. Has the sheriff made any headway in his investigations?'

'Not as far as I know.'

'What of Gervase?'

'He told me that he was going to the lord Nicholas's manor house.'

'Why?'

'He did not say, Ralph.'

'Gervase rarely does anything without a good reason.' He removed his helm and she took it from him. 'Now, my love. Let me hear about your accident again.'

'But that is old news, Ralph.'

'Not since I spoke with Walter Baderon. Where was it that the horse threw you? Near the East Gate?'

'Yes. Berold will confirm the exact spot.'

'I will make him take me there, Golde.'

'For what purpose?'

'To satisfy my curiosity.'

'About what?'

'I will tell you when I have been there. Remind me, my love. Your horse took fright and suddenly reared, you say?'

'Yes, Ralph.'

'Did it hear a noise or see something which frightened it?'

'I do not know. It happened so quickly.'

'And Berold came to your rescue?'

'Immediately.'

'Yet I seem to remember your telling me that he was not pleased to take you to view the siege tunnel. Why was that?'

'I have no idea.'

'Then I will ask him directly,' he said. 'Before I do that, I need to shave this beard from my face and put some food into my belly.'

'What you most need is some sleep.'

'That will have to wait.'

'But you are sagging with fatigue.'

'I cannot sleep while there is a murderer at liberty,' he said, making an effort to sit upright. 'Hervey de Marigny was a good friend. I owe it to him to keep on the tail of his killer and I cannot do that if I am slumbering in that bed. I merely wanted to let you know that I had returned before I go to find Baldwin.'

'That was very considerate,' she said.

'I wished to see my wife.'

'Well, she is delighted to see you safely returned.' She hugged him again and he revived enough to rise to his feet. Holding her by the shoulders, he gave her a kiss on the forehead.

'What has been happening in my absence?' he wondered.

'Very little.'

'No more visits from Bishop Osbern?'

'He is far too busy at the cathedral.'

'So what have you been doing, Golde?'

'I have spent most of my time in here.'

'What about the lady Albreda? Has she been to see you again?'

'No, Ralph. I was able to visit her apartment.'

'Why did you do that?'

A look of guilt came into her eyes. Ralph saw it at once.

When he returned to the city, he sent his escort back to the castle and headed straight for Saewin's house. Gervase Bret was in time to catch the reeve as he was coming out of his front door. He remained in the saddle as he spoke to him. 'One moment, Saewin. I need your help.'

'I will be happy to give it to you, Master Bret.'

'Does Engelric reside in the city?'

'Only until this dispute is settled. He is too old to ride back and forth to Exeter so he chose to stay here with a friend.'

'Do you know the place?'

'Very well.'

'Advise me how to reach it.'

'I will do more than that,' said Saewin obligingly. 'I will

conduct you there myself. It is difficult to find and you may well get lost.'

'Then I accept your offer,' said Gervase, dismounting to fall in beside him as they set off in the direction of the High Street. 'Have all the claimants been advised of the delay?'

'Yes, Master Bret.'

'Did you speak with them personally?'

'Only with three of them.'

'Who were they?'

'The abbot of Tavistock, the lady Loretta and Engelric.'

'You did not call on Asa, then?'

'No,' he said smoothly. 'I sent a man to deliver the news to Asa and a second one to explain to Tetbald why the proceedings were postponed.'

'I know. I have just visited him and the lady Catherine.'

'You *saw* her?' said the other in surprise.

'We conversed at some length.'

'Why did you ride all that way, Master Bret?'

'To ask a few questions of her and her steward.'

'In connection with the dispute?'

'Indirectly.'

Saewin was worried. 'Does that mean that you and the other commissioners have already come to a decision?' he said. 'Were you visiting the lady Catherine in order to give her some sort of unofficial confirmation?'

'That was not the purpose of my errand.'

'But her claim must surely be the strongest. I dare say Tetbald presented it to good effect at the shire hall yesterday? I am told that he is an able speaker.'

'By whom?'

'Tetbald himself for one,' said Saewin with a smile. 'He is not the most modest of individuals. Did he impress you with his advocacy?'

'Why do you wish to know?'

'No reason, Master Bret.'

'Then I have no reason to answer your enquiry,' said Gervase with a meaningful glance at him. 'Let us put Tetbald aside for a while and turn to Asa. You did not see her yesterday, then?'

'No. I told you. I sent a messenger.'

'Did you call on her for any other reason?'

'Of course not.'

'How well do you know Asa?'

'I had never met her until this dispute began.'

'So it was not she who asked you to find out how the lady Catherine's claim had been received by us?'

Saewin flinched slightly. 'No, Master Bret.'

'Who did?'

'Nobody.'

'Are you quite certain?'

'Yes. I am the town reeve. I must be impartial in such matters.'

'I am glad that you remember that, Saewin.'

Gervase wondered why the man was lying to him. Honest and reliable before, the reeve was showing hints of darker qualities. They walked in silence for a while until a stray thought brought Gervase to a halt. Saewin stopped to look enquiringly at him.

'Did you ever visit the lord Nicholas, Saewin?'

'Yes, Master Bret.'

'How often?'

'Two or three times at most. The lord Nicholas liked to know what was going on in the city and I was able to inform him. It is part of my job to make myself available to important barons in the area.'

'What did you think of the manor house?'

'It is a beautiful dwelling.'

'Had you been there before when Engelric owned it?'

'Several times.'

'And spent a night there, perhaps?'

'Only once. Why do you ask?'

'Curiosity.'

'It has not made me prejudiced in favour of Engelric,' said the reeve defensively. 'I was never a close friend of his but he was one of the leading thegns in Devon and one cannot refuse hospitality. Until this dispute began, I had not spoken with Engelric for some time.'

'I believe you,' said Gervase. 'When you visited the lord Nicholas, I wonder if you saw him with a large wooden box?'

Saewin's face was motionless. 'A box?'

'One in which he kept business documents.'

'I do not recall seeing such a thing.'

'But you would recall it had you done so.'

'Naturally.'

They set off again. Gervase waited until they turned a corner before he sprang the next question on him, watching closely for a reaction.

'Do you live alone, Saewin?'

'Yes, Master Bret. My wife died some years ago.'

'I am sorry to hear that. No children, then?'

'None, alas.'

'Do you have nobody to keep you company?'

'A few servants.'

'Nobody else?'

'Only my dog.'

Gervase's interest sharpened. 'Your dog?'

'Yes,' said the reeve. 'I have always loved dogs.'

Berold was almost surly when Ralph Delchard sought him out. The jester was eating a meal in the kitchen and was not at all pleased to be hauled away from his food. When they reached the stables, Ralph made sure that he took the horse which his wife had been riding when she was thrown. Berold led him along the route which he and Golde had taken on that occasion. The jester was uncommunicative.

'Where is the sheriff?' asked Ralph.

'Who knows?'

'I was hoping that you did, Berold.'

'No.'

'Is he still at the castle?'

'He may be.'

'You are usually at his side wherever he is.'

'Am I?'

'Have any arrests been made in connection with the murders?'

'Ask him.'

'I have no idea where the sheriff is,' said Ralph in exasperation, 'but I suspect that you do, Berold. Am I right?'

'Right to suspect me, wrong to harry me.'

'What has been going on here in Exeter?'

'Turmoil.'

'Why are you so infuriating today?'

'I try to be infuriating on most days, my lord.'

'Be warned,' said Ralph. 'I am in no mood for prevarication.'

'Good. That means you will not prevaricate.'

Ralph stifled a protest as the East Gate came in view. He recalled what Golde had told him about her own visit to the siege tunnel.

'My wife tells me that you were not eager to show her the tunnel.'

'No, my lord.'

'Why not?'

'I can think of much more interesting things to show a beautiful woman than an ugly hole in the ground.'

'You did not go near the tunnel, she told me.'

'Why should I?'

'Were you afraid of something?'

'I am always afraid.'

'Of what?'

'Life. Death. Benedictine monks. The sheriff's rage. Forked lightning. Being forced to listen to a sermon from Bishop Osbern. Marriage. The smell of lavender. Poisoned food. Bad ale. Jesting before an assembly which does not laugh. I am afraid of everything.'

'Then you would do well to fear my temper,' said Ralph, grabbing him by the scruff of the neck, 'for it has been shortened by a ride to Tavistock and back. I am looking into the murder of my friend, Berold. Turn that into a jest and I will crack your head open.'

'You will find it empty, my lord.'

'Why were you so reluctant to visit the siege tunnel?'

'Because I am superstitious.'

Ralph released him. 'Go on.'

'The place is believed to be haunted.'

'By whom?'

'Men who fought and fell during the siege.'

'Norman soldiers?'

'Saxons. There were incidents.'

'What kind of incidents?'

'The kind that mean nothing in themselves, my lord, but which build to a pattern when taken together. Some boys were frightened away when they tried to play in the tunnel.'

'By what?'

'A weird noise, they claimed. One man was found lying unconscious there. A second was thrown from his horse, as your good lady was. A third swears he saw a ghostly figure at night. A fourth claims that he saw a flame coming from the entrance. And so it goes on.'

'Why did you not warn my wife?' said Ralph angrily.

'Nothing would have stopped her wanting to see the tunnel.'

'But it might have saved her from an accident.'

'She saw my reluctance.'

They came out through the East Gate and approached the siege tunnel. Berold hung back once again, but Ralph nudged his horse forward until it was close to the mouth of the tunnel. The animal did not shy or back away. Ralph dismounted and peered into the cave. It was almost three feet in height and wide enough for a man to scurry along underground in a crouched position.

'How far does it go?' he asked.

'It went all the way to the city wall at one time,' said Berold, 'but they filled much of it in.'

'Did nobody search the place after the incidents of which you speak?'

'Yes, my lord. Nothing was found.'

Ralph took out his sword and ducked low to enter the tunnel. It was dark and dank. His shoulders brushed the walls and dislodged dust from the rock. He struggled on, using his sword to tap the ground in front of him. When it met an obstruction, he came to a halt and reached out a hand to feel a large boulder which had been rolled into the tunnel. It stopped him going any further but he had no wish to do so. The stench which hit his nostrils was foul. It made him hold his breath and back hurriedly away. Coming quickly out of the tunnel, he grimaced violently and inhaled fresh air as if his life depended on it.

Berold was highly amused by his expression of utter disgust. 'With a face like that,' he said, 'you could have been a jester.'

Troubled and embarrassed, Golde went in search of the lady Albreda. She found her walking around the perimeter of the courtyard for exercise with a gentlewoman in attendance. When she saw the urgency with which Golde was hobbling towards her, she came to a halt and dismissed her companion immediately.

'What ails you, Golde?'

'We must talk again about that letter, my lady.'

'I have been doing my best to put it out of my mind.'

'You must show it to your husband,' said Golde, 'as soon as

possible. It is the only way to stave off the threat of blackmail and it will also spare my blushes.'

'I do not understand.'

'In taking me into your confidence, you oblige me to lie to my own husband. When Ralph asked me if I had seen you while he was away, I was forced to hold back the truth from him. He sensed it at once and taxed me with dishonesty. That has never happened before.'

'I am sorry I put you in such a position, Golde.'

'Your problem is mine writ large, my lady. Conceal something of importance from your husband and he will surely catch wind of it in time. His fury will be all the greater. Tell him now.'

'I dare not, Golde.'

'Then let me tell him on your behalf.'

'That would make the situation even worse,' said Albreda, wringing her hands. 'Baldwin would be enraged if he thought I had discussed with someone else an intimate matter between husband and wife.'

'Would you rather submit to blackmail?'

'I must.'

'Is it worth the cost?'

'I would give everything I have to get those letters back again.'

'But how do you know that you *would* get them?' said Golde. 'A person who can enjoy making you suffer in this way can hardly be trusted to honour his side of the bargain. You may end up paying a large amount of money and being betrayed in return.'

'That is a risk I will have to take.'

'It is not necessary.'

A roar of anger interrupted them. Their gaze drifted to the other side of the courtyard where the sheriff was berating one of his men. His voice echoed round the whole castle. When the man tried to argue back, Baldwin struck him to the ground, kicked him hard, then marched away. Mounting his horse, he led a posse swiftly out through the gates. Golde was appalled by the sudden violence she had witnessed. When she turned back to Albreda, she was met by a wan smile.

'Would you tell the truth to such a man?' said Albreda.

'You will need to wait, my lady. To choose the right moment.'

'There will never be a right moment with Baldwin.'

'Then we must get those letters back ourselves,' said Golde. 'You must have some idea who is behind this blackmail.'

'None. I have been racking my brains to think who it might be. My husband is the sheriff and that means we have many enemies simply by dint of his office. Any one of them could want to drive a wedge between us.' She gave a forlorn sigh. 'You told me to find the blackmailer but I do not even know where to begin.'

'With the letters themselves. Where were they kept?'

'I do not know. The lord Nicholas promised to destroy them.'

'But cherished them too much to do so. They would have been hidden somewhere at his manor house so that his own wife would not see them. Someone must have found them after his death.'

'Or stolen them,' said Albreda as a possibility dawned. 'Baldwin mentioned that there had been a robbery at the house. It did not strike me at first but now I begin to wonder. Suppose the thief broke in to steal my letters to the lord Nicholas?'

'How would he know that they were there?'

'Because he delivered them.'

'What do you mean?'

'I could never trust anyone from the castle to bear such letters to the lord Nicholas. We had to use someone else. Someone whose discretion could be relied upon entirely,' she said as she delved into her memory. 'An honest man who would never dare to open any letter which passed between us, however curious he might be, and would divulge to nobody that he had been employed by us on like errands.'

'Did you know such a man?'

'The lord Nicholas did.'

'Who was he?'

'Saewin the Reeve.'

Loretta was in the garden, walking slowly between the well-tended beds of flowers and noting with pleasure the complete absence of weeds. Birds were perched in her fruit trees, hopping from branch to branch beneath the foliage. Insects were buzzing in the sunshine. When Saewin was shown out to her, she drew his attention to her pond. 'Do you like fish?' she asked.

'Only when they are on a plate, my lady.'

'They are beautiful creatures when you get to know them. So much more dependable than human beings. They never lie to you.' She gave him a look of disapproval. 'Why have you come?'

'You asked me to make enquiries of the commissioners.'

'And?'

'I spoke with Master Bret a while ago,' said Saewin, wilting slightly under her censorious gaze. 'No decision has been reached and there is no tilting in favour of the lady Catherine. On the other hand, Master Bret did ride out to the manor house today. I gather that he spoke with the lady Catherine herself.'

'This is sour news.'

'I felt that you should hear it all the same, my lady.'

'What did they talk about?'

'He would not tell me.'

'Did you press him?'

'Too hard, my lady, and it earned me a reprimand. That is one of the things I came to tell you. I can no longer ferret out information about this dispute for you. My integrity is being compromised.'

'What integrity?' she said with scorn.

'That is unkind!'

Loretta subjected him to such an intense scrutiny that he began to feel uncomfortable. Beads of sweat broke out on his brow. Her voice was low and accusatory. 'You have betrayed me, Saewin.'

'No, my lady!'

'I hoped that I could count on your loyalty.'

'And so you can.'

'My husband helped to put you in the position which you now hold,' she said with withering contempt. 'I am glad that he is not alive to see how unworthy and corrupt you have become.'

'I am neither of those things!' he protested.

'Then why have you turned against me? You know how important it is for me to regain the holdings that were tricked

277

out of my son. You know how long I have waited for this opportunity. It means everything to me.'

'I appreciate that, my lady.'

'Then why do you favour my rivals?'

'I do not.'

'Why did you visit Engelric yesterday and spend so long in his company? What plot were the two of you hatching against me?'

'I merely went to tell him that the commissioners had suspended their sessions. He was entitled to know that, my lady.'

'But was he entitled to have so much of your company?'

Saewin hesitated. 'We had . . . other matters to discuss.'

'So I have gathered.'

'But they are nothing to do with this dispute.'

'I have only your word for that, Saewin.'

'You have always found it reliable in the past, my lady.'

'That was before I heard about the other visit you paid.'

'Other visit?'

'Last evening,' she said quietly. 'You called on Asa, did you not?'

'No, my lady.'

'Called on her and stayed there well into the night. Why, Saewin? What kind of blandishments did she offer you? Why would you visit that harlot if not to claim your reward for helping her with her suit?' She raised a hand to silence his reply. 'Engelric and Asa. The two fellow Saxons involved in this dispute. Your two soulmates. Yet you have the gall to talk about integrity!'

'I confess that I visited Engelric,' he said quickly, 'but mostly on business unrelated to this dispute. I went nowhere near Asa's house. I spent last evening alone in my own home. Ask her. Asa will confirm that we never even met yesterday.'

'I have a more reliable witness than Asa.'

'Do you?'

'Yes, Saewin. He saw you enter and leave her house. So you are guilty of lies as well as treachery.' She looked over his shoulder. 'While you were there, he also saw a candle being lighted in her bedchamber. Why was that, I wonder?' She gave a nod. 'There is my witness. He stands behind you, Saewin. You were caught by one of your own.'

When the reeve swung round, Eldred gave him a vacant grin.

Chapter Thirteen

Gervase Bret had a long wait before Engelric returned, but he did not mind. It gave him time to reflect on all the information he had gathered that morning and to decide what to do next. He was left alone in the parlour of the house where the old Saxon was staying with his friend. Small, bare and dark, it presented a stark contrast to the luxury of the manor house he had visited earlier. The contrast would not have been lost on Engelric himself.

When the old man came back, he was surprised to find Gervase there.

'Why have you come?' he asked.

'I need to ask you some questions.'

'I told you all that I could at the shire hall.'

'Yes,' said Gervase respectfully, 'but we only discussed the ownership of the holdings at Upton Pyne. I wish to touch on the wider issues.'

'Of what?'

'Murder and conspiracy.'

Engelric did not blench. 'You lay these charges at my door?'

'No. I merely want you to understand the seriousness of my enquiries. At the shire hall, you spoke under oath. I would like equal honesty here.'

'You will have it, Master Bret,' said the other, eyes glistening.

They sat opposite each other in the gloomy parlour. The house was very similar to the one in which Gervase had been born and brought up. He felt at home, but Engelric's pride was clearly hurt at being found in such a mean dwelling. He had a faint air of embarrassment. Gervase took note of it, then plunged straight in.

'What sort of relationship did you have with the lord Nicholas?'

'A frosty one.'

'Did you exchange hot words with him?'

'From time to time.'

'What about your sons?'

'They found him as cruel and selfish as I did.'

'Cruel and selfish enough to drive them to thoughts of killing him?'

'Yes,' said Engelric readily. 'We wished him dead many a time, but that does not mean we lifted a hand to kill him. Normans can be vicious masters, as you must know. Cross them and your family will suffer for generations.'

'How well were you acquainted with the lady Catherine?'

'Not well at all. I only saw her once when I called at the house.'

'Did you feel bitter to see your former home occupied?'

'Bitter but resigned, Master Bret. It is the only way.'

'Do your sons share that view?'

'My sons are no more involved in this murder than I,' said the old man with spirit. 'And what is this conspiracy you allege?'

'Conspiracy to pervert the course of justice.'

'With regard to the dispute?'

'Yes, Engelric. Someone sent me letters in order to discredit one of the claimants, trying to secure unfair advantage over that person. And there have been other indications of conspiracy.'

'None point to me,' returned the other firmly. 'Justice is the one thing I seek. That is what my claim stands or fails upon. To pervert the course of justice would be folly on my part.'

'I accept that.'

'Then accept this as well, Master Bret. We may be poor, and resentful at what happened to us, but we are not criminals. We abide by the law of the land even when it goes against us.' He straightened himself on his stool. 'Though we shed no tears over the lord Nicholas's death, we want his killer to be caught and punished.'

'So do we all,' said Gervase, 'but let us not forget that there is a second murder here. That is the one which weighs most heavily on my mind.'

'Quite rightly. The lord Hervey was your colleague. I did not know him but he questioned me fairly at the shire hall and I took him for an upright man.'

'That is a good assessment of him.'

'I work on instinct, Master Bret.'

'It is very sound.' Gervase changed his tack. 'Tell me about Saewin. How well do you know him?'

'Fairly well. I have lived in these parts a long time.'

'Would you call him a personal friend?'

'I would.'

'Have you had many dealings with him in the past?'

'Yes, I have.'

'And would you describe him as an honourable man?'

'Extremely honourable,' said the other defensively. 'Saewin is very single-minded. He works hard and is always ready to offer free advice to his friends.'

'Did he offer you advice concerning this dispute?'

'No.'

'Why not?'

'He has high principles, Master Bret. I suspect that you do as well, so you will understand. Saewin showed me no favour at the shire hall, but he has advised me on another matter.'

'Oh?'

'I have been thinking of moving to the city.'

'Why?'

'My bones are too old to withstand another cold winter in the depths of the country. A dwelling in Exeter would be far more suitable, something akin to this house. Small, humble but snug.' His smile sent new waves of wrinkles over his face. 'Saewin promised to let me know when a property fell vacant. He has been very helpful.'

'Have you ever been to his own house?'

'Many times.'

'He has a dog, I believe.'

'It is more like a human than an animal, Master Bret. The reeve has taught that dog things which a child could not learn. Saewin has a way with dogs. I prefer pigs and cattle myself.'

'Why?'

'You can eat them.'

Gervase waited until his cackle died away. 'When you went before the first commissioners who visited the county, how were you received?'

'Justly but unsuccessfully.'

'You and the lord Nicholas were pitted against each other.'

'He called many witnesses in his support. I had none.'

'Yet you must have impressed our predecessors,' said Gervase, 'or they would not have asked us to take a second look at the holdings in Upton Pyne. This time, of course, we have five claimants instead of two. I wonder why some of them did not come forward earlier.'

'Did you tax them with that question?'

'Yes, Engelric. According to the abbot of Tavistock, he was cunningly misinformed about the date of the session here and arrived to find that the commissioners had moved on to Totnes.'

The old man cackled again. 'Do not expect me to feel sorry for the abbot. It was he who seized my land in the first place by means of a fraudulent exchange. Who else failed to come forward?'

'The lady Loretta.'

'What was her excuse?'

'That she was away in Normandy when the returns for this county were being taken.'

'Who told you that?'

284

'The lady Loretta herself.'

'Then either she is deceiving you or she has a very poor memory.'

'What do you mean?'

'When the first commissioners visited this county, she was at her home in Exeter. I remember seeing her when she attended a service at the cathedral. The lady Loretta is a handsome woman,' he said with grudging admiration. 'Even I am not too old to notice that.'

'But she swore under oath that she was in Normandy.'

Engelric was unequivocal. 'Then she lied to you.'

Geoffrey, abbot of Tavistock was not deterred by the presence of the sheriff. His voice was loud, his tone acerbic. He was alone in the hall at the castle with Baldwin and Ralph Delchard, but so large were his gestures and so passionate his rhetoric that he might have been addressing a vast assembly.

'This is one of the most shameful acts that I have ever had the misfortune to encounter,' he said with rising fury. 'I have never had such disrespect shown to me before. You, my lord Ralph, went off behind my back to speak to one of my knights in Tavistock. And you, my lord sheriff, much to my dismay and, I may say, astonishment, condoned this rash conduct. Walter Baderon is my man. My permission should have been sought before he was dragged from his bed to answer any questions.'

'Would you have given your permission?' said Ralph.

'No!'

'That is why I did not bother to seek it.'

'You had no right to ride off to Tavistock like that.'

'I had every right, my lord abbot,' said Ralph unrepentantly. 'I am searching for the man who murdered the lord Hervey and I will go wherever I wish in pursuit of the villain.'

'I support the lord Ralph to the hilt,' said the sheriff.

'Then you are not the man I took you for, Baldwin,' retorted the abbot. 'I provide fifteen knights for the defence of Exeter. They perform their duties well. They do not deserve to be treated like suspects in a murder investigation. I demand an apology from both of you.'

'You will not get one from me,' vowed Ralph.

'No apology is needed, Geoffrey,' said the sheriff, trying to calm him down. 'We took what action we felt was needed at the time.'

'Walter Baderon is an innocent man!' insisted the abbot.

'Innocent but dishonest,' said Ralph. 'He had valuable information to give and it took me time to wrest it from him. Had you left the fellow here in Exeter, I would not have been put to the trouble of galloping all the way to Tavistock. You are to blame here, my lord abbot.'

Geoffrey simmered. 'I have sole authority over my men.'

'Until they commit a crime.'

'Walter Baderon did not do that, my lord Ralph.'

'He withheld vital evidence and that is a crime in itself.'

'There is no point in bickering about it,' said the sheriff wearily. 'I suggest that we put the matter aside.'

'I will not do that!' yelled the abbot. 'If I do not have an abject apology from both of you, I will take my complaint to Bishop Osbern.'

Ralph was scornful. 'Take it to the Archangel Gabriel for all I care!'

'That is blasphemy!'

'It is the closest you will get to an apology.'

'Report this to Osbern, if you wish,' said Baldwin levelly, 'but I think you will find him more worldly than you. When murder takes place, I am entitled to take any steps I deem fit even if that means upsetting an abbot. Be grateful that my lord Ralph did not haul you out of bed in the middle of the night to face his interrogation.'

'That is a monstrous suggestion!'

'We bid you farewell, Geoffrey.'

'I'll not be dismissed before I am ready to go!'

'Depart now while I still have a hold on my temper,' cautioned the sheriff, 'or I will summon my men to assist you out of my castle.'

'You would lay violent hands upon an abbot!'

Ralph beamed at him. 'Given the opportunity.'

The prelate rid himself of another torrent of denunciation, then he stalked out of the hall with his arms waving like the sails of a windmill. They could hear his imprecations as he was crossing the courtyard.

Ralph chuckled. 'The abbot is a more comical jester than Berold.'

'I would sooner my own fool than that one.'

'I will happily dispense with both. Berold and I fell out when I learnt that he might have saved my wife from being injured in an accident.'

'How so?'

'He took her to view the siege tunnel by the East Gate but omitted to warn her about all the strange things which had happened there in the past. He should have kept her away.'

'I agree. The lady Golde's injury could have been far worse.'

'Indeed it could, my lord sheriff. But he is an odd fellow.'

'Berold?'

'He seems to flit between misery and elation.'

'He is a creature of moods.'

'I caught him in a bad one today,' recalled Ralph. 'It was almost as if he would do anything rather than help me. It was perverse.'

'Yet you did see what you wanted.'

'Saw and smelt. A vile place.'

'It is like an open sewer at times.'

'Yet that is where the lord Hervey was heading. I am certain of it. Walter Baderon admitted that he watched him go, turning out of the North Gate and walking along in the lee of the wall towards the East Gate. He must have been going to inspect that siege tunnel,' insisted Ralph. 'He talked of it on our ride to Exeter.'

'Someone must have intercepted him on the way.'

'Or when he left the tunnel. If he left, that is.'

'How did he finish up so far down the river?' wondered the sheriff. 'You would have expected him to leave a trail of blood but my men searched every inch of the bank and found none.'

'Perhaps the body was wrapped in something.'

'The man who did the wrapping would have been smeared in gore.'

'He will be when I catch up with him.'

'Or them,' said the other. 'Confederates may be at work here. On the other hand, maybe the rumours about that siege tunnel are well founded. Maybe it is haunted. Perhaps the lord Hervey was the victim of a Saxon ghost.'

'This ghost is made of flesh and blood,' decided Ralph. 'He does not only lurk around the siege tunnel, remember. He was waiting in that wood to ambush the lord Nicholas. No, he is here somewhere, my lord sheriff. We just have to look a little harder before we find him.'

Asa had never seen the reeve in such a state. There was no sign of his characteristic ease and calmness. Saewin was pale and drawn. When he was shown into her parlour, Asa saw that his hands were trembling. 'What is wrong?' she asked with concern.

'I had to see you at once, Asa.'

'Why?'

'To urge you to withdraw your claim.'

'Withdraw it?' she echoed.

'It is no longer valid.'

'It is as valid as it was when I first advanced it, Saewin. Those holdings are mine. I earned them and I'll not be cheated out of them. Nothing on earth will persuade me to drop my claim.'

'You must,' he pleaded.

'For what possible reason?'

'There are several, Asa. To begin with, you have little chance of success. A letter from the lord Nicholas can hardly compete with his last will and testament. You are nowhere mentioned in that.'

'He promised that I would be.'

'He promised many things to many women.'

'No,' she said, leaping up from her seat. 'I was the only one, Saewin. I loved him truly. That was why he was so eager to show me the strength of his own love. By bequeathing those holdings to me.'

'Renounce your claim, Asa!'

'Never!'

'You will have compensation,' he said wildly. 'I will pay you.'

'Why should you do that?'

'Because I am involved here.'

'How?'

'If you appear at the shire hall again, I stand to lose my office.' He gave a hopeless shrug. 'I was seen, Asa. When I came here last night, I was seen coming and going. Even the light in your bedchamber was noted.'

'What does that prove?'

'Enough to see me disgraced.'

'Deny it,' she said boldly. 'Deny that you ever came here and I will swear that you speak the truth. Goda will support our story.'

'It is too late for that, I fear. The truth is out. I have been given an ultimatum. Persuade you to withdraw or lose my place when this is reported to the commissioners. They are bound to think the worst.' He ran a worried hand across his throat. 'Master Bret asked me if I had been to your house and I told him I had not. He will know me as a liar. That in itself will be enough for him to push for my removal.'

Asa paced up and down the parlour as she tried to take in the enormity of what had happened. Still confident that she had a chance of influencing the commissioners to take a favourable view of her claim, she was mortified at the thought that it should now be withdrawn unconditionally. All her hopes would founder. She turned on Saewin with a savagery that made him back away a few paces. 'Why are you doing this to me?' she demanded.

'It is not my fault, Asa.'

'Is this the reward I get for granting you my favours? I endured it in order to get your help yet you now tell me that I must abandon all interest in the dispute. Is this some cruel game, Saewin?'

'No!'

'Did you take me in order to cast me contemptuously aside?'

'You know that is not true!' he said with quivering sincerity. 'I have waited so long for you, Asa, I have put up with all your rebuffs and all your excuses. You are the one who played games. Did you not send Goda to tell me how grateful you were to me? And what happened when I called here to receive gratitude in person? I was spurned, Asa. I was sent away with my tail between my legs.'

'I wish I had spurned you again last night.'

'But you did not and we will both suffer as a result.'

'Who saw you?' she asked.

'It does not matter.'

'Of course it matters. If someone is trying to rob me of my inheritance, I want to know who they are. Tell me, Saewin! I insist.'

'I have sworn to keep the name secret.'

'Who was it?'

'I cannot say.'

'Why have they put such fear into you?'

'Because I am in danger of losing my place and my reputation,' he said with desperation. 'You are the only person who can save me, Asa. Do you not see that? I am begging you.'

'Then you are wasting your breath.'

'Abandon your claim and I am safe.'

'What do I care about your safety?'

'You will suffer also,' he warned. 'I will be displaced but blame will also attach to you. It will blight what little hope of success you have.'

Asa struck a pose. 'I will take that chance.'

'This will ruin me!'

'You should have thought of that before you came here last night.'

'I had to see you, Asa. You know that.'

'Goda will show you out.'

'Please. Reconsider for a moment. We both stand to lose here.'

'No, Saewin,' she said with studied coldness. 'You are the only person at risk. People know what I am. I do not hide it. Men are seen to visit my house from time to time. There will be neither surprise nor condemnation when the commissioners learn that I entertained someone last night. You are finished, Saewin. Resign your office and avoid the scandal.' She gave a laugh of triumph. 'I do not need you. I will fight this battle on my own and be victorious.'

Gervase Bret returned to the castle and searched for Ralph Delchard. Unable to find him, he went up to the apartment at the top of the keep, but Golde was there alone and had no idea where her husband might be. Gervase was about to leave when she reached out on impulse. 'Wait a while,' she said, hand on his wrist. 'I would value your advice.'

'On what subject?'

'Marriage.'

Gervase smiled. 'You know far more about that than I, Golde.'

'I know about it from the woman's point of view, it is true. But I can only guess how a man sees it.' She indicated the chair. 'Sit down. I would like to describe a situation to you to see your reaction.'

'But I am not even married.'

'You soon will be.'

'Not if our work here moves at such a lethargic pace.'

'You will be back in Winchester in time to marry Alys. I am sure of it. Besides, you have been betrothed to her for so long. What is betrothal but a form of marriage with certain restrictions?'

'I know all about those restrictions!' he said, sitting down. 'I look forward to the day when they can be cast away.'

'It is at hand, Gervase.'

'What is this situation you mentioned?'

'Let us suppose – for the sake of argument – that Alys had another admirer before she had the good fortune to meet you.'

'She had many admirers.'

'I am talking about a special person in her life. Someone she loved.'

'Oh.'

'Not in the physical sense,' explained Golde delicately. 'This would be a man who worshipped her from afar and accepted that she was for ever unattainable.'

'It would still be a profound betrayal,' he said seriously. 'A love that is confined to the heart can still threaten and wound. I know that Alys would never harbour such feelings.'

'I only ask you to pretend that she might, Gervase.'

'Very well.'

'Now,' she continued, moving to the window. 'Supposing that you and she then get married in Winchester.'

'If only we could!' he sighed.

'You live happily together without anything to cause the slightest ripple in the pond of domestic life. Until one day. When you become aware of a letter she once wrote to her admirer, couched in the warmest of terms and suggesting a closer relationship than in fact existed. How do you think you would feel?'

'Shocked and hurt.'

'Even though that friendship took place long ago?'

'Even then, Golde. Alys should have told me about it.'

'She was too shy and fearful to do so.'

'Then she did not enter honestly into the marriage.'

'All people have some kind of secret,' she argued.

'Not of this order,' he countered. 'Marriage vows are the most solemn that we take. They must be honoured. A woman cannot do that properly if she comes to the altar concealing a dubious past.'

'There is nothing dubious here. She loved the man.'

'Then she should have confessed it.'

Golde gave an affectionate smile. 'You expect a perfection that few of us can manage, Gervase. Let us forget Alys, for I see that you take this too personally. Imagine two other people in the situation I have outlined.'

'Well?'

'The embarrassing letter comes out of her past, given to her by an anonymous hand. It is clearly a warning that her husband will be told the truth of her former love if she does not pay dearly to keep the intelligence from him.'

'Is that what has happened?' said Gervase worriedly. 'Someone is trying to blackmail you, Golde?'

'Not me. A friend.'

'Here in Exeter?'

'Perhaps.'

'I need to know. This may be important.'

'It is highly important to the lady in question. I have told her that she must tell her husband the whole truth or she will for ever be at the mercy of the blackmailer.'

'What was her reply?'

'That it would be suicidal to confide in her husband. If he learns the truth, she fears, he will fly into a rage.'

'When was the letter given to her, Golde?'

'Does it matter?'

'Very much. Was it in the last couple of days?'

'Yes.'

'Then she is the second victim.'

'Second?'

'Compromising letters of a slightly different kind were handed to me at the shire hall.'

'By whom?'

'I have no idea.'

'What sort of letters were they?'

'The kind that are extremely damaging to one of the claimants involved in a dispute. That is why they were sent. Though this is not a case of blackmail, I believe that the person who passed on those letters to me was also in possession of the one given to your friend. I would go even further,' said Gervase, thinking it through. 'I would hazard a guess where those letters were found.'

'Where?'

'In a box stolen from the house of the lord Nicholas.'

Golde started. 'But how could anyone know they would be there?'

'They did not. The box was taken because it contained something else. When the thief discovered it also contained those letters, he saw a means to exploit them.' He looked up at her. 'Was your friend in any way involved with the lord Nicholas?'

'I fear that she was.'

'Then she is the second victim of the thief. There may be more,' he said with a roll of his eyes. 'The lord Nicholas seems to have had many such romances and to have kept fond mementoes of his conquests.'

'So what should my friend do?' asked Golde. 'Tell her husband?'

'Not yet.'

'Then what?'

'Hope that I can find the man behind the blackmail before he can do even worse damage. What you have told me has been an immense help,' he said, getting up and moving to the door. 'And the truthful answer to your question is this. If someone was trying to blackmail Alys, I would forgive her any past indiscretion in order to free her from his power.' He opened the door. 'Tell that to your friend, Golde.'

'I will,' she said. 'Unfortunately, she is not married to a Gervase Bret.'

* * *

It was a fruitless search and it took them well into the evening. Under the supervision of Ralph Delchard and the sheriff, the men spread out in a line and walked slowly from the city to the spot where the body of Hervey de Marigny was found, poking about in the grass and among the bushes for any clue left behind by the killer. There were none. When Baldwin called off the search, he was annoyed and depressed. He and Ralph rode disconsolately back towards the city.

'You were wrong, Ralph,' he concluded.

'I do not think so.'

'It may well be that the lord Hervey was murdered in the river itself and left at the spot where he died. That would explain why there are no traces of his having been taken to the river from the city.'

'There is another explanation, my lord sheriff.'

'What?'

'The killer was thorough. He knew how to cover his tracks. How many clues did he leave behind when he ambushed the lord Nicholas?'

'None.'

'It is so here.'

'Is it?' said Baldwin. 'I begin to believe that the villain is no longer anywhere near Exeter. He was only here to commit the murders before fleeing the city altogether.'

'No,' said Ralph. 'There is no chance of that.'

'How can you be so sure?'

'Because of the way the two crimes were committed. They had to be the work of a man who knows the area extremely well. He lay in ambush at the perfect spot in that wood. He hid the lord Hervey's body in a place which took us an age to discover. No, my lord sheriff. We are looking for a local man. And he is still here,' said Ralph, wrinkling his nose in disgust. 'I can smell him!'

By the time they reached the castle, Ralph was drooping with fatigue as the cumulative effect of endless hours without sleep began to tell on him. He was not cheered by the sight of Canon Hubert talking to Gervase Bret close by the castle gate. Ralph dismounted and walked slowly across to them.

'Before you ask me, Hubert,' he said, lifting a hand, 'there has been no progress, I fear. We have found nothing. The cathedral will have to shake in its sandals for another night.'

'It is no jest, my lord,' said Hubert.

'I do not see it as such, believe me!'

'You need some rest, Ralph,' observed Gervase.

'Stop sounding like my wife.'

'There is nothing more you can do this evening.'

'Oh, yes, there is, Gervase. When I have seen Golde and poured a jug of water over my head to wake me up again, I will take another look at that siege tunnel. It worries me. Berold escorted me there earlier but it was bright daylight. I wonder if it takes on a different character by night.'

Hubert was puzzled. 'What has a siege tunnel to do with the murder of the lord Hervey?' he said. 'It is outside the city.'

'So was he when he was killed. Will you come with me, Gervase?'

'No,' said the other, 'I have a call to make on my own account.'

'To whom?'

'The lady Loretta. She perjured herself before us.'

'Can this be so?' said Hubert. 'An honourable woman like that?'

'According to Engelric.'

'Is he the source of this slander?'

'I do not think that it is slander, Canon Hubert.'

'Well, I do, Gervase. If it is a case of Engelric's word against that of the lady Loretta, I know whose I would believe. She is highly respected in the city and in the cathedral. Her generosity to the foundation is well known.' He gave a flabby smile. 'She even sends along her servant to cure a problem that returns to worry them.'

'What sort of problem?' asked Ralph.

'Bats, my lord. Bats in the belfry.'

'How does the servant help?'

'He can charm them into a sack, it seems,' said Hubert, 'then he takes them to the wood to release them. He must be a rare fellow to have such a skill with bats. The wonder of it is that he is dumb. Dean Jerome tells me that he has a gift from God. Eldred is able to commune somehow with almost any animal.'

'Eldred?' repeated Ralph.

'The servant who brought the lady Loretta to the shire hall.'

'I remember the man well.'

'Yes,' said Gervase, mind racing. 'So do I.'

Loretta was seated at the table, studying the charter in the bright candlelight and envisaging the time when the property would once more be in her possession. Certain of her success, she allowed herself a smile of self-congratulation. Then she put the charter aside and picked up one of the letters that lay beside it. She was reading it again and mocking its sentiments afresh when she heard the distant knock at the front door. The maidservant answered it, asked the caller to wait, then tapped on the door of the parlour before entering.

'A gentleman has called to see you, my lady,' said the girl.

'What is his name?'

'Master Gervase Bret.'

'Show him in at once,' she said with pleasant surprise.

'He has two companions with him, my lady.'

'Canon Hubert and Ralph Delchard?'

'No, my lady. Men-at-arms.'

Loretta's face hardened but she did not rescind the order. Gervase was soon stepping into the parlour while the two soldiers waited behind in the hall. She gave him a polite smile.

'This is an unexpected visit, Master Bret.'

'We did not only come to see you, my lady,' he explained. 'We wish to see your servant as well. Eldred.'

'He is not here.'

'Where is he?'

'I am not sure,' she said evasively.

'Will he return tonight?'

'At some point.'

'Then the lord Hervey's knights will wait for him.'

'I do not want two men-at-arms lurking in my hall,' she said with disdain. 'Send them away at once.'

'If you wish, my lady,' he agreed. 'But I will ask them to dispatch six of the sheriff's men in their stead. Eldred will be taken one way or another.'

'Taken?'

'For questioning.'

'On what grounds do you arrest him?'

'That is what I have come here to establish.'

Gervase's eye fell on the table and he saw the letters. Loretta moved the charter on top of them to hide them from view but she was too slow. He had seen enough to spark his interest. He strolled calmly across the room to confront her. 'I called at Saewin's house on the way here, my lady.'

'Indeed?'

'He was telling me more about this gift of Eldred's. The way he seems to have of talking to animals even though he is himself mute. When the reeve's dog was sick, it was Eldred who medicined him. He cured the creature. Saewin says that it was he who recommended Eldred to you.'

'That is true.'

'When nobody else would employ him, you took him in.'

'He is a loyal servant.'

'That is how Saewin described him as well, my lady. He said that Eldred was so grateful to you that he would do anything you asked.' Gervase moved in closer. 'Without hesitation.'

'I expect obedience from a servant.'

'You demanded more than that from Eldred. I recall how he sat beside you at the shire hall, aware of what you wanted even before you voiced a request. You and he seemed to have a kind of understanding, a form of speech that did not rely on words.'

'What are you trying to say, Master Bret?'

'I believe that your servant may have been responsible for two foul murders, both involving the use of an animal. A fox, perhaps. Or some kind of dog. Or a wildcat. A man who can

301

charm bats out of the cathedral belfry can tame any creature.' He watched her face but it betrayed no emotion. 'I also suspect that he stole a box from the manor house of Nicholas Picard, using his skill with animals to placate the four dogs who were on guard there in the night.'

Loretta gave a laugh of disbelief. 'What possible reason could a peace-loving man like Eldred have to kill someone? And why should he want to break into someone's house?'

'To retrieve something for you, my lady.'

'Me?'

'Yes,' said Gervase, sweeping the charter aside and snatching up the letters with his other hand. 'Who wrote these? Asa? Or some other woman you are going to persecute?'

Loretta got up and tried to grab them, but he was far too quick for her. Stepping back smartly, he held the letters behind him so that they were well out of her reach. Loretta extended an imperious palm.

'Those are mine. Please return them.'

'They are stolen property, my lady,' he said with a nod at her chair. 'Sit down again. We have much to discuss.'

'You have no right to be in my house!' she snapped.

'Send for the sheriff and have me evicted. Not that I would advise it, my lady. He is much more likely to invite you to the castle to continue this conversation there. Now – are you going to sit down?'

Seething with controlled anger, she slowly resumed her seat.

'You have plenty of strange ideas, Master Bret,' she said, regaining her poise. 'Strange ideas and wild accusations. Yet no proof whatsoever.'

He held up the letters. 'Except these.'

'What do they prove?'

'That you ordered Eldred to steal the box which contained them. It also contained some letters from Asa to lord Nicholas. They were sent anonymously to me so that her claim was imperilled.'

'Her claim!' sneered Loretta. 'It was totally worthless. Did she tell you that the lord Nicholas had been nowhere near her for over a year? Asa was discarded. He would hardly bequeath those holdings to a woman he could no longer bear to see.'

'You seem to know a lot about the lord Nicholas,' he said quietly.

'I heard all the gossip.'

'You do not strike me as a person who listens to gossip.'

'What *do* I strike you as, Master Bret?' she taunted.

'A woman who would stop at nothing to secure her ends.'

'All I wanted was my legitimate right.'

'Achieved by illegitimate means.'

'Or so you imagine.'

'You committed perjury before us,' said Gervase. 'That was what first made me wonder if the lady Loretta was all that she appeared to be. You told us that you were in Normandy when the first commissioners came, and that was why you made no appeal before them. Yet Engelric saw you at a service in the cathedral during the time they were here. So did Dean Jerome and Saewin. I took the trouble to confirm Engelric's comments with them.'

'You have been diligent,' she mocked.

'Not quite as diligent as you and Eldred. But let me see if I can suggest the real reason why you were silent when our predecessors were here. You advanced no claim then because the lord Nicholas was alive. There was some bond between you which forced you to hold back.'

'Oh, yes!' she murmured. 'There was a bond!'

'What exactly happened, my lady?'

'You tell me, Master Bret. You have such a colourful imagination that I could listen to your tales for hours. What other hideous crimes are you going to lay upon me? What other weird motives did I have?'

'There is nothing weird about the desire for revenge. Nicholas Picard cheated your son out of the holdings at Upton Pyne – or so you allege. It is no wonder that you wanted them back so much.'

'They were mine – they *are* mine!'

'Not any more, my lady.'

'I have a prior claim.'

'Murder cancelled it.'

Loretta stared at him with undisguised loathing, then her eye fell on the charter in front of her. It no longer lifted her spirits. She brushed it aside and rose to her feet.

'Yes,' she said. 'I had a bond with Nicholas Picard. The strongest bond a woman can have. When I could not get my property back from him by legal means, I chose another way. I seduced him.' She smiled at the shocked expression on Gervase's face. 'It was not difficult. He had a weakness for a pretty face and I flatter myself that mine can still turn a man's head. Besides, he had been sniffing around me for years and his attentions became more obvious after my husband died. He was such a vain man, Master Bret. He thought he would be doing me a favour. It never crossed his mind that I was only letting him enjoy *my* favours in order to get my property back.'

'But you never managed that.'

'I came close,' she said. 'Very close. He promised to restore those holdings to me a number of times but always drew back at the last moment. Then he made his mistake.'

'He told you that you would never secure that property.'

'In effect. He lost interest in me. He came to break off our romance, though he lacked the courage to do that properly. I have my pride. I am no Asa to be cast off like a dirty garment. The lord Nicholas betrayed me. He had to pay for that, Master Bret.'

'So you gave instructions to Eldred?'

'He will let nobody harm me.'

'Did you order him to steal that box?'

'I had to,' she said simply. 'It contained letters which the lord Nicholas made me write to him. I had to flatter his vanity. He told me that they were safely locked away in a box in his bedchamber and that he carried the only key on his person. It was important for me to retrieve my letters before someone broke open the box and found them. You and your colleagues might not have looked so favourably upon my claim had you known of a romance between the lord Nicholas and myself, especially as my letters contained more than one reference to the holdings in Upton Pyne.'

'Had Eldred been to the manor house before?'

'No, but I had. I described it to him in detail.'

'Then he charmed his way past the guard dogs and took the box.'

'It was more than a box, Master Bret,' she said with a high laugh. 'It was a treasure trove. There were letters in there from over a dozen women. The lord Nicholas had an obsession about keeping trophies. Some of the letters were from Asa. I got Eldred to translate them. He may not be able to speak but he can read and write. When I realised what I was holding, I used them to the best advantage by sending them to you. Asa's claim was fatally weakened.'

'So is yours now, my lady,' he reminded her.

Loretta gazed at him with a mixture of hate and resignation, then she turned away and moved across to a large wooden chest which stood against the wall. There was an air of defeat about her now. Gervase moved up behind her. Loretta's shoulders sagged.

'The rest of the letters are in here, Master Bret,' she whispered. 'I will show you what was in that box.'

Lifting the lid of the chest, she slipped a hand into it and felt around for something. When it came out again, however, it held no letters. Loretta had a dagger in her grasp and she swung round to strike wildly at Gervase. He leapt back with a cry but the point of the dagger ripped its way through his sleeve and drew blood. Gervase hurled the letters into her face then grappled with her, twisting her wrist until she dropped the dagger. Alerted by his yell, the two men-at-arms came in from the hall to lend their aid. Loretta was quickly overpowered.

Gervase was panting but relieved as he stood before her. 'These men are from the lord Hervey's retinue,' he said. 'They would like to know why he was killed as well.'

'It was none of my doing,' she protested. 'He stumbled on Eldred by complete chance and learnt more than was good for him. I was sorry to hear of his death. Had he lived, I might now be the rightful owner of the property that was taken away from me. It was within my reach.'

'Not any more, my lady. Take her to the castle. The sheriff will wish to hear more about that chance meeting.'

The men escorted her out and Gervase became aware of the blood which was seeping through his sleeve. The wound was not deep. He tore a strip of cloth from his apparel to bind it up. Ignoring the pain, he picked up the letters and began to read the first of them. As soon as he realised that it was from the lady Albreda, he remembered his earlier conversation with Golde. He was holding the correspondence with which Loretta intended to blackmail the sheriff's wife. Gervase intruded no more into her past. Holding the letters over the candle one by one, he let them burn until they floated harmlessly to the stone floor.

Albreda was safe. He would ask Golde to tell her that.

When Ralph Delchard and his men reached the North Gate, darkness was falling. Two of the four knights who accompanied him were carrying torches. The guards on sentry duty were surprised that they wanted to leave the city on foot at that hour. Ralph brushed aside their enquiries and led his men out through the gate, determination keeping fatigue at bay. They walked in the direction taken by Hervey de Marigny after his talk with the captain of the guard. It was almost pitch-dark in the shadow of the city wall and they needed their torches to guide their footsteps as they scrunched through the grass.

Eventually, they came to the siege tunnel on the eastern side. It looked quite eerie now, a gaping wound in the earth. When Ralph peered into it, he expected to see a forbidding gloom but instead noticed a faint glow. He remembered Berold's mention of someone who claimed that flames had come from the hole. Taking a torch from one of his men, he bent double and went into the tunnel. In the confined space, the flaming torch gave off an acrid smell but it did not completely hide the stench which came from the end of the tunnel. Ralph moved on to the point where the boulder had stopped him earlier and was amazed to see that it had been rolled back and eased into a large cavity in the side of the tunnel. He was able to work his way forward for twenty yards or more.

A slight bend was ahead of him and instinct warned him of the danger that lay around it. He drew his sword in readiness and moved on. The stench grew stronger and hissing noises filled his ears. When he came round the bend, he saw that the tunnel widened into a cave and his torch illumined a number of wooden cages around their walls. Animals of all kinds crouched and growled in their lairs but it was the wildcat which caught his attention. When it saw Ralph, it let out a screech of anger. Its cage was suddenly opened by a man's hand and it came hurtling out to attack him.

But Ralph was no careless rider, returning home alone through a wood. Nor was he a curious soldier, wishing to take a nostalgic peep at a siege tunnel. The element of surprise which had rendered both Nicholas Picard and Hervey de Marigny vulnerable to their killer did not exist here. As the wildcat leapt for his face, Ralph knocked it away with the torch, then put it out of its wailing misery with one jab from his sword. The death of his beloved pet enraged Eldred. He came out from the corner where he was lurking and flung himself at Ralph, knocking him to the ground and sending both sword and torch rolling from his hands.

Eldred pounded away at his face with both fists but Ralph reacted swiftly. Summoning up the last reserves of his strength, he pushed his attacker off him and rolled on top. Amid the pandemonium of the watching animals, they fought with great ferocity, punching, kicking, gouging and drawing blood. Eldred snatched a dagger from its scabbard and went for his adversary's throat. Ralph was ready for him, seizing the man's wrist and applying such irresistible power that the weapon was turned back upon its owner until it pierced his head between the staring eyes. Only when it had been sunk to the hilt did Eldred stop struggling.

The animals accorded their master a deafening requiem.

Epilogue

It took no more than a morning for the commissioners to reach their decision. Loretta's arrest simplified the proceedings. Since her claim was summarily withdrawn, and since neither Asa nor the abbot of Tavistock commanded any support at the shire hall, the dispute became a battle between Engelric and the widow of Nicholas Picard. Representing the latter, Tetbald the Steward was so certain of success that his arrogance overflowed and he tried to lecture the commissioners on the laws of inheritance. It was a foolish mistake. Ralph Delchard put him firmly in his place and rejection was added to reproach when Tetbald heard that the dispute had been resolved in favour of Engelric. While the old Saxon was celebrating the return of his property, the steward had to ride home to what he knew would be a frosty reception at the manor house.

As they took refreshment in the shire hall, the commissioners were entitled to feel that they were making progress. Ralph was jubilant.

'Exeter is indebted to us,' he said, chewing a piece of bread.

'We have solved two murders and a burglary, arrested those responsible, saved a number of ladies in this city from embarrassing revelations and settled the most complicated dispute which faced us. At this rate, we will have Gervase back in Winchester a week before the marriage.'

'As long as I am home on the day itself,' said Gervase with a smile. 'That is all that Alys will want. To have me there.'

'Wait until your wedding night. Alys will want much more than simply having you there. A marriage has to be consummated.'

'God forbid!' cried Brother Simon, choking on his food.

'These are unseemly remarks, my lord,' chided Canon Hubert. 'Holy matrimony is a solemn undertaking. Do not soil it with vulgarity.'

'You are right,' said Ralph cheerfully, 'and I apologise. I would not thank anyone for making coarse remarks about my own marriage. It has brought me nothing but joy. It is a delight to ride beside my wife when we visit each new county.'

'Golde is a charming companion,' said Gervase, 'but she is also an asset to us. Something she confided in me proved extremely useful.'

'What was that, Gervase?'

'It does not matter now. The whole matter has gone up in smoke.'

'The real credit must go to you and to the lord Ralph,' said Hubert. 'You solved crimes which left the sheriff quite bewildered. Brother Simon and I congratulate you.'

'Yes,' said Simon before gulping down some water.

'Do not forget your own part in this, Canon Hubert,' said Gervase. 'That information about Eldred was critical. If you had not seen him coming to deal with the bats at the cathedral, we might never have known that he had a gift with animals. My own suspicions had settled on Saewin.'

'Mine were on that loathsome steward,' admitted Ralph. 'I thought that Tetbald might have killed his master in order to enjoy the favours of the widow. He behaved almost like a second husband to her.' He gave a chuckle. 'I would love to be there when he reports his failure to the lady Catherine. He will be fortunate to retain his office. It is pleasant to be able to sow a little discord in his life.'

'Do not blame the steward,' said Hubert. 'It was the lord Nicholas who was chiefly responsible for all the chaos. When he was alive, he was a monster of promiscuity. When he died, a wife and two mistresses fought over his remains like animals. They were the true wildcats of Exeter.'

'And all three of them failed,' observed Simon.

'But not before they left a few scratches,' said Gervase, rubbing his injured arm. 'I am glad that this dispute is behind us.'

'So am I,' said Ralph. 'Hervey de Marigny's death has been avenged and his body has been sent back to his widow for burial. It is time to put the tragedy behind us and work our way through all the other disputes we have come to investigate. Call in Saewin.'

One of the guards at the rear of the hall went out and returned with the reeve. Saewin was relieved that the threat to his own position had now been lifted and there was an even greater willingness about him than before. When Ralph gave him instructions, the man nodded obediently before hurrying off on his errands. Gervase watched him go and decided that Exeter would be served by a chastened town reeve from now on – and one who might no longer be welcome at Asa's house.

When they had finished their repast, the commissioners resumed their seats and looked through the documents relating to their next case. A great weight had been lifted from their shoulders. Each of them was enjoying a new sense of freedom.

'Baldwin is delighted by our work,' said Ralph.

'That is a surprise.' remarked Hubert. 'I had the distinct impression that the lord sheriff was not pleased to have us in his county. His welcome, as I recall, was short on warmth and sincerity.'

'All that has changed, Hubert.'

'Has it, my lord?'

'Yes,' said Ralph. 'Now that we have helped solve the crimes and clean up the city for him, Baldwin cannot do enough for us. He is to hold another banquet in our honour tomorrow as a mark of his favour. You are both cordially invited, Hubert. You and Simon.'

'In that case,' said the canon, recalling the excellence of the food that was served at the castle, 'I take back my strictures. We would be happy to accept the invitation.'

'I would rather decline it, Canon Hubert,' said Simon sheepishly.

'Why?'

'Banquets hold no appeal for me.'

'Think of it as the Last Supper,' Ralph teased him.

'I would rather eat humbler fare at the cathedral.'

'Then so you shall, Brother Simon,' said Hubert.

'Though you may find yourself short of company,' warned Ralph. 'I know that Bishop Osbern is coming to the banquet. So is Dean Jerome and others from the cathedral. You may well be the only person who does not attend the feast.'

'That will content me,' said Simon.

'What about the abbot of Tavistock?' asked Gervase. 'Will he be there?'

Ralph grinned. 'I doubt it. My guess is that he has ridden off in a fit of pique. Saewin tells me that he was outraged when he heard that he would not be called before us again because we felt his claim did not merit further attention. He used some very unmonastic language.'

'I refuse to believe that,' said Hubert.

'I do not,' said Ralph. 'The chances are that he complained of us to the bishop, then sent off letters of condemnation to the king and to the archbishop of Canterbury, calling for our instant removal. Geoffrey, abbot of Tavistock has not mastered the art of being a gracious loser.'

'I have some sympathy for him,' said Hubert. 'There is nothing gracious about the seizure of one's land.'

'Engelric endured it with more dignity,' Gervase pointed out.

'Yes,' added Ralph. 'Of the five claims, I have to confess that

I thought his was the weakest at first glance. I have learnt better.'

Hubert gave a complacent smile. 'We all have, my lord.'

'Where are they!' yelled an angry voice.

The mood of calm was shattered by the appearance of a figure at the rear of the hall. Flinging open the door, Bishop Osbern stood there in his vestments and raised a finger of doom. He shook with indignation.

'How dare you insult Geoffrey, abbot of Tavistock!' he howled. 'I have come to speak on his behalf and censure you most strongly for your appalling treatment of him. His claim has been disregarded when it should have been upheld. I demand that you restore the property to the abbey and apologise to the abbot for your gross mistake.'

Simon was rigid with fear, Hubert was momentarily dumb-founded and even Gervase was taken aback at first, but Ralph's rich laughter soon made all three of them take a closer look at the bishop of Exeter. Taking off his mitre, he bowed low then strode towards them with a wide grin. Berold the Jester bestowed a friendly wave upon the table.

'I came to give you my blessing,' he said airily.

'Take off those vestments at once!' ordered Hubert.

'Would you have a naked man standing before you?' said Berold.

'No!' cried Simon.

The jester nudged him. 'Then I will bring a naked woman instead.'

'Peace, good Berold!' said Ralph, controlling his mirth. 'We appreciate this episcopal visitation but we have serious work to do here.'

'I came with news that you may not have heard, my lord.'

'I spy another jest.'

'No, my lord,' said the other solemnly. 'This concerns the man you killed, Eldred. As strangers to the city, you may not know his history.'

'What do you mean?'

'He was not born mute. He was a soldier here during the siege and earned himself a place in the records for his bravery. When King William and his men surrounded the city, Eldred stood on the battlements and lowered his breeches to tell them what he thought of them.'

'Saints preserve us!' said Simon in horror.

'Hervey de Marigny told us this tale,' recalled Ralph. 'But he could not remember what happened to the man.'

'He was caught,' said Berold, 'and taken before the king. His life was spared but King William exacted a just punishment. Because Eldred preferred to speak through his nether regions, the king ordered his tongue to be cut out. That is how he came by his name.'

'What name?' asked Hubert.

'Eldred the Fart.'

Hubert spluttered and Simon hid himself in his cowl. Only Ralph and Gervase realised that Berold was once again jesting. Had he been the soldier in question, Eldred would never have been so devoted to a Norman lady like Loretta. They were sorry that Hervey de Marigny was not there because he would have appreciated the jest more than any of them. When they had calmed Hubert down, they thanked Berold for bringing some amusement to the shire hall, then sent him on his way.

'That fool should be whipped for his insolence,' said Hubert.

'Berold is an important man in his own way,' said Ralph. 'He puts a smile on the face of the castle and that is a major achievement. I do not think that Bishop Osbern would have been offended. It was a flattering portrait of him.'

'Flattering!' echoed Hubert. 'It was demeaning!'

Ralph became brisk. 'Whatever it was,' he said, 'let us put it aside and address ourselves to the task in hand. It is high time we remembered what we are doing in the county of Devon.'

'Climbing our way up a mountain of disputes,' sighed Gervase.

'Suffering all kinds of blasphemy,' complained Simon.

'Bringing the sword of justice to this part of the kingdom,' said Hubert with more than his usual pomposity. 'Rewarding honesty, weeding out corruption and punishing any irregularities that we uncover. We are the privileged scribes of the Domesday Book. That is our main purpose here.'

'No, it is not,' said Ralph.

'Then what is, my lord?'

'Making sure that Gervase gets to the altar in time,' he said with an arm round his friend's shoulders. 'His lovely young bride must not be disappointed or Gervase may have another wildcat on his hands.'